THE BONES OF SANTORINI

AN EDWARD TYRINGTON MYSTERY

JONI SWIFT

SP

SPIRANTE PRESS

Cover by Miblart

For V

who changed my life with four words

Contents

Chapter One

March, 1863 - Port Said, Egypt

Edward sat alone and wondered whether his father was looking down on him from heaven, transcribing all his mistakes in some great galactic ledger where no erasures were permitted. He stared at the myriad stars shining beyond the dark outline of the ziggurat pyramid before him and pushed the anger he felt away. *I will not think ill of the dead, no matter what he thought of me or the situation he left me in.*

He stood and the desert sands shifted beneath his polished shoes as he meandered back to the grand ball, bitter about having to keep up appearances as the wealthy son of Lord Tyrington when in truth, nothing about his current circumstance that could be construed as "wealthy." *I have a wealth of debt*, he thought, smiling sardonically.

Edward had left the ball after his friend Henri had secretly arranged for a musician to hand Edward his violin to force him to play for everyone. Edward had played poorly, he thought, and he rubbed his fingertips, which still stung from the violin strings. The ball was Isma'il Pasha, leader of Egypt in the Ottoman Empire's first ball since his father, Said Pasha, had died. The lavish event was to convince all investors that the new pasha was as committed to the Suez Canal project as the former pasha. Isma'il was younger and more impetuous than his father, which became clear when he insisted that a traditional Ghawazi dancer join Edward on stage. Her deep decolletage, bare midriff, flying purple skirts, and shaking hips with gold coins broke his concentration. Never mind how her kohl-colored eyes bored into his or how scandalously she shook and danced. He pushed the images of her lithe, mostly naked, body from his mind and resigned himself to one more hour before he could, by protocol, acceptably leave.

As he returned to the ball, the cool desert night was rent by the sound of a woman's scream. It was a hysterical scream that repeated three times with the same intensity and came from somewhere toward town. The quiet that followed brought Edward a sense of foreboding. *What silenced her?* The thought drove his heels across the sand, past the lanterns that lined the entrance to the ball, and onto the cobblestones of town.

When he reached a small square, he found a crying woman with a footman walking her to a carriage. Behind them, a man lay motionless on the ground. The copious blood on the cobblestones told the tale of a life extinguished and that it was futile to check for a pulse. Edward had heard how lawless the canal work zone could be, but none of the rumors were anything as brutal as what lay before him.

The woman was wearing a claret ball gown with white lace accents. Her hair was pulled back from her face, but along her back it tumbled in long strawberry blond curls. Edward recalled admiring her when he saw her across the room speaking to the pasha. He had wanted to ask her to dance, but was chosen to play the violin. When he finished, she had already left.

Edward asked, "What happened?"

The woman tried to speak but could not. Instead, she pointed at the body. The footman said, "Please get into the carriage, miss. I will speak to him."

She nodded and wept as he handed her into the black hansom. The footman closed the door and joined Edward.

"What happened?" Edward asked again.

"I don't know, sir. I was driving the lady home when she told me to stop. She saw this man from the window and asked me to check on him, thinking perhaps he'd had too much to drink. I found him just like this. While I was investigating, she came over. It is quite a sight for a lady."

"Indeed," Edward muttered as he scanned the area. If the footman's story was true, the murderer might be lurking nearby. They were at the edge of a courtyard surrounded on three sides by closely spaced, brown, two-story buildings, with three rather dark alleyways leading away from them. Each building had a single long balcony across the length of the second floor. Each balcony was spotless, devoid of any signs of habitation. It was all too immaculate. Based on the small size of the buildings, this part of town seemed to be for the small army of low-level Egyptian managers that oversaw the canal's construction. Edward guessed that someone had ordered them to remove their possessions from the balconies to give an appearance of order and cleanliness for the guests of the pasha.

The nearest lamppost was unlit, but light came from a flickering lamp across the street. He saw no one, and nothing moved in the darker corners of the square.

Two French police officers arrived. Edward could tell the Suez Canal Company employed them by their blue uniforms with shoulder tassels and blue pill-box caps. They checked the body. "Merde!" said the first officer. He was short, with a mustache that was tightly cropped.

"What is it?" Edward asked.

The officer pointed at the body. "This is Monsieur Dupont."

Edward had read the name on dozens of orders authorizing personnel, materials, equipment, absolutely everything that he had requested for his dig site. "The operations director?"

"Yes."

This will back up work for weeks, if not months. Edward thought.

"I am Officer Girard and this is my assistant, Rogett. And you are?"

"Edward Tyrington. Chief archeologist for the company."

Girard grunted, wrote Edward's name in a small book. "Why aren't you at the ball?"

"I went outside for a breath of air when the woman in the carriage screamed, so I ran here to help. I arrived only a few minutes before you did."

"Did you hear a gunshot?"

"No. Only her scream."

Girard went to the carriage and asked the woman. "What is your name? Is there someone at the ball we should collect to escort you home?"

"I will escort her home, if that is agreeable to her," Edward offered.

She locked her gaze with his and pursed her lips. "No. Not you." She took a deep breath and turned to Officer Girard. "Please retrieve my father. His name is John Briggs. I could not find him when I left the ball."

Her rejection stung, but he decided not to press the issue. As Officer Rogett was about to leave, Edward spoke up. "You should collect the French Foreign Minister Jacques Thouvenel, as well."

Girard cocked his head "Why?"

"This is shaping up to be quite the international incident. Thouvenel will need as much warning to deal with it as possible." Inwardly, Edward cringed at the stern authority of his voice. His words had the clipped tone of his father, barking orders, knowing that they would be followed without question.

It was not long before Officer Rogett returned with Mr. Briggs and Monsieur Thouvenel. Mr. Briggs was an older gentleman with sunken cheeks who, despite his apparent years, moved faster than Edward would have imagined. In stark contrast, Thouvenel's corpulent physique, ruddy nose, and the beads of perspiration bore out his reputation for a love of food and drink as he came panting up behind the officer.

Mr. Briggs entered the carriage and held his daughter, who cried on his shoulder. Edward turned away from them and saw Thouvenel check Dupont's pockets. Thouvenel handed Dupont's watch to Girard. He asked the group, "Did anyone hear a shot?"

Girard responded, "No. He was likely murdered during the pasha's fireworks." He returned to the carriage and questioned Miss

Briggs. “I’d like to hear your account of what happened here, Miss Briggs. Were you acquainted with Monsieur Dupont?”

“No...I... only saw him lying there and thought perhaps he had too much to drink. I did not know— ” Her voice trailed off.

“Can we continue this in the morning? She is distraught and should see a doctor,” Mr. Briggs snapped.

“Where are you staying?”

“The Pharaoh Inn.”

“We will visit tomorrow to continue our questions.”

Mr. Briggs nodded, and they left.

Thouvenel left to notify the pasha and Ferdinand de Lesseps, the owner of the Suez Canal Company.

Chapter Two

Girard knelt to inspect the body, then ordered the officer Rogett to take his lantern and inspect the area. He mopped his brow as he inspected Dupont. Edward watched his tentative work from a distance and held his tongue. The officer's scrutiny of the body lacked understanding of the scientific method or any investigation techniques. Girard barely examined the bullet hole, nor did he check under the body. He checked Dupont's pockets, and clearly he was interested in being as perfunctory as possible.

Finding nothing of note in Dupont's pockets besides the watch Thouvenel had given him, Girard straightened as Officer Rogett returned and reported that he found nothing out of order. "The rooms are empty. They must be at Sham el-Nessim."

Edward asked, "Sham el-Nessim?"

"The Spring Festival. It's one of the few holidays the pasha allows the canal workers to celebrate. The celebration is across the canal."

A wicker basket fell from a balcony and crashed on the east side of the courtyard. Girard shot Rogett a scorching look, and they ran toward the noise, leaving Edward alone with the body.

Edward pushed his shoulders back, approached Dupont, and exhaled as he stared at the blood across the man's shirt. His previous experience finding a dead man was years before, and he felt unprepared for this moment. He had also seen corpses in his university science classes, but they were washed clean and laid out under a white sheet. Even then, he had not grown accustomed to the sight. This scene, with Dupont's arms and legs splayed and blood spilled across the paving stones, differed vastly from the cold dissemination of knowledge in a schoolroom. This was a life removed, a future erased, loved ones in mourning black for a year or more, with friends who meant well but stayed away due to their own awkwardness. Edward remembered his lonely days of mourning as he hung his head. He wondered what Dupont's last thought was, and thought of his own brother Thaddeus. He wondered if Thaddeus had met a similar fate, given the life he chose.

Stop it, Edward. Just stop.

Edward steeled his nerves and examined Dupont. The bullet entrance wound in his chest was ringed by a scorched area that smelled of burned gunpowder. *He was shot at close range.* Edward thought. He rolled him over and examined the bullet's exit wound. Edward's stomach lurched at the carnage the bullet left in its path, with shreds of cloth and skin hanging from the outer edge. He inhaled through his mouth as the cobblestones swirled before his eyes and the buildings wavered at the edge of his vision. He choked back the bile that burned his throat and stepped away.

Once Edward had regained his composure, he continued his inspection. Blood had drenched the stones under Dupont's body and flowed along the pattern of crevices between them toward his head like some bloody geometric halo. The metallic scent caught his nose, and he turned his head and exhaled. Dupont had faced whoever shot him, and the exit wound indicated a large-caliber bullet, not a typical-size weapon for a woman to carry. *Not that I suspect Miss Briggs, but I feel better about dismissing her as a murderer.*

Edward laid Dupont on his back again and inspected his hands and arms. The skin was still warm. The well-manicured fingernails had a few short brown hairs under them, and his wrists were scratched.

A small prayer buoyed up from the depths of Edward's mind. He did not consider himself a religious man, and the prayer surprised him at first, but the solemnity of a man so violently losing all of his tomorrows overcame his hesitation. He bowed his head and made the sign of the cross. *Godspeed, Dupont. I am sorry I can not do more for you.* He opened his eyes and looked around.

The silence of the square was chilling. He wondered where the officers had gone. In the gloom, he saw a figure creep down the stairs from a second-story balcony. Edward slipped into the shadows and stayed out of sight as the man made his way down. The man wore a white galabia, the loose-fitting robe of the Egyptian workers, making him obvious as he came down the stairs.

Edward approached the entrance of the alley as the person reached the bottom of the wooden stairs and ran. Edward took up pursuit, the heels of his dress shoes clattering on the cobblestones as he chased him down the alley to the next street. Turning the corner, Edward cursed his slick soles as they slid and he almost fell. Breathing hard, he stopped.

The long, narrow road lined by dwellings was dimly lit, and the person he chased was gone. There was no movement, no sound. All seemed peaceful and empty. He twisted the locked doorknobs of the first two doors. The knob on the third door turned. Edward looked up and down the alley one last time, saw no one, and entered the building. He closed the door, and the darkness engulfed him like a shroud. The dark was welcome to hide him, but also dangerous for whom it might hide.

A square of light came through the small window to his left, but it was not enough to illuminate the room. As he waited for his eyes to adjust, he pushed himself against the wall, held his breath, and listened. He heard nothing but the hammering of his own heart. When his eyes grew accustomed to the darkness, he saw a cot in the corner, a cooking area with pots and several water jugs, two chairs, and the dim outline of the first few rungs of a ladder at the back of the room that went to the upper floor.

Edward approached the ladder and climbed halfway up when it pitched away from the landing, throwing him onto the ground with a thud. A person on the second floor ran as Edward scrambled to his feet, reset the ladder, and climbed up. He followed the sound of footsteps through several connected rooms and saw a person flee to another balcony before the door to the balcony slammed shut. As Edward came outside, the fugitive jumped off the balcony, stumbled, then ran away.

Edward jumped off the balcony, his feet screaming as they slammed onto the cobblestones, and ran. His quarry was halfway down the alley when another man turned the corner and walked toward them from the far end of the street. Edward screamed, "Stop him!" but the bystander ran back from where he had come, and the fugitive entered another building. Edward followed, and as he crossed the threshold, a chair crashed down on his head.

Chapter Three

As the chair hit him, Edward fell to his hands and knees, his head aching from the blow. He grabbed the splintered leg of the chair as he watched the man who attacked him run away. Edward shook his head and ran through the house after the man. The Egyptian came to a locked door and pushed his body against it. Edward closed the gap and sliced the chair leg through the air to hit his head with a thud. The criminal crumpled to the ground like a pile of old sheets.

Edward grabbed his wrists, pulled him out to the alley, and yelled for the police, hoping Girard or Rogett were close enough to hear him. The officers arrived soon after, and Edward explained he had caught the man running from the scene of the murder of Monsieur Dupont. The police lashed the prisoner's hands as the Egyptian awoke. He shouted at the police in a mix of French and Arabic that vacillated from anger to pleading and back again. From what Edward understood, the man accused him of attacking him as he slept in his house.

Girard told him to be quiet. Turning to Edward, he said, "I'm glad you captured him. We thought we saw someone, but we lost him."

The Egyptian continued to protest his innocence until Girard threatened him with a gag.

The police searched the worker for a weapon but found none and returned to the square with the prisoner in tow. Edward followed them.

Girard said, "Mister Tyrington, thank you for your help. I think this settles the situation. If we have any more questions, we will contact you."

Edward thanked them and left just as more officers were arriving. He dusted the sand off his dark suit and straightened his hair as best he could as he walked back to the ball to collect Henri. His shoes were badly scuffed, and his jacket needed to be laundered, but there was nothing to be done about it. Hopefully, the partygoers would be too drunk to notice.

The ball was inside an elaborate network of luxuriously appointed tents that formed a large hall. The former pasha frequently held parties in this manner. It was an homage to their Bedouin culture and a way for the pasha to appear connected to his people, although, Edward noted by the luxury of the tents, that was far from the truth.

Despite the events of the past hour, Edward was in awe when he re-entered the ball. The tents were twenty feet tall, with colored tapestries lining the walls and Persian rugs on the floor, which gave an exotic softness to the rooms, as if none of their surroundings were real. Potted palms and large candelabras gave enough light and enough seclusion to deepen the dreamlike impression and grant the attendees a sense of warmth and intimacy. A chamber orchestra played while the attendees sat or stood in small groups, drinking and talking. Their secrets, their plans, their relationships were all safe in these tents, so far from their normal society. This was no more clear than the clutch of Europeans in the far corner lazing on couches smoking opium. Some appeared asleep and others looked half dead, with only two scraping or lighting their pipes.

As he scanned the room for Henri, a familiar voice sneered from behind him. "Young Edward Tyrington, how unexpected to see you here. How have you been faring in the year since your father's funeral?"

Edward turned to see Lord Livingstone. Edward was careful to keep his face neutral as he checked the frisson of contempt that skeltered up his spine, and his reply was smooth as silk. "I am well. What brings you to the Suez Canal, Lord Livingstone?"

Livingstone was a short man who wore his excesses around his middle like a pudding that he could never quite stuff into his clothing. Edward looked down at him, using his own height to intimidate the doughy man.

Livingstone waved his hand in a manner that, for anyone else, would give the impression of lightheartedness, but from him, it reeked of over-privileged disinterest. "Oh, several things. You know how busy the life of a lord can be. I am surprised to see you here, though, so far from the safety of London." His words, his tone, dripped with derision.

"I am here on business. If you will excuse me, there is someone I must meet. Good evening." Edward bowed at the neck and walked from the entrance where Livingstone had intercepted him. He searched the room for Henri and finally found him speaking to

Ferdinand de Lesseps, the mastermind and sole driver of the Suez Canal project.

As he approached, de Lesseps leaned toward him. "I understand the events of the past hour were quite trying." He waved to a couple who were leaving through the door across the room and said to Edward through his clenched smile, "I would appreciate discretion regarding the Dupont situation. I cannot fathom how we will replace him, but this whole venture has been doing the impossible, so I am sure we will persevere somehow. And of course, I mourn him as a friend. However, I would hate to have the confidence in the project—and investor interest we achieved tonight—marred by these unfortunate events."

"I will maintain the fullest discretion regarding the situation." Edward nodded.

"Thank you." De Lesseps waved at another couple and called to them to have a safe journey. Edward and Henri bid de Lesseps a good night.

When Edward and Henri arrived at Henri's house, they cloistered themselves in his study. Darkness cloaked the books on the shelves and the light of the small fire barely outlined the furniture. Henri crossed the room and lit an ornate candelabrum and then poured them each a large glass of whiskey.

Henri raised his glass. "To the memory of Pierre Campion Dupont. He was a good man and a pleasure to work with. The world is dimmer without his light."

Edward raised his glass and echoed Dupont's full name.

Henri drank the full measure of whiskey, handed his glass back for a refill, and collapsed into a chair by the fire. "Now, tell me what happened."

Edward took a deep draught of his own drink, its smooth peaty taste steeling his nerves. He refilled Henri's glass for him, then paced the room and told his account of events as Henri stared at the fire and wiped his eyes.

Henri asked, "Why would a worker kill him?"

"Robbery? Revenge? I do not know. How did the workers feel about Dupont?"

"The workers had no animosity toward him. Most did not know him, and the ones that did had no quarrel with him. The workers complain about three things: the pasha who forces them to work, the managers who directly oversee them, and each other for whatever petty squabble arises. Also, if a worker got his hands on a pistol, why would he need to rob someone? They are worth a small fortune here."

Edward nodded. "They did not find a gun with the worker they arrested, but he certainly had ample opportunity to hide it between when the murder occurred and when I spotted him. I assume the police will look further for the weapon. What concerns me most is Dupont's post. As operations manager, it is possible that someone shot him to impede the progress of the canal. His position is vital, and already the canal is years behind schedule. Given how many countries frown on this project and the advantage it may give French shipping and business, murdering a key man in the operation is not beyond the realm of possibility."

Henri's jaw dropped, and he handed Edward his glass to be refilled again. "If that is the case, others could be at risk as well—including me, as the procurement officer."

Edward inhaled slowly. "Possibly. But before we jump to that conclusion, if the captured man is guilty, I am sure his motive will become clear after the police question him."

Edward opened the decanter, then paused and held the glass stopper in his hand as he stared out the darkened window, his own rather ruffled reflection more visible than anything outside, but he did not see it. His mind's eye looked beyond the present, into the past.

He shook himself from the memory and refilled Henri's glass. "There is another thing that is bothering me. I had completely forgotten about it until now. You may recall that before my father died, he was investigating potential sources of British military secrets that have landed in the hands of the French."

"Yes, but I did not believe he had uncovered any actual evidence of wrongdoing."

Edward sat in the chair opposite Henri by the hearth and handed him his glass. "Yes, and no. There was insufficient evidence to determine who the traitor was, but there was substantiation of his misdeeds. My father never identified the criminal."

Henri leaned forward. "But the official inquiry from the House of Lords said nothing was discovered."

"Politics. The inquiry took too long, and some felt the continued investigation was too damaging."

"But your father would not let it go."

Edward rolled his glass between his hands, watching the firelight dance in his drink. "You knew my father. He was a loyal servant to the truth. I found a few scant notes on the subject in his effects. Most make no sense to me, but one stands out in particular. It said, 'See Dupont. Hadad Street, Damietta, Egypt.'"

"But Dupont was not in Damietta."

"I do not know how old the note is or if it is the same Dupont. Perhaps he used to work in Damietta, or perhaps it is someone else."

Henri sat back and sipped his drink, ruminating as he stared at the fire. "Dupont spoke little about his past. Before coming to the Suez Canal, I believe he worked in Algeria for a time, but that is all I know."

Edward stood and put his glass on the spirits table. "I have to go to the port in Damietta tomorrow to collect my surveying equipment. It was mistakenly delivered there, along with other company supplies, and I need to retrieve them before I return to Santorini. I plan to see what I can find out while I am there. I would like to finish my father's investigation, if I can."

"It is unlikely the two Duponts were the same person." Henri was already in his cups, and his words slurred into an unbroken smear of consonants and vowels.

"Hopefully tomorrow I can find out and be certain." Edward bid him adieu for the evening and walked home. Despite the late hour, his own home was brightly lit, since his man, Davis, had waited up to prepare him for bed. Davis had been his father's valet before him, and although he was quite spry for his age, his years were evident in the sandy gray of his hair that encircled his expanding bald spot.

Since Edward's father died, he had become something more than a valet. Edward considered him more of a trusted companion, but Davis would never deign to assume he was anything more than his title proffered.

Despite how tired he was, Edward tossed and turned after retiring, and sleep was elusive until deep in the morning. A few hours later, with dreams still tugging his eyelids, he awoke, staring at the hinged, double-framed photographs of his mother and father. The photographs were years old, taken when they were both alive, and Edward was a teenaged boy. As a grown man, he saw his features in their faces: he had his father's strong jawline and his mother's green eyes and dark, wavy hair. He smiled at the amusement caught in his mother's eyes, as if having her photograph made was great fun.

The smile slipped from his lips, and he forced himself to rise while trying to focus on the day ahead. After Davis dressed him and he ate a small breakfast, he walked through the morning, which was already far too bright for his mood, to the train station.

The station was a one-story building that was serviceable and solid, but lacked comfort or style. The stucco walls highlighted the grime of a million hands that had pressed the archway edges and the places where tired workers leaned against the wall for a few moments of rest. It was clear dignitaries rarely, if ever, came through this station. The pier was far more opulent and designed to impress potential foreign investors. The train station, despite its recent construction, already showed signs of age and wear from the hundreds of thousands who passed through here to dig and work in the canal. Like the workers, even a short term of service had noticeably aged the building. He purchased his ticket and crossed the hall to his departure track when his jaw fell open. There was Henri, who looked like Death's ghost.

Chapter Four

Henri's countenance was paler than Edward had ever seen it, with dark, puffy circles under his bloodshot eyes. He had finger combed his dark hair away from his face with little care. He sat half-sprawled on a mahogany bench in the train station with his head tilted back, looking at the giant portrait of the pasha on the far wall. As a point of contrast, his impeccably pressed gray Cheviot jacket and knickerbockers, along with his polished leather gaiters, showed the competence and care of his valet, who must have had quite a time dressing him given his current state.

The station was busy this morning, and people rushed about with luggage and freight, but Henri was an island of stillness in all the movement, imperturbable in the wake of humanity that passed before him.

Edward said, "For someone who is considered such a catch amongst the fairer sex, you look dreadful."

"Shh. Do not yell."

"I did not yell," Edward whispered as he sat next to Henri. "What happened to you?"

"My friend Dupont was murdered in cold blood, so naturally I finished the bottle of whiskey."

"You seemed to be bearing up all right when I left.'"

Henri sat up, pulled a bottle from his pocket, and uncorked it and drank a slug.

Edward grabbed the bottle from him and read the label. "Dr. Bodrum's Restorative Nervous Cordial. You must be on death's doorstep to drink that."

"Indeed." Henri took it back and swallowed a healthy dose. "Now let us board the train so I may sleep."

The crowd on the platform was thick. Locals crowded around the third-class cars and shoved each other in, fitting as many as possible. Crews of Egyptians had been released from their service to the canal, and they were heading home, soon to be replaced by fresh workers. Edward guided Henri through the shifting patterns of galabia-clad crowd to their first-class car, and his friend stretched his legs and closed his eyes to sleep off his hangover. The whistle blew, and the last of the crowd boarded as the steam engine crawled the train out of the station. Once outside of town, they rolled through the Egyptian countryside, and Edward mused over the sharply contrasting landscapes—on the one side, a narrow strip of cotton fields hugging the shore of the Mediterranean, and on the other, the sandy desert landscape. The complete lack of water on the sun-drenched dunes so close to the Mediterranean where the fishermen were casting their nets was startling. It reminded him of the contrasts of feast and famine in his own life.

As the train approached Damietta station, Henri opened his eyes and whistled as he set about straightening his hair and clothing.

After he had made himself presentable, Edward joked, "You almost make me believe that Nervous Restorative did you some good."

Henri checked his reflection in the glass one last time. "I swear by it. You should try it."

Edward gave him an incredulous look before disembarking.

It was a delicious shock as he stepped off the train into the bustle of Damietta, which had a different feel from the Suez Canal construction zone. This was Egypt without the influence of colonization. This was the Egypt of Egyptians, the place of their own determination, their own design, and that renewed Edward's sense of adventure. Rather than being a British citizen visiting the world that Britain and France had conquered or influenced, he was simply a foreigner here, an outsider. In Port Said, from whence they came, the French had designed and constructed the entire town and had such an overbearing influence on everything from the town architecture, to the placement of where people stayed, that it was easy to be lulled into a sense that you were in some warmer annex of France rather than Egypt. Damietta was established centuries earlier, as was clear in every aspect of the town. The very smell reminded him that everything he had ever known was far away. His heart beat faster, and he knew his wits were his only compass. Even something as mundane as crossing the street could become an uncertain proposition in such a foreign place. His smile grew at the thrill of it.

Edward squinted in the late-morning sun as hawkers haggled with buyers throughout the square at the station entrance. Everything was for sale here, from the cheapest trinkets to food, livestock, and clothing. Several men sold cotton shirts, galabias, and bolts of cloth.

Egyptian cotton was by far the highest quality, and Edward lingered to feel the softness slip between his fingers but refused when the seller tried to goad him to buy something.

He and Henri walked to the edge of the square, found a carriage, and directed the driver to Hadad Street. The ride was bumpy and choked with dust and throngs of people. When they arrived, they asked several people standing nearby if anyone spoke English or French.

A young man was sitting on the ground next to a building. His galabia was grimy and torn at the bottom, but his hair and face seemed clean. "You need someone to speak French?"

"Yes, we need help to find a Monsieur Dupont who lives—or previously lived—on Hadad Street."

"I help. Worked on canal. Speak good French. First, *bakshish*!" A demand for payment. Edward gave him a coin.

The young man nodded, finished the last of the dates he was eating, and worked his way down the street, asking everyone if they remembered Dupont. Head after head shook as people walked by. A group of boys ran over with hands out, begging for whatever Edward and Henri would provide, but the older boy shooed them away, apparently claiming ownership of them in his rebuke of the beggars.

Finally, where the street opened to a small square with a beautiful view of the Damietta Branch of the Nile River, they found a woman who remembered a Frenchman. She was older, with a leathery face, heavy eyelids, and wrinkled hands. She told them that the Frenchman had left years before. Another woman, wrapped in black from head to toe and pushing a cart of fruit, stopped to argue with the first woman. It was not long before their words came fast, punctuated by waving arms and gestures.

Edward could not imagine what the trouble was until the boy said, "They are arguing over whether he died."

Henri's jaw dropped. "How did they..."

Edward said, "It may be someone else that they are thinking of." Then he turned to the boy and asked, "They think he died?"

The boy tilted his head toward one woman. "She say he move away, but she doesn't know where. Other lady say he died, and both think the other is talking about someone else."

Edward tried to interject, but to no avail. Once the women had spent enough energy getting nowhere, they turned to him and spoke.

The boy translated, "They want to know who you are and why you want to know about him."

Henri said, "I am a friend."

There was another exchange between the ladies and the young man. He translated, "The woman with the cart said, 'Not such a good friend that you did not know he died.'"

The women started bickering again, and Edward felt a tap on his shoulder. There stood a rotund man with a flowing beard of black and white who quietly asked a few questions in French about the person they sought. The man leaned in a whispered, "You will not find him here, but I have a friend who might know where he is."

Edward touched Henri's arm and beckoned with his other hand.

Henri thanked the boy, bowed to the women, and followed. "Who is he?"

"He has a friend who might know where Dupont is."

The stranger turned with a grin. "Yes, my friend used to work for a man named Dupont. A pleasant fellow, by the way he spoke of him. But he moved from here years ago, if it is the same man I am remembering. My friend will know where he is now."

He led them to a rickshaw. "Not as fancy as a carriage, but he will get you where you are going."

"Which is where?" Henri asked.

"A popular place for fun here. There will be a man in the center of the crowd taking money. He knew Dupont."

He spoke to the driver in Arabic, and Edward and Henri were on their way.

Chapter Five

Henri tapped his right foot on the wooden floor of the rickshaw while making verbal notes of any obvious street or business names they passed. When Edward asked what he was doing, Henri answered, "We must be careful. We do not know where we are going or what we will find when we get there."

Every alleyway seemed to have laundry hanging from lines above the street and was full of people, making the entire scene a shifting painting of tan buildings and white, black, or gray cloth flying in the breeze. Only the occasional market seller seemed to break up the monotony. Edward used the sun to determine their direction of travel and noted anything that stood out. They wheeled past vegetable stands and small plazas, until they reached a square with two-story buildings lining three of the sides and dilapidated wooden dovecotes, lining the fourth side, where the pavement dissolved into endless desert. Far ahead on the dune was a caravan of wagons set in a straight line, their long, blue shadows stretching toward Edward like a carpet across the sands.

As they arrived, the excitement of the crowd electrified Edward. Henri smiled and Edward asked as they exited the rickshaw, "What is going on here?"

"Pigeon races. I should have known. They are quite popular in Egypt." Henri jumped out.

There were birdcages lined up along the caravan, and men inspecting the various birds that would compete. The cacophony of birds and men was deafening, and the bets were shouted and accounted for in a near constant stream. When the noise subsided and people lined up, it was clear the race would begin. Henri found a place at the edge of the crowd with a view of the start and finish lines. Silence fell as a flag rose at the starting line.

When the flag fell, the birdcages opened. The roar of beating wings as the birds rose as a group in the air was unnerving. Time slowed for Edward as he stood in awe of the expansive beauty of the late afternoon and the view of the horizon—the reddish-tan hue of the desert contrasting the deep cobalt of the sky. The birds flew past, a continuous mass of beating feathers, bird calls, and men yelling encouragement, until they reached their dovecotes. A flag rose with the pattern of the owner of the winning dove, and the crowd erupted in a cry of celebration and disappointment. Money changed hands again, with one tall man in the center of it all.

As the last bets were paid, and the crowd dispersed, they approached him. Edward introduced them and told of their search for Monsieur Dupont of Hadad Street.

He glanced up briefly at Edward with hazel-green eyes, then returned his gaze to the money he counted. "I worked for a Monsieur Dupont five or six years ago making sails."

"Then where did he go?"

"I don't know, but he went to work on... What is the word..." He said something in Arabic to himself, then snapped his fingers. "A ship. He went to work on a ship, I think. He spent little time with the workers, but I heard a rumor about where he went after he left."

Edward looked across the dispersing crowd. "Does anyone else here remember him?"

He looked up and scanned the few remaining men around them. "No."

"Is the sail company still here?"

He stopped counting his money and looked Edward in the eye. "No, it went out of business. We all moved on. Now, I have other business to attend to."

They thanked him and walked back toward their rickshaw. Edward was crestfallen. "Well, that was a dead end."

"I can tell you this: Dupont knew nothing about being a sailor. He studied management and efficiency. But even if our Dupont was not the one your father was looking for, I would like for you to look into our Dupont's death."

"Why?" Edward pushed a lock of hair off his forehead. "The police are far more capable at this kind of thing."

Henri stopped, squinting in the afternoon sun as he turned to face Edward. "Are they? They are thugs and ruffians who excel at keeping order in the ranks of workers sent here, but they do not know how to investigate a murder. If Dupont was murdered to slow the progress of the canal, then I worry about my safety as well as the safety of others. The police will pin this on the first person they can. I feel sure they stopped investigating the minute you captured that worker. And what if it was someone else? A person from his past, perhaps? Someone trying to stop our work? Someone who got away with murder because the 'police,' if you can call them that, were too indolent to look past their noses for a motive or a reason."

Edward searched Henri's eyes for a long moment. He understood the helplessness of having no reason for a loved one's death, the yearning to understand why they were not there to talk to, to comfort you, or to share your days. "You want to know why he died. And worker animosity is not enough of a reason for you. This isn't about justice as much as it is about understanding why."

Henri shook his head in frustration. "It is both, and it means everything to me right now. I need your help. You have always excelled at puzzles and you solved the mystery in Cadiz. This is just another mystery to solve."

Edward sighed and continued toward their rickshaw as the sand surrounded his shoes and made walking difficult. He gave Henri a sideward glance. "I will do what I can, but I doubt I will discover anything useful. Besides, I am bound for Santorini soon."

"Thank you. All I ask is that you try. Perhaps between both of our efforts, we will be successful."

They went to retrieve Edward's new theodolite for surveying. The company warehouse was a long, low, nondescript building designed to go unnoticed near the activity of the rail station. Inside, there were long aisles of shipping pallets and crates of every imaginable piece of equipment the project might use.

Edward opened his crate, examined the instrument to ensure the glass was whole, and showed it to Henri. "This will help me measure exact locations of the walls and buildings within the archaeological site and get a better understanding of the layout of the village we are uncovering. It is crucial for the maps I am creating."

Henri distractedly mumbled something as he filled out a requisition for shovels and tents to be delivered with the theodolite to Port Said on their train.

They arrived back at Port Said at the mouth of the canal in the early evening. Henri went to the office to finish some neglected paperwork and to ensure that someone properly delivered their equipment. As the sun sank low on the horizon, Edward visited the canal to watch the twilight descend on the Mediterranean. He sat on the bluff above the sea and watched the army of men, thousands of them, digging the channel by hand, carving what would be a hundred miles of waterway one shovelful at a time. It was as if an army of ghosts from an old fairy tale had descended to earth for the project as they moved about vaporously in their white galabias with their faces covered.

The lines of men and boys sang a cadence song, and sections of them seemed to work as one man, digging and lifting the sand in one fluid motion. The younger boys hauled the sand away, moving in a line behind the men. Further on he could see a lone steam shovel excavating huge amounts of sand and dumping it nearby. De Lesseps had purchased two steam shovels the year prior, and reportedly the project was making better headway with them, although Edward had heard the one stationed south of Timsah consistently broke down in the rockier soils there. The steam shovel was loud where he was and was surely deafening for the workers laying track ahead of it and digging nearby.

Edward turned his back to the canal and looked to the sea. White-sailed Felucca boats were returning to shore with their catch for the day, chased by dozens of hungry seagulls diving for whatever morsel they could snatch. The fishermen unloaded their haul as the sun crept lower in the sky, and they prepared the fish for market and the boats for the next day's work.

He stared out across the sea and tried to turn his mind away from the swirling thoughts around Dupont. It would be good to get back to Santorini and his archaeology, and leave this madness behind. He only hoped he was wrong about someone trying to sabotage the canal by killing Dupont. Regardless, those who knew de Lesseps knew he would carry on.

When the sun had dipped below the horizon in shifting shades of orange, red, and blue, he rose and walked home. At the edge of town, a hand clapped over his mouth and pulled him into a dark alley.

Chapter Six

Edward was pushed face-first against a brick wall, and his right arm was screaming in pain from being wrenched high along his back by his attacker. Edward tried to break free, but there was no room to rotate between the thug and the wall. Small bits of mortar scraped Edward's face as an unshaven cheek scratched his left ear.

"Did you think you could leave town and he wouldn't know, *Mister Tyrington*?" The man sneered his name with utter contempt. "Did you think he wouldn't have someone keep an eye on you?"

Edward shriveled from the stench of ale and rotting teeth that surrounded him. "I... I... came for work. You... you... must know I am working."

Edward felt the man's breath on his ear as he whispered, "Aye, that we do. But men who work halfway around the world forget their obligations, and our employer thought you should know he has a very large group of friends."

Edward scraped his left foot down the front of his attacker's left leg, then stomped on his foot as hard as he could. The man yelped in pain and let go of Edward's arm. Edward turned and punched the side of the man's head, and his attacker returned with a punch to the eye that flung Edward back against the wall. He fell sideways to the pavement.

Another man joined the fight and hit his attacker, who ran off. "Did he rob you? Do I need to chase him?"

Edward rejoiced at hearing Henri's voice. "No."

Henri reached down from the darkness to help him up. "I cannot leave you alone for a minute without you finding trouble."

"Thank goodness you arrived when you did."

"Are you sure he did not rob you?"

"Yes. Well, in a manner of speaking, I suppose." Edward dusted off his coat and trousers and touched his eyelid, which was already swollen. "Let us go to my house."

They walked the rest of the way in the gathering darkness near the cotton fields. By the light spilling from Edward's windows, Henri said, "Your eye looks painful. Can you see?"

"Not well. It is swelling fast."

"A cold potato will cure that."

Edward turned to him and cocked his head. "I am starting to believe you should be a physician rather than a procurement officer."

"It works. Try it."

As Edward opened the door, his valet's eyes grew wide and his jaw dropped. Under normal circumstances, Davis appeared as the physical manifestation of fastidiousness and calm resolve, and his clothing always included some small tasteful addition that completed his ensemble uniquely, which tonight was a cerulean silk pocket square that had been a gift from Edward's father.

Remembering himself, Davis straightened his shoulders, closed his mouth, then asked drolly, "Have you taken up boxing, sir?"

"If I had, I would clearly need more practice. Henri and I will be in the study."

By the light spilling from the hall, Edward crossed the study to the spirits table, where he drank two slugs of whiskey in quick succession. Then he handed Henri a glass.

The study was cold and dark, and Davis moved about the room lighting lamps. The light revealed one wall with large windows, two small bookcases, a desk that appeared to be unused, a small sofa and two chairs. Despite the coziness of the décor, the room felt like cold refuge, a place to hide, devoid of comfort or any sign of human habitation or use.

Davis knelt to light the fire. "I apologize, sir. I was not expecting you until after dinner."

"A fire is unnecessary. Please leave us," Edward said.

"Of course, sir." He stood, bowed, and closed the door behind him.

Henri stood near the spirits table and stared at Edward as he sipped his whiskey.

"What?" Edward stared at him.

"I am waiting for you to explain why I had to pull someone off of you in an alley."

"How did you come to be there?"

"I was coming to see you. Why were you there, and who was that man?"

"It was nothing." Edward walked to the cold hearth. "I was returning home. Another minute, and I would have had the situation in hand."

Henri walked to the bookshelf next to the fireplace. He stared at the volumes of books for a moment, then turned to Edward, his voice a low growl. "If you cannot tell me why that man was accosting you, then I question the veracity of our friendship."

Edward ran his hand through his hair pointed to a chair. "Sit." Then he drained his glass in one gulp.

His friend perched at the edge of the chair, holding his breath as Edward poured himself more whiskey.

At length, Edward sighed. "I am sorry. More than anything, I owe you a deep debt of gratitude for this job. You see, I am a bit...down on my luck."

"What do you mean 'down on your luck'? You do not gamble."

Edward sat in the blue wingback chair across from Henri, tilted his head back, and closed his eyes as if to ward off the blow of what he was about to say. "Unbeknownst to any of us, father spent a significant portion of the family fortune on his investigation. Once the House of Lords decided there was insufficient evidence, they dropped the matter. But you knew my father. He would not give up, and he kept funding the investigation from his own account. That is why I had to follow the last lead to Damietta: to close the book on the entire episode. I inherited the house in town and nowhere near enough money to cover expenses. I released most of the staff and have sold most of my valued possessions, and I even had to borrow money from a disreputable character to keep the townhouse and

Davis. The thug who accosted me tonight was one of the henchmen under my loaner's employ, sent to remind me of my debts."

Henri's jaw was slack for a moment before he spoke. "I did not know things were so difficult for you. Can your brother not help you?"

Edward shook his head. "Despite being accelerated to the earldom, Charles is in a similar situation. His lot will improve over time with judicious management of the Essex estate; however, he is not currently in a position to help."

Edward stood and paced the room. "However, it occurs to me I should be thankful for my lot. The inheritance was simply money earned by others; I produced none of what there was to inherit. I have no proper right to it, and certainly after what happened with Thaddeus, this loss seems just and fair."

"Nonsense. Do you have any idea how many lords and ladies have fallen on hard times? You will be a self-made man regardless, and the sciences will be better for it. And stop blaming yourself for Thaddeus."

Edward sighed. "I am only glad that you thought of me for this work before things got too terrible."

"Of course I thought of you." Henri looked incredulous. "You studied under Giuseppi Fiorrelli, for God's sake. There is nobody who knows more about an archaeological excavation in volcanic ash than he does after his work in Pompeii. He is the only other person I would have considered for this project. Had I known you were in trouble, I would have found a position for you earlier. Could the Earl of Mar help you?"

Edward smiled at the thought of his father's friend, who had become so dear to him as they grieved their loss together. "I would not dream of requesting assistance from James. He is a good friend and has given me strength when few could. Besides, I have tried to keep my current situation as close to the vest as possible."

They sat in silence for a few moments, absorbing the situation.

Henri stared at the darkened windows as if something would become clear from the night sky outside, or perhaps he was studying his own reflection. "I am still shocked that your father is gone. He was always so full of life. I am so sorry. I am sure he planned to regain his fortune before his demise."

Then his eyes brightened as he leaned forward, and Edward steeled himself for whatever would come next.

"Could you marry your way into a better fortune?"

Edward almost choked on his whiskey. "No, I cannot."

"Of course you can. There must be a dozen wealthy young ladies who would drool to be styled as Mrs. Tyrington. I know there were several who would have jumped at the chance the last time I was in London. Who was that one in the beautiful amethyst ball gown you danced with at the Lyon's ball last year? She was quite stunning, as I recall."

"First, a fortune is not the proper foundation for a marriage."

Henri scoffed. "Many marriages are built on less, and then you could take a 'wife in watercolors' or even two. That would take the sting out of marrying for money; we French do it all the time. Perhaps my sister Joelle has a friend."

"The French recommendation notwithstanding, I have no mind to marry and take a mistress—or mistresses." Edward stared at Henri. "Nor, under any circumstances, are you to share this with Joelle, or anyone else, for that matter. Besides, I am unsuitable to be a husband."

Henri scoffed. "What?"

Edward paced again. "The girl in the amethyst gown was Anna Presslar, and you are right, she was quite stunning and also quite kind. I asked Mr. Presslar to court her, but he refused, saying I was unsuitable due to my recent expeditions and 'general nomadic lifestyle,' despite my assurances that I am planning to use my talents to cultivate a professorship as my father wanted me to do."

"A professor? You?" Henri drank his whiskey in one swallow and pointed at Edward with the empty glass. "You despise classrooms. You were always happiest hiking in the forest or rowing on the river."

"Life has a way of changing people. Now, why did you come to see me?"

Henri frowned at the floor. "I came to visit you for two reasons: first, to inform you that the police searched Dupont's home. They found nothing to implicate anyone in his murder. His desk drawers were unlocked, which the butler said was unusual, but nothing else was amiss. And second, to request your help in packing Dupont's effects tomorrow. I cannot face the task alone."

"Of course I will help." Edward returned to his seat across from Henri. He remembered how helpful James had been with packing his father's effects and all the anguish that went with filling those boxes with memories that had no future.

There was a light knock on the door, and Davis entered, carrying a silver tray with a small beefsteak. "I am sorry to bother you, sir, but you should put this on your eye."

"Henri suggested a cold potato for it."

"With all due respect, sir, Henri is a gentleman. I have used this treatment to great effect in the past."

"On whom?"

"I would rather not share that in front of company, sir."

"You may speak in front of Henri."

"Very well. Your father." He placed the tray on a nearby table and continued, "The apple did not fall far from the tree for pugilistic skill." The thinning of his lips was the only sign of his struggle to keep a straight face.

Henri chuckled and bid Edward good night as he placed the beef over his eye. The raw meat was soothing, and he relaxed into his chair. "Thank you, Davis."

It was still early enough for dinner, but Edward had no appetite. Instead, he sat before the fireplace and brooded about his situation as Davis laid a fire for him. The clatter of the wood and tearing paper did not deter him from starting to doze almost as soon as the fire was lit.

But it wasn't long before a knock on the front door awakened him.

Chapter Seven

Davis answered the door and said in a whisper, "I am sorry. He is indisposed."

Edward chafed at being mollycoddled and called to him, "I am not indisposed. Whoever it is, send them in."

"It is Miss Catherine Briggs, sir." Davis allowed her to enter and took her cloak as Edward stood and removed the beef from his eye.

Edward regretted his outburst but welcomed her regardless of the impropriety of a woman visiting him alone, especially this late in the evening. "Miss Briggs, this is an unexpected pleasure."

Catherine turned to face him and gasped. "What on earth happened to your eye?"

"I am sure it appears worse than it is. I am quite fine."

"You need comfrey root." She came into the study and inspected his face. The scent she wore was floral, and he inhaled as she approached. She was quite tall, only a few inches shorter than Edward, with golden-red hair that glowed in the lamplight. With many women, the straightness of their stance was due to a combination of finishing school and corset. With Miss Briggs, that posture extended into her eyes, which shone not with submission, but a sense of self-esteem. Edward found her eyes captivating with their gray-blue color ringed by a darker shade of navy, a dark ocean held within a circle of night, and he wondered how tumultuous that ocean could be.

He handed the beefsteak to Davis and wiped his eye with a handkerchief. "Comfrey root? What about beefsteak?"

"Oh, that is an old wives' tale. I saw a Wild West show some years ago, and they had an American Indian medicine man. He was so tall and quite striking, with his long black braid and his leather outfit. He gave a lecture on natural remedies from the forest. It was hard to understand his accent at first, but as I became accustomed to it, I found he was quite eloquent. He recommended comfrey root smashed into a poultice for swelling and bruises."

Edward arched the eyebrow of his good eye at Davis, who turned and left the room. "Now, what could bring you to my abode at this hour of evening? Is everything all right?"

Catherine sat in the chair nearest the fire. "Yes, everything is fine. I came to apologize to you and thank you for your help last night. It was an awful experience."

"Apologize?"

"Yes. I judged you unfairly because I thought you had planned to play the violin at the ball with the dancer. Today I heard you did not know you would play, and that the dancer joined you at the behest of the pasha."

"And..."

"And, well, the comments I heard whispered by the men seated near me were rather scandalous. Leave it to the French to be that lowbrow. I found the objectification of her to be reprehensible, and you seemed to abet, or at the very least, condone, that behavior. Today, I realize I had wrongly judged you, and I apologize."

Edward could still see the dancer's bare midriff, flying purple skirt, and black eyes. He had tried not to stare, but she was impossible to ignore, and his eyes had wandered over her body as much as any other man's during her performance. The memory of her played in a loop in his mind. He pulled himself from his reverie. "No apology is necessary. But if I may ask, what happened when you saw Dupont?"

"It was as I told the police. I was returning to my lodgings from the ball, saw him from the carriage window, and asked the driver to stop. I thought perhaps he had too much to drink. When I arrived, he was exactly as you saw him since I arrived only a few moments before you." She looked at her lap, smoothed her skirt, and continued, "but I came to tell you about my investigation into his murder."

"What would possess you to investigate a murder?" Edward sat across from her. "That is a job for the police. Besides, they have already made an arrest."

She raised her eyes to meet his. "Yes, with your help, I understand. But the worker claims he is innocent and Dupont was unknown to him. There is no motive for murder."

"Except robbery. Dupont was a gentleman walking alone at night."

Catherine dipped her head as if asking a great favor. "Please. Let me tell you what I learned."

Edward crossed to the spirits table. "Excuse me. My manners have failed me, Miss Briggs. Would you care for a glass of sherry?"

"Yes, please."

As he handed her a glass and sat across from her, she sipped, taking a moment to collect her thoughts before looking him in the eye and speaking again. "I questioned Dupont's housekeeper and learned someone had threatened him and his wife six months ago."

"The housekeeper shared that with you, a total stranger?"

"She did not think I was a total stranger. She thought I was Dupont's office maid."

"How on earth could she mistake you for a maid?"

Miss Briggs gave a triumphant smile and said in the most rural French Edward had ever heard, "I borrowed my housekeeper's clothes and slipped into my old cook's accent."

He gaped at her. "That was French straight off the farm. Why do you speak French with a farmer's accent?"

"The only one who could coax me to eat after my mother died was our cook. She was such a kind woman. I sat in the kitchen and listened to her whenever I could. The accent is almost as natural to me as my own."

Edward stood and paced the length of the carpet. "The housekeeper told you Dupont had been threatened, but by whom?"

"She remembered the name Reginald Broussard being discussed. She is a local woman who understands more French than one might guess, and she admitted she used the assumption that she did not speak French to eavesdrop on the family conversations. I have had dealings with Reginald. He is the son of a shipping magnate, Andre Broussard. He is, shall we say, less effective than his father in the shipping business and is possibly an embezzler. His father once allowed him to run the company for three months while he went to attend to his mother's estate in France. During that time, Reginald lost several shipments, including two of ours, and a sum of money went missing."

"When was this?"

Catherine relaxed against the back of her chair, a catlike laziness overcoming her demeanor as she sipped her sherry and pondered. "About two years ago. Andre Broussard returned from France and paid us, and several others, for the lost cargo. He knew he would lose a large amount of business if he did not set things to rights."

"Were the ships lost or only the cargo?"

"That was the strangest part. The ships made their destinations, but without the cargo. When we questioned why our agents had not received the goods, Reginald said our agents lied and had stolen from us. That kind of thing can happen, although we take precautions. We might have chalked it up to poor employees, but my father and several competitors were playing cards one evening, and the subject came up. They discerned that only certain types of goods in certain ports disappeared, such as textiles in Madeira and food stuffs in Fos-sur-Mer. They discovered a pattern of theft. My father confronted Andre Broussard about it. He investigated and found something amiss, although he never said what, but he paid us for our lost shipments and informed us that he had fixed the issue. And now it seems his son threatened Monsieur Dupont and his wife on the street a few months ago."

"Do you know of any connection between Broussard and Dupont?"

"The housekeeper did not know of one, but she is a local woman supplied by the company, not someone who would have traveled with the family."

"Can you think of any way in which Broussard might stand to gain if the canal project is stopped?"

Catherine's jaw dropped. "You think this was a crime to stop the canal?"

"Dupont was the operations manager. It is not beyond possibility that the canal is the motive. Have you shared what you discovered with the police?"

"Yes, but they had no interest. They already arrested someone. The case is closed as far as they are concerned."

Edward sat across from her. "So, why are you telling me?"

She leaned forward. "Not to put too fine a point on it, but my father knew your father and described him as a man dedicated to justice, a fair-minded man who used his power and influence to ensure fair balance in the law. I hoped his son might share those qualities and would be interested in pursuing this information further. As it should be."

"Miss Briggs, I am a scientist." He set his drink on the table. "And although I possess skills that may be helpful to an investigation, I am quite busy working on my archaeological excavation on Santorini."

"Please, Mister Tyrington, Dupont deserves justice, which arresting the nearest worker does not serve, and the police will not give this case another thought."

Edward stood. "I appreciate that you have shared this with me, but I am bound for Santorini soon. I will see what I can do, but it is unlikely I will have much time to investigate this information before I leave."

Catherine rose, looking both crestfallen and galvanized. Her prim words took on a clipped edge. "Thank you for your time. I appreciate whatever you can do. Good evening."

Chapter Eight

When Edward awoke the next morning, he chided Davis for letting him sleep in, but in his heart, he was thankful for it. The crisp white sheets and deep-gold comforter were warm and soft and encouraged general laziness. The sun streamed through the pivot blinds, and the thin slats of light across his bed beckoned him to rise before the day became too warm. He hid from his responsibilities as long as he could and wondered how he would keep his word to Henri and Catherine to investigate in the little time he had left at the canal. He arose slowly, wishing he were already in Santorini and away from the volatility of Egypt. As Davis dressed him in his tan walking suit, the question of whether Reginald Broussard was responsible for Monsieur Dupont's murder plagued Edward.

Once Edward was dressed, Davis brought him a silver salver. "You received a letter, sir."

Edward recognized the perfect penmanship as James's and ran his finger across the wax seal of the Earl of Mar before opening the envelope. He read:

Dear Edward,

Thank you for your letter of January 7th. I am heartened by your invitation to excavate the archaeological site for the Suez Canal Com-

pany. It was clear from your letter that this opportunity means quite a lot to you; however, are there no English excavations you could lead? I would be happy to recommend you to any you deem suitable. I want what is best for you, and considering the tensions between England and France over the construction of the canal, it seems wiser to work in a capacity that will leave the question of your loyalties unimpeachable. I simply loathe anything that may limit your future options. Please consider it, and remember, I have great faith in you and your abilities. and know your father would be proud of you.

I remain with Sultan Abdulaziz and the Ottomans on the business of England and plan to travel to Athens for King George's coronation once the Regency Council approves a date, and I hope to visit you on my travels to, or from, Athens, as time allows. I look forward to seeing you then.

With warm regards,

James

Edward smiled. Seeing James would be welcome indeed. He had few genuine friends in the world, but the Earl of Mar was among them. Despite their political differences, Edward's father and James were quite close. He had been a steadying influence for Edward after his father's passing. In some ways, he had filled the void left by his father's death as a trusted counselor, but he was kinder than his own father, which made him a dear friend.

After breakfast, Edward walked into town, and although it had not been his intention, he returned to the square where Dupont had died. He stood alone, an island in a sea of bustling people, mostly Egyptian women, on their way to somewhere. Some carried baskets on their head, others tugged children along in a rush. They moved swiftly, with a purpose. It seemed everyone here had too little time to do whatever was needed, and by comparison he felt unmoored with nothing to demand his time or attention as he strode at his own ambling pace.

What became clear in the light of day was that there were several blocks between where he found the body and the workers' tent encampment area, which was a large expanse on the sands along the Sweet Water Canal built to bring fresh water to the workers and crops next to the Suez Canal channel.

Edward inspected the spot where Dupont's body had fallen. It looked no different from the rest of the area. Even the blood was gone. Someone had gone to some length to clean the paving stones, but the sand on the breeze and the footsteps of hundreds of workers had erased any sign of the life lost here just hours before. No evidence that might have helped him remained, and he reprimanded himself for not paying closer attention at the time. But as he looked at the spot, he remembered each detail. There had been nothing to find then, and there was nothing now.

He walked down the alley where he had chased the worker. Today it was lively with people moving about, carrying laundry, cooking food, living their life as best they could despite the pasha's required service. The smell of seared meat and warm pita bread made his mouth water. It was clear that if he had not seized the fugitive where he had, the man might have escaped into the sea of tents within a few blocks. There were thousands of tents in straight rows, almost as far as the eye could see. Edward knew he would have never caught the culprit if he had made it to the encampment.

As he stood musing, an argument between two women broke out near the Sweetwater Canal. One yelled in Arabic, and the other in English.

"Give it to me!" was the only phrase he heard clearly.

Edward ran toward the voices. As he left the pavement, his shoes sank in the moving sands and made running more difficult. The argument continued, and other people, all Egyptian, also came to see what the tumult was about. When he arrived there stood Catherine Briggs in a white walking dress that looked remarkably like a galabia, with a shawl over her hair. Another woman was shouting at her.

This is an unwelcome pattern. The Egyptian woman held something in her hands as Catherine tried to wrest it from her grasp. A small crowd had gathered, and Edward broke into the circle.

Catherine said, "Thank goodness you are here. This is Monsieur Dupont's drenched wallet, but some papers inside are still legible."

Edward took the wallet from the other woman and checked the contents. He found no money, but everything else seemed in order. "Where did you find this, Miss Briggs? And what are you doing here?"

She turned to the woman who had shouted. "Nenet found it when she filled her bucket in the Sweet Water Canal."

"Nenet? How do you know her name?"

"I came to talk to some workers."

"You did what? Do you know how dangerous this place is for a woman alone? Are you mad?"

She squared her shoulders. "The only way to discern the treatment of the workers is to talk to them."

Edward took her elbow and pulled her away from the crowd. "Does your father know where you are right now?"

Catherine shook her elbow loose from his hand and dusted off her sleeve where he had touched her. "No, but I expect he will soon enough."

His face was fiery with anger. "Oh, there is no doubt about that. You should leave now. You want nothing to do with this."

"But the police will need to question me. I was here when she found the wallet."

"I will talk to them and send them to your hotel if they need to speak to you." Edward looked around at the sea of workers. He knew no one there. "Miss Briggs, there is no one here that I trust to escort you home. It is not safe for you to travel alone, so you must stay, but I ask that you allow me to speak to the police when they arrive, and do not contradict me. It is best if you are not involved. If you even breathe loudly while the police are here, I will make your father rue the day he brought you to Egypt."

She glared at him but said nothing.

He convinced a worker to retrieve the company police, and while they waited, Edward dispersed the crowd except for Nenet.

When the officers arrived, he recognized Officer Girard. Edward wondered if he had really seen him previously running after a suspect for the apparent laziness in his gait today.

"I am surprised to see you again, Mister Tyrington."

Edward explained they came to see the square again when some women began arguing over the wallet. They questioned the Egyptian woman, who spoke to them in broken French, saying that she found it in the water. The officers thanked her for her help and took the wallet. Edward warned Catherine with his eyes to keep quiet. She chewed her lip in silence, glaring back at him.

"How do you think the wallet got into the canal?" Edward asked.

"We thought we chased someone else that night. He must have had the wallet, taken the money, and tossed it into the canal."

"Do you think this crime was something personal to Dupont, or a crime to slow the progress of the canal, given his position?"

The incredulous look on the officer's face spoke volumes. "We are very remote here. It seems a long way to come to murder one man to stop the unstoppable canal." Officer Girard chuckled and walked away.

Chapter Nine

Edward did not relish being rebuffed in such a manner, nor did he enjoy dealing with Miss Briggs, but he escorted her home. As they walked through the sand, Catherine chastised him for implying she had been with him. "You lied to the police."

Edward muttered through clenched teeth, "I would not have had to if you had not been foolish enough to come to the worker area unescorted."

"If I had not been there, the police would not have his wallet. And aside from that, I am determined to assist the workers. Have you seen the conditions in which they live?" She kept her tone even, but her shawl had fallen to her shoulders, and a lock of hair loosed itself from her bun and stood in the air like a flame as she spoke. "They are treated as slaves. Hundreds, if not thousands, of them die each month because of the extreme heat, disease, poor sanitation, and lack of proper food, let alone the dangerous working conditions. If there is no credible witness to their plight, it will continue, and thousands more will die. Perhaps it was not wise for me to come here unattended, but sometimes one must take chances to obtain one's goals."

As they gained the cobblestones, Edward walked forcibly through his anger. There was something admirable in her goals, but her methods were unsafe and unorthodox, and he vacillated between awe, bewilderment, and frustration as he strode. Catherine had to hurry to keep up, and they walked through the narrow streets to her hotel in silence.

When they arrived, he insisted on meeting with John to explain his daughter's whereabouts. Catherine directed him into the front room and went to retrieve her father. It was a drab room that smelled slightly of curry, with little in the way of decoration with a desk, a small sofa and a table. The furnishings tended toward functionality, not comfort – perhaps to dissuade guests from dallying too long. Edward took his cue from the furnishings and planned to be as succinct as possible.

When John arrived, his apparent age struck Edward. Frailty seemed to ooze from his body and stooped shoulders, but his eyes shone as a man who knew how to wield power and would not hesitate to do so.

Catherine tossed herself onto the sofa with her arms crossed and an unwavering look that said she was ready for battle. Edward introduced himself and shared the events of the day. Hearing the story, John's jaw clenched, and his brows knitted as he faced Catherine.

When Edward finished, John said, "Thank you for removing my reckless daughter from a dangerous situation."

Catherine spat her response. "For all they knew, I was a French citizen under the protection of Napoleon himself."

Edward stared wide-eyed. "You mean the protection the French citizen Dupont found? You may think this a game, Miss Briggs—"

"Not at all, but causing unnecessary worry for my father is something I cannot condone."

John's voice took a steel-edged tone. "I will decide what is unnecessary worry, child, not you. You may return to your room. I would like a word with Mister Tyrington. Alone."

Catherine left, and John poured Edward and himself glasses of whiskey. Handing one to Edward, he said, "Thank you for looking after her. She is not always so careless, but she is a woman of deep convictions."

Edward's curiosity got the better of him. "Why did she leave the ball alone last night?"

John sipped his drink and turned to look out the small window over the barren landscape behind the hotel. "You played beautifully at the ball."

Edward felt the heat rise in his cheeks. "Thank you."

John continued, "Perhaps you can understand why a proper Englishwoman might be offended by the dancer who performed with you?"

Edward again remembered the dancer, and how she slinked and swayed her coin-adorned hips before the crowd. Her dark eyes had sparkled above her face veil and challenged him as he played. Her stare had dared him to fail, dared him to succeed, dared him to be her equal on a stage where only one could shine. He still was not sure if he was more embarrassed by his own playing or by how she had completely captivated him. "I understand, and you should know that I had no hand in that. The pasha planned it himself. That entire portion of the evening was a surprise to me. But that still does not explain her leaving without you."

"It upset her. She looked and could not find me, so she took the carriage by herself rather than stay."

"A rather impulsive decision."

"Please do not judge her harshly." John's voice was almost imperceptible. Turning back to Edward, he said, "But you are Lord Tyrington's middle son, of course. I should have recognized you last night."

Edward cocked his head and looked askance at him. "Have we met?"

"No, but I knew your father. In the import-export business, the head of the Commerce Committee in the House of Lords is an important ally. I recall your father had a daguerreotype of his children on his desk. You have grown since then, of course, but the resemblance is there. I moved my offices to France ten years ago. I have only rarely returned."

An Englishman typically moved to France because of a financial setback of some type, and Edward wondered what had caused him to move.

John stood next to his desk and sipped his drink. "Tell me, how are Charles and Thaddeus?"

Edward's jaw clenched at the thought of Thaddeus. "Charles is well. He took my father's position as Lord. Thaddeus is well." He lied. He did not know how Thaddeus was, although he wished him well. God knows the last time he saw him he was as far from well as Edward had ever seen a man. Edward hoped to divert the subject from his family, but thankfully, John moved on to the next subject without prompting.

"What brings you all the way from London to the Suez Canal?"

"I am leading an archaeological excavation for the company on Santorini, at their quarry near the town of Akrotiri. We have already found evidence of an ancient civilization there. Santorini is like Pompeii because it is buried in volcanic ash, and much of what we have discovered is in excellent condition."

"Fascinating. I would like to see your work there."

"I am returning tonight, but you are welcome to visit."

John sat behind the desk. "Would you mind if we joined you on your journey? We had planned to quit Suez tomorrow for Damietta. But I have no pressing business there, and we can easily change the arrangements. I would love to see the work on an archaeological site. Historical discoveries have always fascinated me."

Edward gave a gracious smile. *I see where Catherine gets her impulsive nature from*. "Of course, you are more than welcome to join me. I warn you, it is a dusty operation, but we have made some significant discoveries. If you are enamored with archaeology, you will find it quite interesting."

John agreed and began making preparations as Edward left for Dupont's home to question a member of the staff that might have more knowledge of Dupont's past.

Chapter Ten

Dupont's house was one of the largest in the center of town. It was three stories and built of brick, with tall, ornate windows edged in white and a menacing black mansard roof. In every way, this home appeared to be French, except for the plantings along the path, which were more suited to the desert. Edward walked up the cobblestones to the imposing black double doors. The bell pull by the door already had a black crepe ribbon affixed to it to show that the house was in mourning. Edward pulled the ringer and waited. When the butler answered, Edward handed him his card and introduced himself as a friend of Henri's. "Monsieur LeMarchal has asked me to speak to you regarding Monsieur Dupont and the terrible events of yesterday."

The butler was a short man, with gray hair and jowls reminiscent of a bulldog. His scowl told Edward this would not be a simple conversation. "Why would he ask you to come and not visit himself?"

"He sends his regrets that he cannot visit today, but he is mourning as well and trying to keep work on the canal going. He has asked me to look into the circumstances around the events of last night."

"That seems unlikely. The police are already looking into it. Why would Monsieur LeMarchal ask you to get involved?"

His rudeness put Edward off, but he assumed it was grief speaking and pressed on. "Because I know of some things that may be important and of which you might have some knowledge. Please, can we speak inside?"

The butler moved aside and directed him to a small room to the left of the entrance hall. The room was cool, with shuttered windows that left the room rather dark after the simmering brightness of the day. Even in the dimness, the opulence of the room was striking in its mixture of cultures: French rosewood tables with scrolled feet, Persian rugs, embossed brass platters, and Egyptian scarab beetle carvings. There was a faint scent of fire in the room, which was not uncommon, but this was acrid, as if someone had burned something other than wood in the fireplace. Edward glanced at the hearth, but it had been swept clean. The butler made no move to make the room more comfortable and simply stared at him.

Edward cleared his throat. "I understand that there was an altercation six months ago between Monsieur Dupont, his wife, and a Frenchman."

"What of it?"

"So you are familiar with the incident. Who was he?"

The butler hesitated for a moment then said, "Forgive my impertinence, sir, but what difference does it make? That was six months ago, not yesterday."

"Can you tell me one person you know of who was an enemy of Monsieur Dupont?" Edward fixed him with an icy stare.

"Of course not, sir. He was a good man."

"Exactly. That is what I have heard from every quarter, which makes it more inconceivable that someone would murder him."

The butler gasped at the word *murder*.

Edward backtracked. "I apologize for the insensitive wording, but you see my predicament. Monsieur le Marchal believes someone else may be involved. The only person anyone can seem to think of who might have a motive is the Frenchman. I ask your cooperation to help me determine who he was and whether he was involved in this ghastly business."

"Monsieur Broussard was the man who accosted them."

At this, Edward motioned for them to sit on the two nearest walnut chairs by the hearth. "How did Monsieur Dupont know Monsieur Broussard?"

"Before Monsieur Dupont came to Suez, he lived and worked in Algeria for a time. Monsieur Broussard was his former employer. He was the son of the owner. Monsieur Dupont and Broussard never got along."

"Why?"

"Sir, I would rather not air my former employer's laundry to a complete stranger."

Edward leaned forward. "I may be a complete stranger, but I am the only one who is currently trying to solve what happened to him. I think he would want you to tell me so that he may find some peace."

The butler defiantly held his gaze. "Everything I tell you, Monsieur Dupont himself shared with me. I won't have you thinking

I was skulking around, listening at keyholes. I served Monsieur Dupont for over thirty years."

"I understand."

"Did you work with my employer at all?"

"No. But I've been told he was very efficient."

"Precisely. And very early in his career in Algeria, Andre Broussard praised his efficiency. Reginald, the son, did not like that. My employer said Reginald was lazy and felt that Monsieur Dupont's industrious nature made him look bad. There was trouble on and off over several years."

"Until?"

"Until what, sir?"

"What were the circumstances of Monsieur Dupont's departure from the Broussard company?"

The butler said, "I'm sure I don't know, sir."

"It appears Monsieur Dupont confided in you regularly, and yet suddenly you do not know the circumstances of his leaving the company?"

"He had connections at the Suez Canal Company and came here."

"And that was it?"

"Yes, sir." The butler stood, implying that Edward should leave.

Edward remained seated. "Then why did this man accost Monsieur and Madame Dupont in the street here six months ago?"

The butler's eyes flashed, but he maintained an even tone. "Madame Josette had nothing to do with it."

Edward snagged on the breach of protocol. "Josette, eh? That is exceedingly familiar for a butler. What are you hiding, Mister...Say, what is your name?"

"Ellis, and I've nothing to hide. That is how Madame wishes us to address her. And simply because Monsieur Dupont confided some things to me does not mean he confided everything. Now if you'll excuse me, there are preparations to be made, and I must attend to them."

"Of course." Edward knew he would get nothing further from Ellis. As he left the room, he turned. "When will the service be held?"

"Ten days hence, after Madame Dupont arrives."

"Thank you, Mr. Ellis." Edward donned his hat and left for Henri's office to assist him with Dupont's effects.

Chapter Eleven

Edward walked beneath the scorching noonday sun to Henri's office. The office was in a large four-story granite building with two tall spires at each end of the edifice. The front of the building was an expansive covered porch that shaded the front of the entire structure. Marble columns supported the porch roof, and arched doorways led into the building. There were two cleaning women on their hands and knees, scrubbing the day's dust from the porch. Edward heard the scratch of the horse bristle brushes as he climbed the few steps onto the porch and stepped lightly past them, trying not to soil their fresh work. He was thankful for the shade and the coolness of the marble hall as he entered. He mopped his brow as he greeted the receptionist and then climbed the stairs to the fourth floor, and found Henri in an office that was brightly lit, even with the windows half-shaded by louvered shutters. The space was cramped by the large oak desk, two straight-back chairs, a sofa, and a credenza. The room was well organized, but the desk had piles of paper held down with paperweights. Edward told his friend about finding Miss Briggs in the worker encampment, and Henri shook his head.

"Miss Briggs has always been headstrong, but that seems beyond the pale, even for her."

"What do you mean, always? How do you know her?"

"Our families know each other rather well. We spent a portion of the summer with them, and vice versa on several occasions."

Edward's jaw clenched. He was not fond of the idea of Catherine and Henri being such friends. Edward continued. "She also interviewed Dupont's housekeeper and found that Reginald Broussard accosted him about six months ago. This morning, I followed suit and interviewed his butler, who corroborated the story. Are you familiar with Broussard, or have you heard this story?"

Henri thought for a moment. "That name is not familiar, and I have heard nothing about someone accosting Dupont."

"Apparently, Dupont worked for him in Algeria. There was some trouble between them, but the butler would not give me details as to why Dupont left Broussard's employ."

"I will look into it and see if I can find out anything further. Perhaps someone else at the company knows more about it."

Henri showed Edward which drawers contained Dupont's belongings, thanked him for his help, and went to work in a small adjacent room. Edward sat at Dupont's desk and packed a daguerreotype of his wife, Josette, and their children and another of an older woman—his mother, by the looks of her.

"Is his mother still alive?" he called to Henri.

"No, she passed away last year, his father several years before that."

Edward stared at the picture. She was a handsome woman, maybe fifty-five years old in the picture. She looked too young to have passed away, and Edward thought about the similarities of his life and Dupont's: two parents lost, making their way in foreign lands.

With one bullet, all anyone had left of Dupont were a few scant pictures and letters; in one afternoon, that was all Edward had of his father. Henri's voice broke him from his reverie.

"But what of you? How are you handling this?"

"I am fine. It is unfortunate, but as I did not know him..." His voice trailed off, and he set about packing.

Henri cocked his head and looked at him for a long moment through the doorway. "You are not fine. Look at you. Your foot bounces almost as much as your eyes jump around the room. This has you more rattled than I believe I have ever seen you."

Edward avoided his gaze. "It is nothing."

"So we are back to secrets again?"

"The entire event is distressing, but I am simply packing as you asked."

"For several minutes, you simply stared at that picture. Something is wrong, and I will not let you avoid it, whatever it is."

He looked away from Henri's eyes and gazed at the floor. "It is a small thing, not worth mentioning. I worked for Peterson on his ornithological expedition to Zanzibar. We had some difficulty with the locals and faced a dangerous situation, and this reminds me of it. That is all." Edward picked up a blue glass paperweight etched with a camel from the desk and shoved it into the box. He packed several other items in rapid succession and turned his back to Henri.

He felt Henri's stare rather than saw it. Then Henri asked, "Was someone murdered?"

Edward looked for another trinket to pack. "No, there was no murder. Perhaps it is the unpredictability of locals that has me a bit shaken."

"If you think I believe that, you think very little of my intellect. You are a citizen of the world, Edward. I have seen you blend into situations with all kinds of people around the globe."

Edward spun to face him. "You will not leave it, will you?" His voice was rough, almost a snarl, and louder than he had intended. Henri's eyes widened, and Edward immediately regretted the outburst. Henri was in mourning, and Edward was being less than comforting. But it was easier to be cruel than to talk about it.

Edward raked his hands through his hair and turned to face the window. The view of the canal work was lovely from here. He saw the orderly lines of men digging in time, the sand and rubble flying from their shovels in unison as if freed for one moment, only to be snatched by gravity again and forced back to the earth. The steam shovel in the distance seemed a portent of the future. Edward wondered if he would ever be replaced by a machine.

Hearing Henri clear his throat, he returned from his daydreaming, turned around, and sighed. "I apologize for my outburst. Peterson offended the local tribe's leader. It would have been a small thing if Peterson would have apologized and made amends, but as a British subject, he claimed superiority and made the situation far worse. In the end, it was only because of my navigation skills and Davis's bribery of a few of the local boys that we got out alive. One boy had warned us earlier that afternoon that the tribe was coming for us, so we packed what we could carry and ran. When we ascended the hill outside the village, we saw a large fire. I can only surmise it was our huts being burned to the ground. It took us five days of rough travel to get to the next town where we could arrange for passage out. Seeing Dupont was like viewing my alternate fate and what should have become of me that night." Edward opened a drawer and sifted through the contents.

"Thank goodness you made it out alive. Was Peterson chastised by the university for ruining the expedition?"

"Quite the contrary." Edward stopped, squared his shoulders, and looked Henri in the eye. "He placed the blame on me, although it had taken my cunning to get us out of there. He even took credit for my discoveries. It is rumored he promised the others payment and position for not contradicting his story. That was when things well and truly fell apart for me. But it is in the past now."

Henri's jaw hung open in disbelief. "Why would he do that?"

"University politics. I caught him in an unsavory pastime whilst in Zanzibar, and he felt the only way to maintain his reputation was to ruin mine. Universities can be more cutthroat than any corner of Africa."

Edward turned away from him and packed several handkerchiefs, a hat, and two silk cravats into a box, and placed a pair of work boots into a separate box. Changing the subject, he said, "Dupont seemed to have clothes for every occasion."

"I am sorry for your difficulties in Zanzibar. You should have told me; perhaps there was some way I could have helped." Edward shook his head, and Henri nodded toward the silk scarf in Edward's hands. "Dupont liked to be prepared for anything."

Edward continued with as much forced nonchalance as he could muster. “I assume the silk cravats were not for the work area.”

“No.” Henri picked up the blue one with a small, gold fleur-de-lis on it. “This one was a gift from de Lesseps for the success of the first steam shovel working in the canal. The white one was his own.”

Edward took the blue one from Henri and packed them both away. He tried to open the desk drawer, but it was locked. “Do you have a key?”

Henri opened another drawer and removed the key fastened to its bottom. Edward unlocked the drawer and whistled.

“What did you find?”

“A Lefaucheux revolver. He *was* prepared for anything.”

“Careful. I am sure it is loaded.” Henri leaned in to see it.

“I assumed so.” Edward unhinged the cylinder and removed the bullets, then checked the chamber to ensure it was clear. He placed the gun in the box. He took a plain cotton handkerchief from the drawer and wrapped the bullets.

Below the gun was a ledger with a worn, brown leather cover. Edward handed it to Henri, who said, “That must be a personal ledger. I already removed the company ledger from his desk.”

Edward opened it and found Henri was correct. Each entry was recorded and calculated in a neat hand. He read through the entries, tracing his finger down the page as he noted each one. “That is odd.”

Henri came to read over his shoulder, and Edward pointed to the entries. “Each one has a specific date and a rather detailed description of the purchase, except for these, which only list M. R. Services. What is M. R. Services?”

“I do not know.”

Edward flipped through the pages. “There is one entry each month for the last four months under that name, all in the same amount. But nothing for M. R. Services before that.”

“The remaining entries look normal. Payment of his staff, purchase of food and wine, a new hat.”

“The hat you just packed, by the description of it in the ledger.”

“Yes. He went to such an effort to describe each item, down to the color and style of the hat he purchased. But the M. R. Services entries have no information at all.” They looked at each other. Henri’s brow furrowed. “Almost as if he was trying to keep them secret.”

“Help me look for anything that might be from M. R. Services.” Edward closed the ledger.

They packed everything that remained in the desk drawer and scoured the room for other information. Henri methodically looked behind the paintings in the room and under the drawers of the filing cabinet. They both looked through each file to see if there were any secret papers hidden in their midst. Henri even tapped the walls to see if there was a hidden safe.

At the end of an hour, Edward said, “Whatever it is, there is no other information here that I can find.”

“Nor I. Perhaps his wife will know, but she will not be here for eight days or so. Poor Dupont will be buried by then, but they will have a service for him after she arrives.” Henri sighed and looked out the window.

Edward asked. “Where will he be buried?”

"The graveyard at St. Mary's church, in the center of town. He would have wanted to be buried near the canal." Henri packed a set of ink pens and said, "We should finish here."

"Yes. I need to finish preparing to return to Santorini tonight."

"Thank you for your help. By the way, Julian Arnout will come photograph your discoveries as soon as he can break free from his current assignment. De Lesseps wants to use what you have found to raise more interest and investment in the project."

Edward's smile belied his apprehension. "I will expect him soon then."

"Be safe. Greece is still a lawless place, even with the army acting as the police." Henri shook his hand and said, "Oh, and I arranged for the Briggses to be on your ship tonight."

Edward smiled. "Thank you for that."

"You may regret inviting them. As you know, she can be rather trying."

Edward nodded and said, "I have no one to blame but myself. Goodbye, Henri."

Chapter Twelve

After dinner, Edward and Davis boarded a freighter for the overnight journey to Santorini. It was clear Davis was celebrating their return with his deep-royal-blue pocket square, which matched the shutters on most of the houses on the island. As Edward crossed the gangplank, he relaxed, and the stress of the previous days left his shoulders. Davis brought their belongings onboard, and Edward made for the bow of the ship as she left dock.

The sailors coiled the heavy dock lines nearby as Edward basked in the softened blues and golds of evening dusk, and the cool breeze from the Mediterranean seemed a portent of peace. The workers spoke freely in Greek about their day and the passengers, coarsely ribbing one another in fun, assuming Edward could not understand. He turned away from them and soon stopped listening, plagued by concern for Henri. He hoped his friend would fare better in the coming days, but the churning sea before the bow reminded him of how unhappy, how desperate Henri seemed, grasping at any hope to avenge Dupont no matter how tenuous or small. Despite his concern for his friend, Edward was glad to step onto the boat and off the sand of Egypt. With any luck, perhaps Henri could come to Santorini and take a break from the stress of Egypt for a while.

As the ship took to open water, he focused on the horizon. Everything about this moment calmed him. His doubts fled while the salt wind tugged at his hair, the open water ahead his only companion. His focus was on this one moment and taking it all in. Eventually, as darkness shrouded the day, the wind chilled him, and he quit to his cabin to freshen up before he looked for John and Catherine Briggs.

The ship was built for efficiency more than comfort, and his compact quarters were evidence of that. His berth had a bed, a wardrobe, and a washbasin expertly placed into as tight a space as possible. In the glass over the basin, he noted his eye had improved from his fight the other night. Smiling, he was thankful that Davis had had the best treatment all along, despite the assertions of others.

Edward entered the lounge, which was modest but comfortable, with whitewashed walls and navy blue leather chairs set about small tables. There were a half-dozen other men seated around the room, mostly middle managers from the look of them. Several were older Greek men whose leathery faces showed years spent working in the sun. Edward noticed the men's eyes glancing at one table in the far corner—the table where Catherine sat with her father.

He walked over to join them, and John shook his hand. "Thank you for inviting us to come see your excavation."

As Edward kissed Catherine's hand, he was in a reverie of how lovely she looked. She wore a bottle-green dress with cream lace insets. The color of her dress and the emerald dangling from her choker made her eyes appear more gray and stormy, as if Nephele, the Greek nymph of the clouds, had possessed her.

John's voice snapped him back to reality. "I still find it extraordinary that de Lesseps is funding the archaeological excavation when construction of the canal is already so far behind. By their initial estimates, the canal should be complete by now."

Edward sat opposite Catherine as a waiter offered him a glass of whiskey, which he accepted. "There are some who feel that proper excavation of the site will assist with public relations and financial backing for the project."

John lifted one brow whilst furrowing the other. "With all due respect, there is far too much at stake for a few old pots to sway England's disapproval of the project."

"No offense taken." Edward smiled and dropped his voice to a whisper. "I, too, harbor doubts about the efficacy of that premise, but it is not my decision, and I am happy to work on a project such as this. Our findings are quite remarkable, both artistically and sociologically."

Catherine asked, "What is artistically remarkable about the site?"

"Ah. You will see soon enough. It is impossible to describe."

"How mysterious. I look forward to seeing it."

Conversation turned around various aspects of the site, with Edward explaining the mechanics of archaeological excavation, and the types and numbers of laborers the project used.

Edward saw Catherine sit straighter as she asked, "Does your project use labor from the Corvee?"

John's eyes widened. "Now, Catherine, I am sure Mister Tyrington does not want to discuss the details of the contract for the laborers."

Edward smiled, inspected his glass of whiskey for a moment, and tilted his head. "I am surprised you know of the Corvee. Most who work for the Suez Canal Company, let alone an outsider, are not interested in the labor agreement between France and Egypt. However, since the site is in Greece, I do not believe the Corvee applies." In truth, Edward did not know whether the Corvee applied to his work. That was an issue for those above him. Hopefully, deflection would divert whatever storm appeared to be brewing in her. "We are using labor from the local quarry. They assign the workers to me for this project."

"I apologize if I offended you with such a direct question." She looked down at her hands.

John cut in, a touch of velvet to his voice. "I am afraid my daughter is spoiled by so much time with me and the free discourse we share. I have neglected enforcing the more subtle rules of etiquette. She has suffered from my willingness to be so easy on her." He chuckled and gave her a rather patronizing look.

Edward cringed inwardly at John's condescension, but he forced a smile to move beyond the moment. "Actually, candor is an admirable quality, since it is so rare to know what someone truly thinks. Discerning a person's motivations through all the verbiage can be quite tiring, as I am sure you know, Mr. Briggs. Plain-speaking is nothing to be ashamed of and quite worth cultivating."

John's smile grew wide. "I am glad you feel that way. But if you will excuse me, it is getting late, and I should retire. Perhaps you would be so kind as to accompany Catherine on a stroll on the deck? She has always been more of a night owl than I."

Edward saw the briefest flash of surprise in Catherine's eyes toward John and almost laughed. In her haste to recover her own composure, she failed to notice Edward's brief smile and said, "Yes, Mister Tyrington, if you have a moment, I would enjoy the night air."

The evening was cool, and they walked to the aft of the ship to take a respite from the wind. As they strolled, Edward asked, "How do you come to travel with your father on business?"

"I present value to him in that I am careful with numbers and understand the legal framework of business. Since I am his only child, he uses me to my fullest capacity. Father is far too practical to let my sex stand in the way of his use of competent help. It is easier for him than trusting the family business to someone who is not blood."

"Would you not prefer to live a life of ease? Business in the Ottoman Empire seems a rather hard life for an Englishwoman."

As they reached the rail, Catherine turned to him, her jaw set firmly. "Needlepoint was never my long suit, Mister Tyrington; I prefer to be useful in the world."

Sensing her discomfort, Edward abandoned that course of conversation, and they fell silent for a time. The reflection of the low moon over the water, with the sound of the Mediterranean dividing around the ship, was mesmerizing. They watched the ship's wake part white and spread across the still sea. As they stood side by side with their hands on the rail, their hair, and the edging of her dress, tugged about in the breeze. It was not long before a lighthouse came into view in the distance.

Catherine asked, "What light is that?"

"If I am not mistaken, that is Gavdos, off the southern coast of Crete. We should arrive in Santorini by midmorning."

She turned to him. "Thank you for this sojourn, but there are things I must attend to before we arrive. It is time for me to retire."

Edward made to walk her back to her cabin, but she continued, "I can find my way back to my cabin. Stay here and enjoy the night air. Good night."

Chapter Thirteen

The next morning, Edward arose early and stood on the deck peering through the gray predawn mist, waiting for Santorini to come into view. His mind vacillated between what he must do when he returned to work, Dupont's murder, and concern that the wrong man might be executed for the crime.

As the sun climbed higher in the sky, his concerns faded, and he reveled in the surrounding beauty. The water shone a brilliant cobalt blue, fading through a thousand other hues that only Poseidon himself knew the names of. He watched as small islands marched by, some arid hills rising from the water while others appeared as ghosts on the horizon that drifted away into the haze. Something in Edward's heart stirred at the ghostly islands. They reminded him of the past year of his life and how the awkward wedge of grief can smother friendships and acquaintances.

As the boat surged forward, the tiny dot that was Santorini grew. Edward smiled at the contrast of crisp white with the varyingly colored cliffs. He realized, from a distance, the crest of the hillside appeared to be covered with snow that blanketed the upper slopes up to the edge of the cliff. As the boat neared the island, the white blanket showed its true nature as clusters of buildings that rose almost vertically along the wall of rock. The largest of these was a church with a barrel roof and three large bells.

The cliffs before him told a story of hot, volcanic eruptions and flows washing over the landscape as a sea of lava and, at times, as a fall of ash. Successive layers baring their souls in hues of black, gray, and red ignited his desire to study and understand them.

As they drew closer, he saw the small caves carved into the ash of the cliff. Wind had cut some, while others had been hollowed out by men as a place to shelter from the sun near the isolated beaches. He waited impatiently for Akrotiri Lighthouse to come into view high on the eastward cliff. Against the stilled black lava beneath, it stood stark white, still winking into the morning light.

When they arrived at the port, it was a whirl of activity. Workers immediately beset the freighter to unload its cargo as Edward and Davis disembarked with John and Catherine Briggs. The smell of fish hung in the air as fishermen unloaded their early morning catch before sailing out for more.

As their baggage was unloaded, Davis arranged for their trip to the city at the top of the cliff by donkey. It was less than ideal, but was the only conveyance available due to the steepness of the terrain.

Catherine appeared unsettled by the prospect of riding sidesaddle on such a beast up the near-vertical trail that switched back and forth up the cliff, but as the only other choice was to walk, she clenched her teeth and put on a brave face. John had trouble mounting his donkey, but the locals helped and escorted their passengers up the path alongside each animal. Edward tried to make conversation with Catherine to keep her mind off the cliff next to the trail, but she barely responded. It was clear she was focused on maintaining her grip on the saddle horn.

After a half-hour ride on the switchback trail, they reached the top and entered a small city of winding paths and an untold number of stairs that meandered up and down the upper portion of the cliff face. They dismounted their donkeys, paid the owners, and set off into town.

There were no carriages here, as most of the walkways were composed of stairs, but it was only a short walk to their hotel, and with the aid of some porters to carry the luggage, the stroll was lovely, and the views of the small island, Nea Kameni, at the center of the volcano's submerged caldera were breathtaking. After they walked the Briggses to their hotel, Edward and Davis went to the far edge of town to procure a carriage to take to their home, which was tucked into the hillside near the excavation site.

Edward's house was one story, white stucco, with an entry that opened into a small dining area with a thick-plank wooden table and chairs. To the right was a comfortable sitting room with the bedrooms off the far end. Beyond the table was a small but bright kitchen, with a courtyard alongside. The courtyard was larger than most of the rooms of the house. It was clearly meant to be an important area for entertaining, with settees under the olive and almond trees. There was a large table, a small outside brasserie, and a large arbor covered in deep-green ivy. It was grander than most accommodations on his expeditions, and Edward was well pleased with it.

Davis brought the bags in, and Edward left to find Patros, his assistant at the dig site, to see what progress they had made.

Chapter Fourteen

Wildflowers and vineyards surrounded the excavation site at the top of the bluffs above the red sand beach. It was a pleasant walk from his house, with exceptional views of the sea. As he approached, Patros was working with one excavation crew in the eastern portion of the site, while Asim and Gahiji, his Egyptian foremen, worked with a crew further to the north.

Patros was a middle-aged man with a broad, hawksbill nose that ended between two incised lines around his mouth. The sun had been his companion his whole life, and his skin had a leathery texture that reminded Edward of his mother's favorite riding boots. He had more salt than pepper in his hair and the darkest eyes Edward had ever seen. His intimidating appearance was at odds with his gentle spirit, but that did not prevent him from using his looks to great effect from time to time.

The quarry operation had started here but then ceased in this area to allow for the archaeological excavation. Since that time, his crews had found several stone walls delineating various rooms and buildings. Most of the walls they found were rough-hewn from stone, a sharp contrast to the soft, volcanic ash that encased the village.

As the excavation continued, the series of walls revealed a large, ancient settlement with small rooms and narrow alleys. They had begun digging in several areas but focused on two locations early on: the West House and a building they had named Ladies' House due to the feminine theme of the frescoes. These were larger than other dwellings they had excavated and were discovered early on since they towered above the rest of the settlement. Ladies' House was next to the triangular town plaza and was the only building they had discovered with smooth blocks for walls. Edward surmised that someone important had lived there.

The uppermost floor of Ladies' House included frescoes of ladies gathering flowers and water with swallows flying overhead. The ash and dry climate preserved the frescoes, so their colors of deep burgundy, blue, and gold were almost as brilliant as they were the day the volcano erupted. Edward's crews removed layer upon layer of ash by wheelbarrow and dumped it from the bluff onto the beach below.

When Patros walked over, he smiled and shook Edward's hand. "What happened to your eye? I told you to be careful in Egypt."

It surprised Edward that Patros could see the injury, but then again, Patros surprised him in many ways. Edward rebuffed the question. "It only added to the adventure. How have things been here?"

Patros gave him a summary of their progress and then said, "There is one problem that I am concerned about." He called to Asim and waved him over. Asim left his crew and hurried along toward them, his trowel in hand and his galabia floating in the light breeze behind him. When he arrived, Patros said, "Tell him what happened."

Asim said hello and launched directly into his story. "I came to the dig site the other night." Patros shot Edward a meaningful look as Asim continued. "I know I wasn't supposed to be here by myself. But I couldn't sleep, and I didn't think there would be any harm in coming for a walk. I was sitting on the rock ledge overlooking the site when I saw something moving near the West House. It seemed to be a young boy wandering through the site. I figured he was curious, and he didn't seem to do any harm. He wandered through the site and left on the path that goes down the bluff toward the beach. The next morning I was on the scaffolding cleaning the window openings of West House when the scaffolding collapsed. I chalked it up to bad construction—"

"Until I saw the lashing," Patros intervened. He brought Edward to his worktable and pulled a section of lashing from the drawer. "The lashes tying the scaffolding together had been partially severed. You can see where a knife cut through most of the thickness and where it frayed under the weight on the scaffolding."

"Asim, are you all right?" Edward stared at him looking for some sign of injury.

"Yes, I clung to the window ledge, and the workers put a ladder under me so I could climb down."

Edward breathed a sigh of relief. "You think the boy did this on purpose? To what end? The boy was probably just having a prank."

Patros shrugged. "I don't know what to think. But it is not beyond possibility that someone would want to sabotage the work here."

"That seems farfetched. What would be gained by sabotage?"

"I don't need to tell you that the Suez Canal is unpopular in some corners of the world. Sabotage is a possibility."

"I suppose you are right, but for what purpose? We are in Greece, not Egypt. If they want to sabotage the canal, it seems the location of the project would be a better starting place."

"Unless this was simply a convenient place to weaken the operation."

"Patros, we are on a remote bluff on a remote island hundreds of miles from Egypt. There is nothing convenient about this place." Edward smiled for a moment and then scowled. "But I am concerned for the safety of our workers. Should we tell the police? They can guard the site."

Patros let out a great belly laugh. "It's clear you've never met the Greek police. No. Do not breathe a word about this to anyone. Only time will tell if this was a random act or deliberate. In the meantime, Asim and I have kept this secret from the workers. We don't need to make them afraid to work here."

"Agreed. Asim, please inspect all the scaffolding and wall bracing before work each day."

"I have been, sir."

Edward dismissed Patros to his other duties away from the excavation and put Asim and Gahiji in charge of the two crews.

Not long after they got settled on their tasks, the wind rose, and the fine ash blew everywhere. Edward covered his face with a scarf to keep the ash from pelting his nose and mouth as he cleaned frescoes.

The walls were almost ready for Julian Arnout to photograph, but issues with the workers slowed Edward's pace. They needed constant supervision and encouragement, or their work slowed to almost nothing. He wondered if their work would go backward and fill in the site if he were not pushing them to excavate it. Shaking his head, he thought of ways to improve their progress.

That afternoon, the wind stilled, and the air was a perfect temperature. All the workers seemed focused on their tasks when he heard men call out from Asim's group. Their words were a mystery to Edward, but he understood the frisson of excitement that charged their voices. He ran over to join them.

In the pit, they had excavated a stairway to a floor below. At the top of the exposed wall was a portion of a smooth block painted a deep red. He took out his notebook and sketched as he directed them to discover how far the painted wall continued. After several hours, they had discovered a room that had frescoes on each of the walls. Edward used the theodolite to determine the room's location in the village and measured the room's dimensions as they excavated to reveal more of the painting.

As Edward worked, angry shouts rose from the other crew working under a tarpaulin on the West House. Edward ran over as two men squared off, one with a knife, the other with a shovel. The remaining workers had circled around them, reminding Edward of the fights at his boarding school playground. Gahiji seemed at a loss for how to stop the violence.

Edward broke through the circle and stood between the two men, one hand up toward each one as if he were ready to push them apart. He spoke to them in English. "There is no need for violence."

Asim translated, and there was shouting between them. Edward looked at Asim, who said, "They were gambling last night. One claims the other cheated."

The worker with the knife stepped forward to stab around Edward, who grabbed his arm and wrestled with him. The worker was lean but strong after years of mining, and he pushed Edward back. Edward hooked his foot around the man's leg as he fell backward, bringing the worker down on top of him. They rolled on the ground, struggling. Asim grabbed the other man, who raised his shovel to bring down on either Edward or the worker underneath him. Edward pinned the knife-wielder beneath him and felt the blade slash at his side. It was a quick sliding sting, followed by a red gash of blood. As the pain radiated from the wound, he grabbed the worker's wrist and twisted as hard as he could until he dropped the knife and another worker grabbed his arms.

Once both of the quarrelers were under control, Edward checked his wound. It was bleeding, but not quite enough to make him stop what he was doing. He bound each of the fighter's hands with ropes from the excavation. Gahiji found Patros to take them back to the quarry foreman, Baba, who was responsible for all the workers at the excavation.

Asim said, "Sir, you're cut."

A bright red stain had spread quickly across his shirt, and Edward pulled it up to examine the wound. “It is not deep.”

“Patros should look at it. He will know what to do.”

When Patros arrived, he pulled Edward aside and growled, “What did I tell you about people here? What were you thinking? These dogs are not worth you risking your life. It’s a miracle you’re not dead!”

“Someone had to stop them. I was the first one there.”

Patros spit on the ground. “It was stupid, and you know it. Now let me look at your wound.”

Edward sighed and, knowing there was no argument that Patros would accept, lifted the side of his shirt.

“Stupid, stupid, stupid,” Patros muttered and poured water over the gash. He then pulled out a leather pouch of tobacco and pushed some leaves into the wound as Edward winced. “It serves you right that it hurts. It’s deeper than you think. The leaves will help the bleeding stop. You should put a bandage over that.”

Patros put the tobacco pouch in his pocket, collected the fighters from Asim, and escorted them to Baba’s office, muttering to himself in Greek.

Edward tied some of the cotton wadding normally used to wrap artifacts around his waist and turned to Asim. “Well, today is going swimmingly.”

Asim tilted his head. “What is ‘swimmingly’?”

“Never mind.”

Chapter Fifteen

When the dinner hour came, Edward plodded back to his house, as he focused on the stones beneath his feet. The gray of the ashen soil suited his mood. His mind was a cadence of all the reasons why he was a failure: his inability to control his workers, his inability to plan for unruliness. He picked up a large black stone and threw it into the field as he thought of his rejection at Oxford. *Perhaps they were right about me.*

As darkness descended, Henri's words came to him. They were a whisper at first: *Of course I chose you for this project. You studied under Guiseppie Fiorelli for God's sake...* Edward's mind tried to chase the words away, but they came back again and again. Each time louder, each time more insistent. Edward did know more about archaeological excavations in ash than most in his field. As he approached his home, the light through the windows, small at first but growing larger, seemed à propos of Henri's voice in his head.

As soon as he entered, Davis started, "That was a dangerous situation you were in today, sir."

And with that, Edward's doubts returned. He passed Davis to go to his room. "I understand your concern for my wellbeing, but I am fine."

Davis called to his back. “Did you clean your wound?”

Edward stopped and sighed.

Davis came over and helped Edward remove his jacket. “We should clean your wound. Please let me see it.” Davis helped Edward remove his shirt and undershirt. He removed the cotton wadding from Edward’s waist and saw the leaves in the wound. “What is this?”

“Patros put tobacco in the wound to stop the bleeding.”

“More wives’ tales and magic medicine.” Davis clucked his tongue. “Please lie on your stomach on the sofa so I can clean out the wound, sir.”

Edward went to the sofa and lay down, and Davis got a cloth from the kitchen and dabbed the wound. Once he removed the tobacco, the bleeding started again, and Edward held the cloth over it.

“The wound is several inches long and rather deep in the center. It needs to be sutured, sir.”

“Be that as it may, I doubt the medical knowledge here extends beyond tobacco leaves, so we will have to leave it at that.”

Davis rose and went to the other room. He returned with a handsome black leather physician’s bag and a fresh undershirt. Putting them down, he went to the spirits table and poured a large glass of whiskey, which he placed on the table next to Edward.

Edward rose onto his elbows. “Where on earth did you get that bag?”

“It was a gift from your father.” He unpacked the items. “During your first expedition to Africa, your father worried about you. He told me that any minor injury that could be healed in London could be life threatening in Africa because of the lack of medical expertise. The entire time you traveled, he worried—until he devised a plan. At first I was resistant to it, but he made me see the sense in it." He took out a bottle of carbolic acid and rinsed a needle and catgut thread in the solution.

"Drink some whiskey while I finish my story, sir. It will help deaden the pain. Your father's plan was for me to study under Dr. Sanderson."

"At University College in London? You are joking."

"Your father convinced him to take me on as a student and to instruct me at night."

Edward took a large swig of whiskey. It warmed his throat, and he wiped his mouth as the story suddenly made sense. "The endowment."

Davis threaded the needle. "Yes, the endowment to the medical college ultimately convinced Dr. Sanderson. I would visit him two nights a week, and he would teach me medical techniques useful to keep you safe in areas where there is no medical care to speak of. Those included many lessons on how to suture wounds. It was your father's plan for me to join you on your next expedition, which is what happened, but not quite as he had envisioned."

The strain in Davis's voice made Edward roll back onto his stomach to keep his valet from seeing the tears that stung his own eyes. He remembered arguing with his father at length about his expeditions, his father imploring him to abandon his chosen path and settle down with a good woman and prominent teaching position. He had never wanted to teach until his father died and everything changed.

Hearing of the care his father had taken to allow him to live his rather unorthodox lifestyle and still provide him with some relative safety filled him with gratitude and a deep sense of loss. His discussion with Davis only compounded Edward's sadness and anger. They both bore the weight of his father's absence, and in that moment, the room filled with the emptiness he had left.

Edward took a deep swig of whiskey and cleared his throat. "Well then, Dr. Davis, you had best get on with it."

"One of the last nights I was at the college, Dr. Joseph Lister came to visit and showed us a technique of using carbolic acid to clean the needle and suture material to prevent infection. He taught us that foul air is not the source of infection, but rather the presence of micro-organisms discovered by Louis Pasteur. His initial results are promising, and the last I heard, he was continuing the study. The process he showed us is the process I am using now."

He finished his preparations. "This is going to hurt a bit, sir, but the closed wound will keep out infection."

Edward clenched his teeth and winced as the needle entered his skin. He drank more whiskey as Davis worked and finally tied off the sutures. As he dressed the wound with a bandage sprayed with carbolic acid, someone pounded on the door. Edward finished wrapping the wound while Davis answered the door.

Baba stormed into the house. He was a short man with a large belly and a smooth, bald head. His round face was contorted in anger. "What do you mean by fighting with my workers?"

Edward raised his hand in protest, "I was not fighting, I was trying to—"

"I don't care what you were *trying* to do. What you *did* was leave my workers alone to start trouble, and then you got yourself stabbed."

Edward held his side as he stood, then winced as he put on a clean undershirt. Through clenched teeth, he said, "I was not stabbed; it is a scratch. And my intention was to keep them from killing each other."

"Let me make myself clear. These are my workers. I loan them to you because I have to. I don't care who you're the son of, or who has asked you to come here. I have a quarry to run, and you have brought nothing but trouble since you arrived."

"As I said, I was trying to keep them from killing each other."

"You keep them from killing each other by not leaving them alone! Even for a minute. Do you understand?"

Edward knew arguing with him was pointless, and the word *yes* crossed his lips like flint on steel, ready to ignite the fire of his temper. Baba turned and slammed the door behind him as he blustered out.

Edward sighed and sat down. After a few moments, he said, "Thank you, Davis, for your willingness to learn the medical arts and for taking good care of me. It has been a rather exciting day. I think I will forgo dinner and retire."

Davis focused on cleaning his instruments and said, "I would not recommend it, sir."

"Excuse me?"

"More than half the crew thinks you are a meddling Englishman who deserved the injury you received today." He continued his work and spoke without looking at Edward. "The other half thinks you are on death's door because of your wound. To not show your face at dinner will only increase those rumors and the animosity behind them."

Edward ran his hand through his hair and sighed. "Then I suppose you had better dress me for dinner. And I will try not to ruin these clothes."

Davis gave a small smile. "I should hope so, sir. And please do not overexert yourself, or the sutures will come apart."

"I will be careful. Thank you, Davis...for everything."

Once dressed, Edward walked to the cafeteria. His mind was reeling from the events of the day and the knowledge of Davis's surreptitious education. During his walk, he stopped repeatedly to swallow a few extra slugs of whiskey from his flask to keep the throbbing of his wound manageable.

He reached the dining hall halfway through dinnertime. As he entered, most of the workers were there, and they all fell silent. Edward breathed through the loud beating of his heart as he crossed the room. He made his way toward Patros, and the sound began again, first as whispers, then as normal conversation after he sat.

Patros smirked. "Well, you've made quite a name for yourself."

Edward buttered his bread. "That was not my intent, but seems correct."

"Baba was angry with you."

"Yes, I am aware of that. He visited my lodgings."

"He'll get over it. Give him a day to see reason. He is like a thunderstorm, all crashing noise until he finishes, and then the sun comes out."

They ate their meal in silence, and although his side pained him, Edward returned to the work site that evening to continue cleaning the frescoes rather than sit at home.

He lit several lanterns to combat the dark while he worked. No one else worked on this portion of the project, since it was too easy to damage the paintings. He cleaned the ash from the paint with brushes and a gentle wipe with water to remove the finest particles. The wet ash smelled like heaven to him, like the last mile of a long hike when one knows that rest and accomplishment are soon to be savored.

The frescoes were astounding to behold. Each scene covered the entire wall of the room. One wall depicted a woman with dark, soulful eyes that touched Edward at his core and left him breathless. Who was she? He hoped she had left before the volcano had erupted.

The fresco on the west wall depicted a field of grain with birds flying overhead. The birds appeared to be sparrows passing a stalk of grain, one to the next, midflight.

On the south wall was a fresco depicting two women, one of whom had her dark hair pulled back and expressive dark eyes. The other woman's head had a blue scarf with a topknot. They were in a field of saffron crocuses that they harvested into baskets.

However, the north wall was the gleaming gem in the collection. On it was a raven-haired woman with delicate curls that flowed over her shoulders and down her back. She wore a golden, short-sleeved jacket with dark spots and a white-striped shirt. Her left arm had three bracelets and her right had two. She sat on an elevated cushion.

The woman's right hand stretched to receive a saffron crocus from a blue monkey standing on hind legs before her. Behind the monkey, a woman with a look of pure adoration on her face poured saffron crocuses into a basket near the seated woman. After studying the entire room, Edward surmised that the seated woman was likely a goddess receiving an offering.

He sat before her and relaxed. This was his favorite moment. Time spent alone with his discovery, alone with the beauty of the past to catch him in its spell. In one way, every excavation was the same for him. In the coming weeks, there would be puzzles to unravel and papers to write. But tonight it was she and he, alone and bound by a love of beauty across hundreds, if not thousands, of years.

After he absorbed the beauty of it, he began a detailed drawing of the north wall. He measured everything and drew it all in proper proportion. There remained a few feet of ash at the bottom of the wall, but he could add those details once they had excavated the rest of the room.

Late into the night, Edward finished what he could. As he drew, a plan to deal with the slow pace of work at the site finally came to him. He left and made the proper arrangements for the next day.

Chapter Sixteen

The next day around midmorning, Davis arrived at the site according to Edward's plan, with two bags. Edward and Davis unpacked them on a central table used for cleaning artifacts. Edward lined up flat breads, dried meat, and fruit and asked Asim to call the workers together and interpret for him.

"Your work recently is slower than when we started, and it occurs to me that your lack of energy is because of a lack of food. I have purchased fruits and dried meats for you to each carry with you during your day, to eat as you need to keep your strength up. Hopefully, this will increase our pace and allow more work to be completed each day. I will continue this practice as long as I see an improvement in your work. If your work returns to the current pace, I will no longer supply extra rations."

There were smiles all around as the men crowded Edward to get their share. As they returned to work, Asim said, "That was generous of you, sir."

"It is unfair for me to receive twice the rations of the workers. I know asking Baba for more food would get us nowhere, so I took matters into my own hands." Edward prayed this would work and his bribe would give him better control of the crew. Perhaps a personal gift that could be rescinded was the ticket to obedience.

After their break, the workers returned to their tasks invigorated. Edward was overseeing his crew when Gahiji came to tell him a woman was outside.

Edward muttered, "Blast it." Then told Gahiji, "Tell Miss Briggs I will be there in a few minutes."

When he wiped his hands and left the room, his jaw fell open.

There before him stood his Aunt Inez, looking as shocked as he felt. "Edward, what happened to your eye?"

Edward stammered as he squinted in the bright sunlight. "Aunt...Aunt Inez?"

Inez was from short, sturdy stock. Had she worn a plain muslin dress, she would easily be mistaken for a farmer's wife. Her hair was gray with some remnants of mousey brown, and her arms were thick like two ham hocks, but there was strength underneath. There was no corseting her portly midriff and, as Edward recalled, no stopping the tide of opinions that periodically flooded from her mouth.

He recovered and hugged her. "Aunt Inez, what brings you to Santorini?"

"I came to see how you are faring here in the east. I see I am a bit too late to keep you from whatever trouble gave you that bruise. Boys of your station should not be roughhousing."

"I am not a boy, Aunt Inez, and it is nothing. When did you arrive?"

She gave him an incredulous look. "It is clearly something, but regardless, Francine and I arrived this morning. It was a beautiful journey from Marseille. The captain of the ship was handsome and attentive; there is little else a woman of my years requires."

Edward searched his memory and came up short. "Who is Francine?"

"You remember her. Your father and her mother were second cousins. She lives in Bristol and came to the Essex estate for Christmas several years when you were children. It has been too long, and you should get acquainted."

"Is that the sole reason you brought her here?"

"Do not be silly, darling. We are on a grand adventure. She will begin her second season soon, and it is time she saw the world."

His innards rolled. *Courting seasons. How glad I am to be away from England right now.* "How long are you staying?"

She gave him a sideward glance. "Trying to get rid of me already? I will be here for at least a week. I have not yet decided. It depends on how the town suits us, and it has been too long since I have seen you. We need to spend some time together."

Edward's jaw tightened. "Yes. And we will. But right now, I am preparing the site for visitor tours, coupled with a ball to announce the discoveries we have made. The ball is in several days, so we do not have much time left to prepare."

"I know about de Lesseps's ball and have already secured an invitation. We cannot have a gala event in your honor without some family represented."

He clenched his jaw into something resembling a smile. Or at least he hoped so. The words "a gala event in your honor" were enough to make him consider not attending the ball himself. Rather than discuss it further, he changed the subject. "I see you are as efficient as ever, Aunt Inez. Very good. I will have my man prepare a room for you at my home."

She shook her head. "Unnecessary. I have secured lodgings in town. I prefer to stay where I can have a view of the sea and am in the bustle of people. Your lodgings are too remote out here for my liking."

Thank God for that. He thought. She told him the name of her hotel, and they arranged for dinner later that evening.

Later that afternoon, Julian Arnout arrived at the excavation site. He was an average-looking man with gray hair and skin of leather from his years photographing the Suez Canal site. His assistant was a bookish young man, lean and small, who seemed to spring at the merest mention of his name. They arrived at the site with all manner of photographic equipment.

"I hope you do not mind, Mister Tyrington, but I wanted to get started as soon as possible."

Edward showed him some discoveries he had made, saving the frescoes for last. As they entered room after room, Julian remarked on the beautiful discoveries. In the goddess room, Julian gave a low whistle and stared.

At long length, he said, "Edward, this is magnificent! Such detailed artwork, such beautiful ladies." He leaned closer to the wall. "And such expressive eyes."

"Yes, their eyes are..." But words failed him, and it seemed that Julian understood why. They both stood a few moments longer.

Julian turned and surveyed the room. "The light in here is terrible. We will need to gather as many lanterns as we can to illuminate the walls—mirrors too, if there are any to be had."

Edward had Asim and another worker fetch the necessary items. While they waited, Edward and Julian worked to photograph the pottery he had discovered in an outside area where the light was better. Once the lanterns arrived, they arranged them with the mirrors to create the proper light for photographing the room. When they finished, the room resembled the inside of a kaleidoscope.

As the evening darkened, Julian photographed the frescoes. Once he had catalogued two of the walls by individual elements and as a whole, he asked Edward to sit for a photograph. It was a surreal scene in the flickering light and ancient paintings, one that brought to mind how the original inhabitants of this village had lived.

They had completed the last photograph when voices rose in the darkness outside. Edward recognized them as Patros with John and Catherine Briggs.

Edward jumped up and went to the doorway to greet them. "This is a surprise. So nice to see you." He dipped his head to kiss Catherine's hand, and she stared in awe at the wall.

John said, "We planned to be here earlier but were delayed. We saw Mr. Patros in town, and he invited us to visit since he knew you were working."

Catherine took two steps toward the fresco, her eyes opened wide as if to capture more of the beauty before her. "I have never…I…It is beautiful."

John, who also appeared to be rather dumbstruck, nodded.

She turned to Edward. "How old is it?"

Edward smiled. "Absolute dates are impossible to know at this stage. But no civilization like this is described in the literature up to this point, so I surmise it is ancient, one thousand years or more. One thing I know: they traded with Africa."]

"How do you know that?"

He pointed to the east wall. "There are no monkeys in Greece or in the rest of Europe. They must have traded in places where they saw monkeys. Africa is a natural assumption."

John said, "Astounding."

Edward showed them more of his discoveries, including other small frescoes and several urns for grain and wine.

"There are some who believe Troy was an actual place," John said. "Perhaps this place was part of a myth as well?"

"It is possible. I have studied Mediterranean mythos and even asked the locals for their stories, but nothing I have heard seems to fit our discoveries here. It seems these people were here before the Greeks, but who they were or where they came from remains a mystery."

They discussed the various cultures of the region as Edward showed them more of his discoveries. After a while, Edward excused himself to dine with Aunt Inez and Francine, and Patros saw John and Catherine back to their hotel.

When Edward arrived, Inez and Francine were occupying a table by the fire in the dining room. Inez was holding court with an older gentleman who stood at the hearth. She was saying, "...and then there was the time I rode a camel in Egypt—Oh, there is my nephew. Edward, come join us."

She introduced Edward, and seeing his opportunity to leave, the gentleman made a rather hasty retreat under the guise of giving them privacy to reacquaint themselves. Inez then introduced Edward to Francine.

Francine had witch-black hair that tumbled in a profusion of ringlets on her sloping porcelain shoulders. Her dress was a dark navy, which made her pale face and arms almost glow against the darkness of fabric and hair. Her nose was rather turned up in a way that suggested a snobbish demeanor and detracted from an otherwise pleasing face. She greeted Edward, but there was little enthusiasm behind it.

Inez was bubbly and delightful throughout dinner to counteract the quietude of her niece. Inez told of her travels across the Continent since she had last seen Edward and shared several flattering stories about Francine. It was clear from the outset that Inez was seeking a match for her niece. Francine added little to the conversation and almost seemed a bystander as her life was recounted before her.

Pity flooded Edward's heart. *What has she done to be a satellite to Aunt Inez?* He resolved to find out during their stay and perhaps ease her mind a bit. After dessert and a glass of port, Edward excused himself to return home.

On his way, he walked through the excavation site, as had become his custom. His mind was fitful, wandering through thoughts of Inez and her matchmaking, murder, and motive. Finally his mind settled on Catherine. She was by far the most unique woman he had ever known, and although he sometimes found her to be quite maddening, sometimes she enchanted him in ways he had never considered possible.

As he strode across the work area, he noticed a new pot off to the side of the most recent area of excavation. Edward looked it over. It was a small amphora with handles on each side and a design of lotus flowers painted in deep red on the natural tan of the clay. He resolved to look at it in the morning and went home for the night.

The next morning, the sooty smell of the kitchen fires snatched Edward from sleep. *They must be training a new cook who does not know how to light a proper fire.* Although he was thankful for an early start to his day, he had slept poorly, and his mood matched the inky grayness of the predawn sky. Rather than disturb Davis, he dressed himself and took some fruit and bread to eat as he walked to the work site.

He stopped near a cliff and ate figs as he watched the sun struggle from the grip of the Aegean. The sky and the sea were spectacular, bathed in blues and grays, with a shock of orange balanced between them and rising fast. He stood a while longer, pushing his troubles from his mind as he watched the waves move back and forth. The beauty of it settled his mind in a better frame for the day ahead, and he moved on when he heard the voices of workers at the site.

When he arrived, he walked to the pot he had seen the night before. This morning it lay shattered quite a distance from where he'd last seen it.

As he studied the pieces, a shadow crossed his view. He looked up to find Asim.

"Have you taken to breaking pots now, sir?"

Edward stood. "I was going to ask you that, Asim. I came last night and found this pot, whole, over there. And this morning I find it broken over here."

"Could an animal have gotten it?"

"I doubt it. There is no scent to attract an animal, and unless something threw it, I cannot explain how it got over here." Edward looked at the ground. "There are no marks on the ground to indicate they dragged it." Edward sighed. "It was a beautiful specimen too. Oh well. Let us collect the pieces and prepare for today's activities."

He then returned to cleaning more of the frescoes in the room. It was slow, detailed work, but each wipe with a damp sponge, each small puff of air blown through a reed, revealed new beauty in the walls. He had uncovered more crocuses with their delicate stamens in hues of gold when he heard frantic shouts from the cliff where they dumped the excavated ash.

Chapter Seventeen

Edward and several others ran to the bluff's edge and looked over the edge to the beach below. At the base of the cliff, there was a man lying face up, his arms splayed from his body and his legs half buried, his black frock coat a stark contrast to the light gray ash mound that held him perched above the red sand beach like some offering to the ancient gods.

Edward yelled to Patros to get the police as he raced to the nearest path that led to the beach below. He ran across the hard sand and began climbing the ash mound. His feet sank into the loose ash, and the climb took longer than it should have, his mind impatiently willing himself faster. As he approached the body, he saw he was European—an Englishman, from the long muttonchop sideburns and moustache, which seemed to be all the fashion there lately. The coldness of his skin confirmed he had been dead for some time.

A steadiness grew within Edward, as if understanding the circumstances of his death overrode the shock of seeing the body itself. He knelt down and looked at his face. The pupil of the man's left eye was far more dilated than the pupil of the right. There were no obvious cuts, knife marks, or significant blood, but there was a dent on the left side of his scalp. *Did that happen from the fall, or was he struck and then fell?* He looked up to see if there were rocks jutting from the sea cliff and instead saw a line of faces, his workers, looking down at him.

Patros yelled, "Is he dead?"

Edward nodded, and the workers' voices buzzed like a hive of bees. Patros focused on getting them under control as Edward continued to inspect the body.

He searched the jacket pockets but found no watch or wallet, just a red pocket square, a silver pen, and a crumpled catalogue advertisement for a pair of dress gloves, but nothing to identify him.

Edward took the dead man's hands into his own. The flesh was cold, but also smooth. These were the hands of a man of some means, with nails that were clean and well kept. There was a long scar on the forefinger of his left hand. It looked like a burn, healed long ago.

About six feet below him on the ash mound, something small and bright glinted in the sun. Edward half-walked, half-slid down and picked up a dark shell button with a small image of an eagle etched into it. He checked the dead man's clothing. The button did not match the three buttons on the corpse's frock coat nor the buttons on his vest. Edward unbuttoned the vest to inspect his shirt. All the shirt buttons were present as well, and none matched the shell button he held.

He pocketed it, rubbed the back of his neck, and looked eastward down the beach. Julian approached with his photographic equipment. When he arrived, Edward asked, "How did you get down here with your equipment so fast?"

Julian tried to catch his breath as he set up his gear. "I arrived as the commotion started at the sea cliff. Patros told me what happened, so I came here. I thought it would be helpful to take a photograph of the body."

As Julian worked, Edward looked around the area for other clues, but there were none. *Two dead men in a few days, and one at my archaeological site.* This was not a trend that he cared to continue.

After Julian finished his photograph, two Greek army officers who were acting as the local police arrived. It surprised Edward to see the Greek police rather than the company police, but the vagaries of law enforcement on a project this massive were beyond him. They wore the traditional outfit, which included white stockings and short, white pantaloons that puffed out from the thighs almost like a skirt. The outfit was completed with a white tunic, a small purse worn around the waist, and suspenders. Edward's mouth twitched at the sight of them, but he knew to laugh would cause more problems than it was worth. The police were efficient and quickly took statements from Edward and Julian, then prepared to take the body away.

When they reached the top of the bluff, Baba was there with Patros. Patros informed Edward that he sent the workers to the cafeteria for questioning by the police. While Patros spoke, Baba glared at Edward with palpable venom, his arms crossed against his barrel chest.

Edward finally asked, "Why are you glaring at me? This is as much of a shock to me as it is to everyone else."

Baba spit at the ground. "Everywhere you go, death follows. This is what comes of digging up bones."

"We have excavated no bones, so it must be something else." Edward almost laughed. As bad as this situation was, Baba's superstitious nature was ridiculous.

Further work being impossible, he walked back to his house. When he arrived, Davis was dusting the study, and Edward informed him what had happened.

"Two men dead in such a short time," Davis said. "Do you think they are connected?"

"I do not know. I am at a loss to explain Dupont's murder, and this man is unidentified. Patros says there are ruffians who wander the hills at night. Perhaps it was one of them. Although why a European was at the dig site, I do not know."

"You should." Davis stopped his work and turned to Edward. "You do it all the time, sir."

"Are you implying that he was an archaeologist intent on finding out what we had unearthed? That is preposterous."

Davis was quiet for a moment. "Is it, sir? De Lesseps has planned a grand ball to make an announcement about your discoveries. Is it so farfetched that someone might have heard of them and come to see for himself? Perhaps to collect an item or two from the unguarded site?"

Edward's stomach dropped at the thought of other archaeologists prowling around his excavation in the middle of the night. He wondered if this man was involved with the boy who had sabotaged the scaffolding, and he remembered the broken urn. "That still does not tell me who murdered him."

"No, but if you find out who he is, it might lead you to why he was here and who is responsible." Davis returned his focus to dusting.

"True enough."

Edward asked to have his lunch in his room while he worked on his catalogues. As he reviewed his notes, his mind buzzed with questions. He had arranged that work would begin again by midafternoon, assuming that would give the police time to perform their duties and the workers time to settle down. As he finished eating, there was a pounding on the door.

Davis opened it, and Edward could hear Patros say breathlessly, "They've arrested Asim."

Edward came to his bedroom door. "What?"

Patros spoke between breaths. "They arrested Asim for murder. They took him about a half an hour ago. I have a carriage at my house."

Edward grabbed his coat and hat, and they ran to the carriage. As they drove away, Edward saw John and Catherine walking down the path toward the excavation. He had the driver stop so he could speak to them.

"I am sorry. I forgot you were coming today. We are on our way to the police station. We found a dead man at the work site, and the police arrested one of my foremen."

John said, "We will come with you."

Edward winced. “I would not recommend it, especially for Miss Briggs. From what I have heard, a Greek police station is a rough place.”

The ferocity with which she straightened her shoulders conveyed that he should have kept quiet. “I am not afraid of the Greek police, Mister Tyrington. And our presence may be helpful. We would like to come with you.”

If Edward knew anything, it was that there was no refusing them now and to continue arguing would only delay them further.

Chapter Eighteen

The police station was as grim a place as he had imagined. There were few windows. The once-whitewashed stucco walls were now stained with a grayness of unknown provenance and had several bulletin boards with descriptions of wanted men and other information. There was a large room with a few desks in the middle piled with papers, and the stench of stale cigarette smoke filled Edward's nostrils. Offices lined one side of the room, and there was a hallway opposite from where he stood that led deeper into the building. There were several officers at desks in the main room; two were writing, and a third was asking questions of what appeared to be a farm boy. He looked young, and his hands shook as he held them together, almost as if he were praying for mercy. Rough words yelled in Greek from down the hallway startled them all. It was a brief outburst, quickly ended by a thud. Edward cringed, hoping Catherine did not speak Greek.

He glanced at her. She stood ramrod straight, her eyes wider than normal, as if she were trying to take in every potential threat at once and calculate how best to respond. She would never admit that this place frightened her, but it undoubtedly did. Her father stood by her side, looking only slightly less overwhelmed.

Edward asked a passing officer about Asim and was told that he was in a cell and only one person could see him. Edward immediately volunteered. The others found an area to wait in the front room.

Edward followed the policeman back to Asim's cell. What he saw through the bars caused his stomach to drop in horror as the jailer fumbled with the keys. Asim's face and body were bloody and bruised. There were several cuts on his legs, his eyes were swollen shut, and his mouth was bloody. Although finding Dupont was a more gruesome discovery, seeing Asim in this condition was far more horrifying. He thought of the jokes they had shared in broken English, and their mutual love of discovery. It all crashed in on Edward in one simple thought: *I should have stayed. I should have protected him. I should have...*

His heartbeat roaring in his ears, Edward was suddenly aware of how young Asim was, barely more than a boy. The officer finally opened the door, and Edward rushed in and fell to his knees next to his cot. "Asim. Asim. Can you hear me?"

A low moan was the only response.

"Asim, I do not know why they have arrested you, but I swear I will get you out of here."

A man in the next cell said, "He's about dead; don't bother with him. Get me out of here. I'll be more use to you than he ever will."

Edward ignored the comment as Asim moaned and tried to touch Edward's coat. He took Asim's hand. "I am so sorry. I should have never left the site. We will get you out of here somehow."

Edward stood and gripped the bars of the cell as if they were the neck of an officer and yelled for the policeman. A man came to let him out, and he stormed back to the front room, anger driving every stomp of his feet. A man who wore the same white outfit as the others but with the addition of a tasseled vest that seemed indicative of some rank, came out of an office.

Edward blocked his path and growled, "Why was Asim arrested?"

The officer stared at him with dull eyes as if he were swatting a tiresome fly. "He admitted he visits the site of the murder at night. We know from another worker that he was not in his tent last night, and he refuses to tell us where he was, which leads us to the conclusion he committed murder."

"That is preposterous. I was at the site last night, as were three other people. He killed no one." Edward's arms akimbo, fists clenched against his hips, he said. "I am Edward Tyrington, brother of the Earl of Essex, and I demand Asim's release at once. If he admitted anything, it is because your officers beat him bloody to get a confession. I will bring the full weight of the Crown of England to bear on your interference with my project and my workers."

"You were at the site last night, you say? Are you admitting to murder? I'd be happy to take you into custody as well. Do not threaten me. You and your brother have no jurisdiction here, and although it might be difficult to press charges against you in the long run, arresting you for murder would be most...satisfying."

Edward blanched at the implied threat. Patros, who had been watching the encounter, stood as everyone else in the room went quiet.

Catherine looked at her father, then raised her voice. "Section fifty-four part five of the Corvee states that if it is determined that a crime has been committed on company property or by company personnel, then the Suez Canal Company has sole jurisdiction over the investigation and punishment of said crime."

Patros translated her words into Greek, and everyone looked at them with stunned silence. The ranking officer pulled a coworker into an office and closed the door.

Edward looked at Catherine. "Wh... What does the Corvee say?"

"That they have no jurisdiction and cannot arrest Asim. The Corvee gives authority for investigation of crimes to the company police, not the local police, as it relates to company personnel or property."

"How on earth would you know the provisions of the Corvee?"

"I read it."

From his seat near the corner of the room, John interjected, "She does that sort of thing. She is a veritable lawyer when it comes to contracts."

"What interest could you have in the Corvee?"

"My interest, Mister Tyrington, is the treatment of the workers. I felt that, in understanding the Corvee, I could advocate on their behalf to convince managers to provide better working conditions."

Her words struck him like a slap to his face. This was a judgment of his character. An unfair assessment that should not have stung as much as it did considering the source, but it cut him to the quick. Through his shock, he leaned in and whispered, "By 'managers,' you mean me. You think so little of me?"

She held her ground and remained steadfast in her severity. She had prepared for battle in this frightening place, and if Edward had not felt so hurt, he would have admired her tenacity. Lowering her voice as her eyes stared past him, she said, "I did not know you, Mister Tyrington. England and France are colonial powers, and we are raised to treat the locals of any place on the globe as less than us, even to the point of slavery. As much as I had hoped the Corvee would provide some provision of comfort for the workers, it does not."

"And you had hoped to catch me mistreating my workers so you could save them? Never mind, do not answer that." Through clenched teeth, he spat, "You need to leave this place, Miss Briggs. I should have never brought you here."

The officer in charge had gone into his office at the mention of the Corvee and returned to say. "Indeed, the Corvee seems to prevent our involvement. I will release him to his manager."

Edward stood. "I am his manager."

"I will release him to the quarry manager."

Patros breathed. "Baba."

Catherine raised one eyebrow at Edward, her eyes ice cold. "I am sure Asim will be glad to hear they will release him." She swept past Edward.

John followed her, saying, "I am sorry. I will talk to her."

Patros stood. "I will take them back and get Baba."

Edward gave a quick nod and asked the officer to see Asim again. He knelt by Asim's cot and told him what had happened, although he was unsure himself of exactly what had just transpired.

He demanded water and a cloth from the officer and cleaned Asim's wounds. Using his pocket knife, he cut the hem of Asim's galabia to use as bandages for the worst cuts. His hands shook so hard that tying the knots proved a challenge. Asim shifted in and out of consciousness through the entire process.

Once Edward had done what he could for Asim, he waited for Baba's return. Edward's mind was a flurry of anguish but screeched to a halt at the thought of the other worker arrested for Dupont's murder. His heart ached at whether that man was beaten, and he wondered if he was even guilty of murder.

When Patros brought Baba back, Edward had steeled himself for a tirade, but when Baba saw Asim, he seemed to crumple. It was several minutes before he spoke.

He looked at each of Asim's wounds. "You cleaned and bound his wounds?"

Edward nodded.

Straightening, he said, "Since they are your fault, that is the only right thing to do."

Chapter Nineteen

Baba picked up Asim, carried him to the carriage, and laid him across one of the seats. Edward and Baba sat on the other.

Edward told Patros, "We will take Asim to my home. Davis knows the medical arts. He will know what to do." Edward and Baba glared at each other. If Baba blamed him for a fight between two workers, he could only imagine his fury now. No matter what blame Baba laid at his feet, it was far less than what he felt responsible for. *How could I be so stupid as to leave the site?* He had been so naïve to think he could just leave. It seemed he should resign to limit further failure, although he did not know how he would recover his finances without this post. Too many emotions swirled in his heart, and he knew that to speak to Baba would precipitate a fight he did not want, so he remained silent.

When they arrived, Edward carried Asim, and as they entered, Davis retrieved his medical bag. Edward placed Asim in his own bed and closed the door behind them so Davis could tend to him.

Davis was thorough. He identified each of Asim's wounds and treated them in order of severity. Edward assisted as needed, and they worked in silence until there was a bang on the front door. He heard Patros answer and then the unwelcome tone of Aunt Inez's voice.

"I will not leave until I see my nephew!"

Edward and Davis locked eyes over Asim's unconscious body before Edward turned and washed his hands in the basin. He left the room.

Patros stood in front of the bedroom door as staunch as any blockade against Aunt Inez, but he moved aside to let Edward out. Patros then entered to assist and closed the door behind him.

Inez's hair looked windblown and disheveled, and there was a wildness in her eyes that told Edward he must get control of her quickly. He spoke in his most calm and authoritative voice. "Aunt Inez, this is not a good time for a visit."

"I understand there was a murder at your work site. Are you all right?"

He took her hand and held it. "I am fine. Yes. There was a murder during the night."

"This is unacceptable. This is no place for a proper Englishman to work. And what is going on in there?"

"We are tending to an injured man."

"Did he fend off the attack that killed the other man? Why are you tending to him and not a doctor?"

Edward tried to guide her to the front door, but she used her rather considerable mass to her advantage and remained rooted to the spot. "Aunt Inez, a man is injured, and we need to help him. My man, Davis, knows the medical arts, more so than the others here, and he needs my assistance in that endeavor. Please go. I will come and explain things later, but right now my work in there is critical."

She moved toward the door. "You are sure that you are all right?"

He squeezed her hand and smiled as best he could. "Yes, I am fine. I will come see you soon." He hugged her.

Aunt Inez nodded and left.

Edward returned to the room and sent Patros to attend to the chaos that followed Asim's arrest. He helped Davis until they had attended to all of Asim's injuries, and they left him to sleep. When Edward emerged from his bedroom, the sun had descended below the horizon, dimming the world to a deep indigo twilight, which seemed appropriate. Edward was thankful he did not have to face the workers right then. He pulled the stopper off and took a swig directly from the whiskey decanter as he walked outside to drink. He clung to the last words Davis had said—"He will recover"—like a drowning man clings to a branch, while his feelings swept him into dangerous currents.

He walked down the darkened path away from the house. His feet scraped along as he slowed to drink more from the bottle. The whiskey was hot in his throat, but it was only one minor discomfort when he deserved a sea of punishment. The florid blackness of Asim's bruises beneath his dark skin filled his mind as he stopped to drink again.

The path led him to a large boulder at the top of the bluff. He pulled himself up on it and sat, drinking and staring out at the slightly darker sea. He heard the rolling waves, but they did nothing to assuage his despair. At first, they sounded like Baba yelling at him for leaving the workers alone to start a fight. Every time he left his workers alone, something horrible happened. He should have known better than to leave them.

The wind calmed a bit, and he moved closer to the edge of the rock to look down at the beach below. He drank deeply again when the wind shifted and the sound mimicked that of the sneering auctioneer counting his commission for the valuable possessions that he would sell. The footmen loaded carriages of instruments, books, furniture, all in the dead of night to limit town gossip about the fallen status of the Tyrington household. Fallen under his watch. To all outsiders, he was a foolish young man who could not manage the fortune given to him. The whispers of how he was "just like Thaddeus" echoed in his mind.

Thaddeus. He dangled his legs off the cliff side of the boulder, kicking his feet against the stone as he drank the last gulps of the whiskey, then wiped his mouth with a shaking hand. His mind's eye saw Thaddeus as a small boy; Edward was chasing him across the croquet field at Cassionberra House after Thaddeus had stolen his ball in the middle of a game. That was always Thaddeus. If he wanted your attention, he made sure he got it, usually by the least productive but most effective means. Thaddeus was a great lover of nature and had a keen interest in birds, butterflies, and caterpillars. Edward came home late from the pub one night and found him asleep at the edge of the forest, notebook on the ground with a list of animals seen, the candle guttering out beside him. Although he could barely walk himself, he carried Thaddeus back to the house.

It was only a few years later that Edward would bring him to the pub, as something akin to a mascot. The ladies he dallied with in those days thought it was sweet to bring his younger brother along, and there were enough people present that Edward could do as he pleased without his younger brother being too much of a bother. Thaddeus had known just how to ensure they invited him back. It was only later that Edward realized Thaddeus had befriended the proprietors of the best places to engage in the worst vices and no longer needed Edward's invitation. It was then that Edward saw what he had lost control of, and had unleashed. His recalled the last time he saw Thaddeus, in an opium den. Thaddeus lying on his side, his dull sunken eyes regarding him through a pipeful of smoke as he said, *Leave me! I do not need family meddling in my affairs*. Edward's desire for a coconspirator had changed the course of Thaddeus' life. For Edward, it was just a small bit of unruly fun, but it cost Thaddeus everything. .

The wind howled again. All their voices came together as a chorus of failure, a chorus of blame, enhanced by visions of Asim's broken body.

His mind's eye saw the face of the dead man. *His face was peaceful.* The moon was rising. He slid forward on the boulder and looked down.

At the base of the cliff was a field of rocks that led out to the beach. They were sufficient to end it all, even if the fifty-foot drop was not. He took a deep breath and stared at the night sky for a moment. There was no fear now, only resignation. *It is best for everyone, really.* He looked down to plan his final trajectory and slid forward a bit more.

CHAPTER TWENTY

As Edward leaned farther forward, a burst of wind and sand blew up the cliff face and pushed him back. The sand peppered his face, the grit burrowing into his pores and needling his eyes. He covered his face, leaned too far right, and lost his balance. His leg slipped as he threw himself onto his back on the rock and found a small divot to hold with his left hand. He dared not move for a moment and lay listening to the rush of his heartbeat over the wind. He slowly shifted his weight to the top of the boulder and wiped the sand from his face and eyes. When he caught his breath, he thought, *What are you doing?*

He pulled himself further back from the edge of the rock before he sat up. Edward picked up the bottle and put it to his lips, but it was empty. The wind died down, and he looked around, trying to shake the feeling of what he had almost done. He looked down at the rocks below, held the whiskey decanter out in front of him, and let go. The glass smashed on the rocks, and he shivered at the thought of his broken body in its place. When he finally moved, he took his time climbing off the rock, even though he suddenly felt very sober, and walked home.

Edward slept on the sofa since Asim occupied his bed. Davis had offered him his own bed, but Edward refused. He deserved far worse, and despite the discomfort, sleep overtook him quickly.

The next morning, he awoke with his blankets tangled around his legs. Half his body hung off the sofa, his right knee was on the ground, and his pillow was on the floor. The room was dark, with only a hint of dawn seeping between the curtains. His head pounded like a Scottish drum band, and his throat was as dry as the sands of Port Said.

His dreams still haunted him, but he could not remember the details, only that they were dark. The thought of returning to sleep was more unwelcome than rising for the day. As he stood, he swooned slightly from the change in position and the headache that plagued him.

Edward stretched, drank as much water as he could stomach, and dressed himself in the clothes that were laid out for him. A while later, Davis emerged from his room and chastised Edward for dressing himself. Edward only grunted in response as he drank his morning coffee.

Soon after, there was a knock at the door. Two policemen stood on the threshold, with bags under their eyelids and hair that appeared finger combed rather than properly cared for, as if the morning itself had beaten them into submission. The officers looked exactly as Edward felt, and a sort of kinship of understanding caught him for a brief moment. Davis asked the purpose of their call, but Edward invited them in and bade them to sit when he saw one of them was Officer Girard. "What are you doing here, Girard? Are you the only officer for the company? I expected your focus was Egypt."

"As the head of the company police, my focus is wherever my employer needs me. Since there has been a murder, my place is here. We took the fast boat over very early this morning."

Girard introduced his compatriot, Officer Fortier. Fortier was a man of average height, with nothing remarkable about him whatsoever, except that his eyes were close set and pinched, as if he were squinting when he had no cause to be.

Girard skipped the preliminaries and got right to the point. "We are here to take the suspect to a holding cell."

Edward's bloodshot eyes bored into Girard's over the lip of his cup of coffee, which he sipped with an air of deliberation, holding it with both hands, as he gathered the fortitude to deal with this latest challenge. He set down his cup and at length said, "That would be unwise. The Greek police beat Asim for information, and he needs medical attention. My man, Davis, is tending him, and he will stay here."

The officers looked at each other, and Girard said, "He can tend to him in the cell."

"That is unacceptable." Edward stood and glared at Girard. "Asim could die in a cell. He needs medical care, which will occur here and only here, unless you would like to be responsible for the death of an innocent man."

"Our orders are to bring him to a cell."

"If you move him, I will write to Monsieur de Lesseps to have you fired without a reference," Edward snarled.

Girard rubbed his knitted brow. "Let me see him. I will judge whether his wounds are as severe as you say."

Edward sat back down, as much due to his hangover as any agreement with Girard. "Davis, please escort Officer Girard to see Asim and explain his injuries."

Davis did as he was asked. They were in the bedroom for five full minutes before they returned. Girard's eyes were wide, and he was chewing his lip as he exited the bedroom. He said, "We will post a guard. He is not to leave this house. Once he is well enough, we will move him to a holding cell."

Edward stood and opened the door, implying it was time for them to leave. "That will be fine. Now I must prepare for work."

"We may be back sooner than you realize to retrieve him." Girard donned his hat, and he and Fortier left.

Edward sat with his head in his hands, and Davis poured a splash of brandy into his coffee. "The decanter of whiskey is missing, sir."

Edward did not move, shame flooding his mind from his folly the night before. "Yes, it will need to be replaced. Do you have any Dr. Bodrum's Nervous Restorative?"

Davis coughed. "I am sorry, sir, but I did not think you would approve of a purchase from a snake-oil salesman."

"Henri swears by it."

"If you would like me to purchase some..."

"Never mind. Just leave me to drink my coffee."

Later, as Edward left for the work site, a guard stood outside the door. Edward greeted the young man, but the officer only nodded in return.

The morning air shivered up his spine as he walked to the site, which helped his mind clear. He arrived before the other workers and appreciated having the time to organize his notes and his plan for the day. When the men arrived, there was much talking, and despite his initial instructions, the crew was at sixes and sevens as they started work. He asked Patros if the crew knew about Asim.

"They knew before you did."

Edward finally settled them down, and the crews set to work to brace several walls so they could dig deeper without fear of the walls collapsing. Once the bracing was complete, they began excavating again. Soon after, one group found a large round stone with a perfect hole cut in the center. The edge was incredibly smooth, and Edward concluded it was a grinding wheel. His pulse quickened to find an artifact that was so central to the daily life of the people, even as he knew de Lesseps would dismiss it as ugly. Still, it would be a perfect gift for a university in France, which is where Edward would send all the artifacts if it were his decision. He instructed his men to look for more grinding apparatus and more amphorae, which might contain stored grain.

By midmorning, Edward mustered the courage to face Aunt Inez. He sent a runner with a note to inform her he would take his lunch with her at her hotel. When he arrived, he was surprised by the size of the hotel dining room which was large and airy, with several gilt columns and open archways. Although Edward tried to hide it, the thought of dining in such opulence turned his stomach. As if she read his mind, Aunt Inez asked the waiter if there was a smaller room where they could dine privately. The waiter led her to a small room behind the main dining room fireplace. It was cozy, with small windows, a low ceiling, and dark wood tables that suited his need to hide from the world at that moment. They had a quiet lunch, and he explained all that had happened. He did not intend to share the entire story with her, but once he started, the words tumbled from him in an incessant stream until the story was done and he was spent from telling it. As he finished, Inez pulled a flask from her chatelaine and added a healthy dose of whiskey to each of their teacups.

Edward stopped and looked at her. "Aunt Inez, that is not appropriate for a lady of your station.""A lady of my station can do as she good and well pleases."

"Being widowed has given you strange ideas."

She drank a slug straight from the flask to emphasize her point. "On the contrary, it has clarified my mind. And you should not blame yourself for Asim's treatment."

Edward recoiled from her apparent clairvoyance.

"You act surprised that I should know how you feel, and yet your entire story professes guilt and self-loathing. There was no blame spared that you could place upon your shoulders, but I say there is no way you could have known, and nothing you could have done. Your only crime is expecting the police to be less corrupt, which is as they should be but apparently are not."

Edward mentally tried to dismiss what she said, but he knew her words had merit. He relaxed into the back of his chair.

Inez continued. "But returning to your story, nobody knows who the murdered man was or the motive for murder?"

"It appears he died from a blow to the head. Perhaps he simply fell from the bluff."

"Unlikely." She gave him a baleful look. "What was a well-dressed European doing wandering through an archaeology site in Greece in the middle of the night? And if he died from a fall, where is his wallet or his watch? Most men carry those things with them when they leave the house. He was not wandering about in his nightclothes, so it is reasonable to expect he would carry his wallet. It all seems quite wrong to me. And speaking of things that are wrong, tell me why you, a Tyrington, tended the wounds of an Egyptian worker accused of murder?"

Edward rubbed the back of his neck and looked out the small window onto the courtyard behind the hotel, where the bougainvillea was blooming and, in the far corner, a Greek woman chopped vegetables for the kitchen. *This is the attitude Catherine spoke of. Aunt Inez will never accept this.* "He is the foreman of one of my crews. He has been invaluable to me since I arrived. The enthusiasm with which he has taken my tutelage shows a good scientific mind. I have worked with him since my arrival, and I can tell you I know he is innocent, just as I know I am."

"I question whether you have the experience to make judgments such as that."

"That is unfair." He sat straighter.

"Be that as it may, I still question it."

He finished his spiked tea and was glad for the whiskey she added, although he would never admit it. "I must be going. I will see you again when I am able. Losing this day of work has put us even further behind."

"Of course." She held out her hand for him to kiss. "Goodbye, and please be careful."

After lunch, Edward visited Baba. His cramped office was more of a closet with files, papers, and God knew what else piled in stacks along the wall. There were long louvered vents in two walls to provide some light and air, and a small wooden desk with an oil lamp. The room smelled faintly of spiced meat, as if he routinely took meals here.

Baba groaned as Edward entered his office. "You are the last person I want to see."

"The feeling is mutual." Edward removed his hat. "But there are some things I need to know."

"Such as?" Baba sighed and continued to study the papers on his desk.

"Whether any Europeans have arrived recently by company boats."

Baba looked up from his work. "Are you now with the company police? I wasn't aware of the change in position."

Edward leaned over the desk. "There is no love lost between you and me, but Asim's life and future are at stake here. I will do all I can to find the actual murderer. If clearing his name means I must investigate behind the backs of the bungling company police, then so be it. And if you care about Asim at all, you will tell me what I need to know."

Baba's gaze tunneled into Edward's for a long moment, and he leaned back in his chair. "Ah. The strong Englishman come to save the poor worker, is that it? You think we are too deficient without your help to defend ourselves?"

"Against the French police, who care about you less than they care about dirt? Yes. I think any of us alone would be too deficient to overcome their indolence. You may not like me, but regardless of whether you assist me, I intend to help him."

Baba stood. "You are different. Most foreigners would be happy to have the police accuse someone and be done with it. You put Asim in your own bed, have your man tend to him, and now try to bully me into helping you clear his name."

Edward held his breath as Baba paused.

"It is lucky for you I like Asim, and I too want to see the murderer punished, as well as those Greek police who beat him. I can't give you copies of the manifests because the police took them, but I can tell you that over seventy Europeans came here on company boats over the past week. Also, other guests for the ball have arrived at the port in Fira."

"Thank you. I know we have had our conflicts, but I hope we can work together to help Asim. Please let me know if you find out anything useful, and I will do the same."

Baba nodded. "I will, for Asim's sake."

Edward returned to the dig site, where Catherine Briggs waited for him in his makeshift office area in one of the excavated rooms. She sat on one of the wooden chairs by the door. When he saw her, and before he thought better of it, he said, "For a woman in a foreign land, you spend a remarkable amount of time traveling unescorted."

Her lips thinned in response. "My father is indisposed with a headache, and I came to apologize for what transpired between us yesterday, Mister Tyrington. You are laboring under false assumptions regarding my motives, which I wish to set straight. Although my knowledge of the Corvee freed Asim from his imprisonment, I gained my knowledge for another reason. I am heartbroken by the working conditions of this project and can assure you my aim was only to bring relief. I studied the Corvee when we first arrived and saw the canal work area, before I even met you. There was never a question of whether you mistreated your workers, and when I arrived here, I learned you treat them well by giving them extra rations and shade to work under."

Edward stood before her. "How do you know about that?"

Catherine stood, thrusting her chin in the air. "My sources shall remain my own, but it is easy to gather information when people want to share their good fortune with you. I heard the tale from several individuals."

Edward still felt rather truculent. "If you were of a mind with the police, you would suspect me of far worse than mistreating workers." Leaning toward her he continued, "You would accuse me of murder."

"That is preposterous. Why would they accuse you?"

"You must admit I was the first person at both murders, assuming the latest one is a murder and not an unfortunate accident. Apparently, prior to my arrival, there had not been a single death under mysterious circumstances since the project began."

Catherine pulled two chairs together by the wall and pointed to one. "Sit."

He did as he was told, removed his hat, and ran a hand through his hair before fixing her with an inquisitive eye.

She sat next to him. "All they have is circumstantial evidence, and they would never arrest the brother of an English lord over something so flimsy. You know that."

"I suspect it. I also suspect there may be other games afoot that I know nothing of. To disgrace me with arrest, even if it is only temporary, disgraces my brother. I am a scientist, not a politician, and I admit I am beyond my depth with what may transpire behind the scenes."

"Then we must work together to find the murderer."

Edward leaned toward Miss Briggs, their foreheads almost touching. "How do you know I am not the murderer?"

She snorted into the most unbecoming fit of raucous laughter he had ever seen from a lady of her station. It was a full minute before she had regained enough composure to continue. "That is the most ridiculous thing I have ever heard."

He cocked his head. "Why? You admit you do not know me well. Good breeding accounts for some things, but certainly not everything. You know that. There have been very well-bred monsters who have committed murder before."

Catherine wiped the tears from her eyes. "Mister Tyrington, my father's eyes have grown weak over the years, and he suffers from many complaints. As his only child, I have assisted him in matters of business. This goes beyond reading and executing contracts. It includes reading the intentions of the people we deal with, understanding their personalities, their foibles, and their strengths, and distilling that information into a clear picture of who a person is. I can assure you, you would no more murder a man than I would. And that is why I will help determine the identity of the actual murderer."

A slow smile crept across his face. "I appreciate your confidence in me, but your help is unnecessary. I will investigate this situation. Two men are dead, and I will not see you put in danger."

She rose from her chair with a small smirk on her face. "My offer stands, whether you are inclined to accept it or not." He stood as well, and she offered her hand for him to kiss. "Good day, Mister Tyrington."

Chapter Twenty One

When Edward arrived home that evening, he smiled and greeted the young guard who was standing by the door as affably as possible. He asked about his job as an officer and reflected on how proud his parents must be of his position. They had spoken for a few minutes when Edward said, "I am sorry you have had to stand out here in the sun all day. Is someone coming to take the night shift?"

"Yes, sir, someone else will be here this evening."

"This is quite unnecessary, you know. I have no intention of moving Asim."

"I have my orders."

"Of course. I understand." He turned toward the door and then played a hunch. Turning around, he said, "I heard the dead person came over on the ship called *Izmir*. Is that right?"

"Really? I heard they'd accounted for all the passengers on all the boats." Then, straightening up and clearing his throat as if he remembered his official duties, he said, "I'm sure I know nothing about it, sir."

"Oh. I must be mistaken." Edward tipped his hat and walked inside.

Davis took his hat and coat when he entered. "Your Aunt Inez visited today."

Edward sat to remove his work boots. "Here? Why? She knew I was working."

"She came to see Asim and said she would not rest until she had spoken to him herself. She was, shall we say, rather expressive when I spoke with her, and Asim heard some of what she said. He asked to speak with her, and I placed a chair near the door so they could converse without her having to view his injuries. She was agreeable with that plan, and I facilitated their conversation. Otherwise, she would still be here."

Edward sighed. "And?"

"And they spoke for a half hour. She had trouble understanding him at first, but they worked that out."

Edward walked to the bedroom door and knocked.

Asim was awake and sitting up in bed. "Sir, you should not have me sleeping in your bed."

"Nonsense. You will stay right there until you are well. You seem improved today, that is very good. I hear my aunt came to visit. I apologize for her intrusion on your recovery."

"She is a smart woman, sir, and she cares for you. Those are good things for a man to have."

"What did she ask you?" Edward sat in a chair next to the bed.

"She wanted to be sure you were right in trusting me. She never came out and said it, but by her questions, that was her worry. Mothers and aunts can worry so. I have aunts who, if they knew I was here, would question you."

"Me? But I am trying to help you."

Asim looked askance at him. "How many Englishmen help Egyptians?"

"I see your point." Edward sighed. "I assume Aunt Inez was satisfied, then?"

"Ask her."

Edward stood and opened the door. "Get some rest. And thank you."

After dinner, he walked down the road to Patros's house. It was smaller than his, but had a better view of the sea. Patros greeted him and poured two glasses of Retsina as they sat at his well-worn kitchen table. Edward held his glass aloft to view the golden wine in the lamplight. "Your opinion of me must be improving if you will share your Retsina."

"Don't read too much into that. It would be bad manners to offer you something less than what I'm drinking."

Edward smirked and sipped the wine. It tasted of the pine resin used to seal the barrels and, despite its sour bite, he loved it. Savoring his sip, he got to the point of his visit. "So, how would a European get on the island other than by company boat?"

"How do you know he didn't come by company boat?"

"I tricked the guard outside my house into telling me."

Patros tilted his head and thought for a moment. "Well, a person could sail a boat himself, or he could have someone sail him from a nearby island. It would not take much time to sail from Ios, Sikinos, or Anafi. Plus, there are trade ships that come into the chief port in Fira, further north on the island."

"Good Lord. How are we supposed to figure out how this man got here, let alone who he was?"

"We could ask the port workers if they've seen him, although asking if they've seen a European with light brown hair won't get us anywhere."

Edward dismissed his concern. "Julian can make a copy of the photograph of him, and we can show those around."

"It would be surprising if the company police hadn't already done that. They may not be the best investigators, but they are obliged to at least identify the body."

"Yes, but as you pointed out, they are not the best investigators, nor do they have the funding of the Suez Canal company to pay for photographs. They are not exactly economical. I suspect that someone went to some trouble to make sure we could not identify him." Edward knitted his brow. "How would a man travel if he wanted to come to the island anonymously?"

Patros was thoughtful again. "Given that they found him at the archaeological site, I'd say his best bet, if he didn't sail alone himself, would be a smuggler."

"A smuggler? How would one find a smuggler, and what do they smuggle?"

"Well, they smuggle ancient artifacts. There's always a wealthy lord or count who would like his own piece of Greek history in his house. It's a lucrative business and would explain why our friend was at the dig site."

Edward's breath became shallow at the thought of others stealing his discoveries. "That is what Davis thinks as well, that this man may have been selling antiquities. Although nothing is missing from the site, so clearly theft was not the motive. Do you think the company police would focus their efforts on a smuggler?"

"Even the local police have trouble identifying smugglers. I'm certain the company police couldn't catch one if they stole one of their officers. Lucky for us, I might know a person who might know another person who might help us."

Edward leaned in. "When can we contact him?"

"*We* will do nothing. The last thing anyone in that position wants is the attention of a brother of the House of Lords. But if you want me to look into this, convince Baba to live without me for a few days."

The next morning, Baba looked less than pleased to see them waiting by his office door at first light. He was reluctant to excuse Patros at first, but relented when they informed him they knew how the deceased person may have gotten to the island and that the company police could not investigate.

Baba looked Patros up and down. "This involves some shady business if you have to do it."

Edward interjected, "We are trying to clear Asim, and we cannot determine who murdered him until we know who he is and what he was doing on the island."

"Fine, you may go tomorrow. But if you get into trouble, I will not lift one finger to help you. You are on your own, and I want no part of whatever business you're going to get into."

"I understand." Patros stood. "Thank you."

As they left the office, Patros and Edward shook hands. "Thank you, Patros."

"I'm not doing it for you. I'm doing it for Asim. But there is one thing you can do for me: I planned for us to go to lunch at my mother's home today."

Edward cocked his head in disbelief. "Us? Why are you only telling me now?"

"I meant to tell you and then forgot. She looks forward to seeing you again, and I hate to tell her no. I won't be able to make it, but you could. You could even bring Mr. and Miss Briggs. She would love to meet them. I will take care of things at the site today as I make my preparations. Take the day and enjoy town with the Briggses, and then visit my mother."

"But that is more people than she was planning to feed."

"She's Greek. What's another mouth to a Greek mother? Please go. She has enjoyed your visits with the family, and it will mean so much to her."

Edward sighed. "Fine. If the Briggses are not otherwise engaged, I will bring them as well."

Chapter Twenty Two

He returned home to find Davis tidying up. As they talked, he thought his man didn't seem as surprised by Edward's change in plans as he might have been. Nor did he seem as disorganized as one might expect for changing clothes the second time in an hour. It was a testament to Davis's efficiency that nothing about this sudden change of plans caught him unprepared. Edward surveyed himself in the mirror and changed his vest from black to something a bit more colorful and better suited to a day of sightseeing. He chose a deep-auburn vest with thin gold pinstripes, decided his outfit was much improved, and left for town.

It was a beautiful morning, with the sun shining clear. The view of the ocean was stunning, set against the white buildings that became more frequent as he approached town. The narrow, winding streets shaded him as he walked to the inn.

As he asked for Mr. Briggs at the desk, John called, "Edward!" He and Catherine sat at a table near the back of the dining room having breakfast. "Come, join us for breakfast. I thought you would work today. We had planned to visit you later."

Edward strode over to them. "Thank you, but I have already eaten. I planned to work today as well, but Patros had another idea.

He informed me they did not need me today and that we, as in the three of us, should go sightseeing and then join his mother for lunch."

John knitted his brow. "Patros's mother?"

"Yes, he already made the arrangements and failed to inform me of them. Patros is an interesting man, but he tends toward sincerity, and he and his family are very welcoming. If you do not mind, he says his mother would appreciate the company. She is an enchanting woman."

"Does she speak English?"

"Oh yes. Patros's father was an Englishman."

John smiled. "That sounds delightful."

Catherine looked pleased at the prospect. She caught Edward looking at her. "Has she been to the archaeological site?"

"I have not seen her there, but I am confident that Patros has shown it to her at some point," Edward said.

"I am still astonished at the beauty of the frescoes. The discoveries you have made are remarkable. And to have done so in such a short amount of time is astounding. I am sure you will be the envy of many archaeologists when others find out."

Discomfort seized Edward. "The entire world will find out soon. Monsieur de Lesseps, the pasha, and their entourage will arrive soon to see our discoveries and have a fete as well."

"That is exciting. A celebration for your efforts and what you have found," Miss Briggs said.

"It is not a celebration of my efforts, more of a celebration of the Suez Canal Company and their project of preserving ancient artifacts. I was told at the outset that the company's interest in this site is to promote goodwill for the canal project." He leaned back and looked from Catherine to John. "Forgive my poor attitude about the ball. I prefer to work in anonymity, and the prospect of the attention for the site has me nervous. But today is a day to learn the secrets of Akrotiri. Is there anywhere that you would like to visit first?"

"We were just discussing that," John said. "Catherine would like to see the enchanting church in the center of town."

"Ah, excellent. Panagia Church is captivating. It has the most beautiful frescoes."

A waiter brought their breakfast, and Edward ordered a cup of coffee. Miss Briggs asked, "You are not having tea?"

"Somewhere along the way, I developed a taste for coffee, and I have never quite gotten over it. Besides, it can be quite difficult to find good English tea in foreign lands. Coffee is ubiquitous, and there are several varieties around the globe that are quite delicious."

The waiter filled Edward's cup as John said, "I understand that Catherine informed you of Monsieur Broussard's connection with Dupont. With my permission, she invited him here."

Edward frowned. "I find it curious that despite her reckless behavior, you keep her involved in the investigation."

Catherine set her teacup down. "Monsieur LeMarchal asked my father to make the contact before we left Egypt, which my father did. I only wrote the letter for him. Besides, I have been involved in this investigation since the beginning."

John finished chewing. "Catherine is more capable than any woman I have known, even her mother. And after living in far-flung lands for so long, I sometimes forget what the English consider proper."

Edward gave a small laugh. "I would hardly consider myself a judge of English propriety, but I prefer she stay out of such nasty business."

"It does not bother you." Catherine set down her utensils.

He held her gaze, and a slow smile grew on his face. "You are observant, Miss Briggs. Indeed, I enjoy investigating. I am a man of boundless curiosity, and puzzles are irresistible to me. Some would call it a sickness." Changing the subject, he turned to John. "What is your plan with Monsieur Broussard?"

"I plan to get to the bottom of his relations with Dupont and their business together. It would be helpful if you would assist me in questioning him."

Edward leaned forward. "I suppose there is no harm in asking him some questions, but will he answer? It would be helpful to know what is important to him: his family, his reputation, his business, his wife. We will need something that we can use as leverage if it is clear he is hedging."

Catherine drew back, her cheeks coloring as she spoke. "Do you plan to employ emotional bribery to discover the truth?"

"No, nothing so dramatic. But knowing what a man values most is helpful in any negotiation. I am sure you understand that, John."

"Yes. I still hope it is unnecessary." John looked down.

"It may not be necessary, but if it is, we should prepare ourselves. Now, if you have finished your breakfast, let us tour the town."

They stood, and Catherine linked her arm in Edward's. The warmth of her hand on his arm, even with the lightness of her touch, was both unnerving and comforting. It had been a long time since he had walked with a beautiful woman.

The morning was bright, and although Catherine wore a cream-colored hat with blue lace to shade her, he caught her tilting her head up so the sun could strike her face.

He smiled. "You are a singular woman, Miss Briggs."

"How so?"

"You investigate murders, you read and understand business contracts, and you are the only English woman I have ever known who seeks the sunshine on her face."

She looked from his face down to her feet and smiled as she returned her gaze to his. "The warmth of the day is invigorating."

The radiance in her eyes undid Edward. "You will hear no argument from me. I have never understood the English woman's aversion to the sun or her worship of porcelain-like skin."

On their way, they passed the botanical garden near the center of town, and Catherine asked to stroll through it before visiting the church. Edward was more than happy to oblige. John named several varieties that Edward was unfamiliar with, and they discussed their favorites. A curator tended a planting nearby, and Edward said, "Your garden here is quite beautiful. How did you come to have such a variety of plants?"

The curator was Greek, and his hours spent outside showed in his leathery complexion. "The French insist on such things. They want every corner of the world to carry the comforts of home. The Suez Canal Company commissioned me to start and maintain these gardens for the benefit of their French employees here."

Looking around, Catherine said, "Oh, look, bells of Ireland. Those were mother's favorite flowers. Remember how she loved them, Father?"

John looked mildly stricken at the mention of his deceased wife, but he rallied quickly and affirmed those were her favorite flowers.

"*Molluccella laevis*, yes. They are native to this region and are quite easy to grow." Edward held one in his hand. Turning to the curator, he asked, "May I? For the lady?"

The curator nodded. "By all means. Many come to here to gather nosegays or small bouquets for their homes."

Edward removed the flower and handed it to Catherine, who placed it on the brim of her hat. John admired it briefly and then looked away. They thanked the curator and wandered the rest of the garden, noting the unopened blooms on several plants and bushes. Soon after, they departed for the church.

Panagia Church was a picturesque whitewashed stucco building with three large brass bells in arching alcoves that formed the bell tower. The major portion of the church stood under a smooth, domed, azure blue roof of stucco. Somehow, the blue of the roof was vibrant enough to compete with the hues of the sky and the sea in a way to complement both and detract from neither. With the contrast of the white building, it was beautiful.

They slowed to take in the view, and for the first time, Edward's shoulders relaxed as he left behind his own world of worries and responsibilities. As they observed the sea, it felt as if no one had been murdered, there was no work to be done, and there would be no fete of politicians. There was only this beautiful moment painted in hues of blue and white.

When they arrived, Edward opened the heavy wooden door, and they stepped inside. It took a few moments for their eyes to adjust from the dazzling sunlight to the dimly lit interior. Catherine walked her father to a seat along the wall. She asked why there were no pews as there were in western churches, and Edward explained everyone stood during the service, with women on one side of the room and men on the other. The church contained a variety of frescoes, and Edward moved along the wall, gazing at the paintings while Catherine stood next to her father.

John whispered, "Go look at the room, child. I am fine here."

Soon Catherine joined Edward. "The detail is astounding," she said.

"Yes. Look here at the eyes of Mary, so expressive. You can almost feel her sadness."

They continued in silence for quite a while, inching through the nave of the church. John seemed content to view it from his seat, which was fine with Edward. In the dome, there were more spectacular paintings and a round chandelier with detailed, stained-glass depictions of saints.

At length, they left the church. The sunlight was startling, and the day had warmed considerably. A breeze blew up from the sea, which made it more comfortable as they stood near the cliff and overlooked the island, Nea Kameni, at the center of the caldera of the volcano, the sea still as glass around it.

Edward looked at his watch. It was almost eleven thirty. He turned to Catherine. "We should depart for Mrs. Patros's house. It will take some time to climb the hill."

John's pace was slower than before, and his face was a study of repressed pain. "The thought of another meal is not something I relish." Catherine was solicitous of her father, but he brushed her concerns aside. "I will be fine. It is only an upset stomach. You two enjoy the day, and I will return to the inn."

Catherine insisted on walking him back to his rooms before departing for Mrs. Patros's house. After they left him, they walked arm in arm in the shade of the whitewashed buildings and trellises heavy with blooming fuchsia bougainvillea.

"I am sorry your father is unwell," Edward said.

"He will be fine." She fidgeted with the strap of her chatelaine, chewed the edge of her lip, and kept her eyes locked in front of her. It was some time before the warmth of the day and the climb of the hill loosened her tongue. "Mister Tyrington, I should apologize for my father."

"Has he done something wrong?"

"Well, no... yes... I am unsure, to be quite honest. But some of his actions may cause you to labor under false illusions."

"Such as?"

"My father... well, he has developed a habit of late that, well..."

Edward stopped and turned toward her. "Miss Briggs, it is clear this subject is distressing to you, and it is also clear that you would like to say something difficult. I can assure you that I would prefer to hear what you have to say straight out, rather than put politely, as you are so diligently striving to do."

Catherine squared her shoulders, inhaled, and closed her eyes. "My father, of late, has developed the habit of parading me before bachelors with the idea that I should marry. I have no interest whatsoever in marriage and wish to clear the air, lest you believe me to have similar interests to my father's."

She opened her eyes to see the reception of her speech.

Edward endeavored to keep from smiling, but the corner of his mouth twitched before he schooled his reaction. "Miss Briggs, thank you for your candor. Although I had noticed your father's...encouragement, shall we say, I too am not of a mind for courting."

Catherine exhaled. "Thank goodness."

Chapter Twenty Three

Although Edward knew many who would be offended by Catherine's candor, he smiled, offered her his arm, and they strode on to Mrs. Patros's for lunch. Edward knew he should feel relieved. Catherine was more trouble than her beauty was worth, and pretending to be the successful son of a lord was somewhat exhausting. But as they walked, the pain of yet another woman's rejection needled him. Although she was difficult, she was also quick of mind, and he admired that about her. None of the wallflowers he had met at various balls had engendered his admiration half as much. And he enjoyed Catherine's company, which was also a rarity.

At length he said, "How have you managed to avoid marriage thus far? If a father wishes his daughter to marry, a woman is hard-pressed to go against it."

"I have a way of...dissuading my prospective suitors. When I am done, they have decided it would be best if we parted." She gave a wry smile, light dancing in her eyes.

"I am not sure I want to even imagine."

"I know you will find this hard to believe, Mister Tyrington, but I can be somewhat unmanageable."

Edward patted her hand lightly but said nothing.

Abandoning the topic, Catherine said, "The buttercups are beautiful along this path."

"Yes. They symbolize riches, if I am not mistaken."

"Are you a student of floriography as well? I find it fascinating, but need to consult my dictionary of flowers, as my mind seems unwilling to commit all their meanings to memory."

"Yes, it dovetailed well into my study of botany and has proven useful knowledge at times." Edward picked three buttercups and gave them to Catherine, and she added them to the bells of Ireland in her hat.

When they arrived, Mrs. Patros flew out to greet them. Her quickness stood in stark contrast to her white hair and lined face. She gave Edward a kiss to each cheek, and Edward introduced Catherine and explained John's absence. She greeted Catherine and asked her to call her Davina then turned to her daughter who stood by the door. "Come, Elena, greet our guests."

Elena was tall and graceful, with dark hair and a brilliant smile. She strode to offer Edward her hand, and he remembered her as the girl who sang during his last visit with Patros's family. Elena took Catherine by the arm and guided her inside. As Edward and Davina were about to follow, Stephan, Patros's brother, came to welcome Edward.

Edward and Stephan joined Davina in the kitchen, where she gathered the pitcher and glasses on a tray and bid them to walk with her to the courtyard. The courtyard was lined with persimmon, date, and olive trees and arbors of bougainvillea. In the center was a long wooden table with benches. On the right side was a bench nestled under an arbor of passionflower and honeysuckle. There they found Elena and Catherine speaking in low voices.

Catherine looked more alive and animated than Edward had ever seen her. Several strands of hair had escaped her bun and framed her face with delightful curls. Her eyes shone with delight as Elena said something that made Catherine laugh. It was the laugh of sisters, of confidantes, the laugh women share when they are free with themselves and think no one is watching. Joy filled Edward's heart to see it. He had no idea what this visit could mean for Catherine, but realized working with her father likely left her without much in the way of female companionship.

They sat and drank lemonade in the shade, discussing the beauty and history of Panagia Church.

Soon Davina and Elena went inside and returned with trays of bread, meats, olives, and cheeses for lunch. The food was delicious and the conversation even better, and Edward could not remember a more agreeable time since he had arrived to work.

After lunch, Davina said, "You should visit the market this afternoon. There is nothing like our market anywhere in the world. You can buy fruits, vegetables, jewelry, clothing, and animals—whatever you want. It would be fun."

Elena jumped in. "I could escort you and help you buy anything you like."

Edward smiled. "Davina, may we have the pleasure of your daughter's company this afternoon?"

"She is a grown woman and can make her own decisions. But it so happens that I won't need her help this afternoon, so there is nothing for her to do here."

Elena looked pleased, and after lunch they departed. The market was close to the center of town, nestled in along a cobblestone alleyway that rose into the hills.

The entrance had an archway across the road and a large banner of painted cloth welcoming customers, under which stood a man hawking figs. He was entertaining and had a beaming smile as he juggled four of his figs to entertain the ladies. Catherine was ready to buy some until Elena cautioned her that this was the most expensive seller in the market and that other fig stands were far more reasonable. Cloths of many colors draped over the alley to provide shade for the market. There were some stalls in the cobblestone street, while others had permanent shops along the sides.

There was little order to the chaos: a seller of pots next to shawls, next to others who sold instruments. The foodstuffs and animals were kept around the edges of the market, the smell of warm fruit and fresh hay pervaded the air, and the voices of many animals mingled with the call of the salesmen.

They walked along until Elena stopped at a scarf shop, while Catherine and Edward stopped across the alley at a blanket on the ground with jewelry pinned to it. The jewelry had themes of Greek crosses, ancient gods and goddesses, ships, and a variety of geometric designs.

As they perused the items, the jeweler beside the blanket greeted them while he heated something in a crucible over the hot coals of a forge. Edward asked what he was heating, and he explained that he was melting silver to make a ring as he squeezed the bellows to stoke the fire. Edward studied the process as he poured the molten metal into a mold of a ring. He filled two more molds of different sizes while they observed.

After the seller had finished his work, Catherine decided to buy a pin depicting Eos, the winged goddess of the dawn and hope. As they settled on a price, Edward paid before Catherine could open her chatelaine. It was an impulsive decision that he could ill afford, but that did not matter.

"That is quite unnecessary. I have the funds to purchase the pin."

"I meant no offense, Miss Briggs, and I have no doubt of your funds. But I ask that I may have the pleasure of purchasing it for you."

It was improper for a man to purchase jewelry for a woman he was not courting. Yet decorum dictated that she not refuse such a request.

She looked at him for a long moment before relenting. "If that is what you wish."

When Edward attached the pin to her dress, she avoided his gaze and whispered, "Thank you."

"We meet again," said a man's voice. "Tell me, do you do any actual work for the company or only attend balls and shop?"

Edward's skin crawled across his skull when he heard Livingstone, and he slowly turned toward him. "First, I see you at the canal, now in Santorini. Do you perform any work in the House of Lords, or have you also taken a position with the Suez Canal Company?"

"No I have not, but I see your issues in Zanzibar forced you to run from England as fast as you could." He leaned in close to Edward. "Tell me, did the villagers try to murder your expedition there, as Peterson said?"

Catherine gasped.

"Oh, I do apologize, Miss..."

"Catherine Briggs."

"Miss Briggs, I am sorry, but you must ask Edward about his exploits. They are quite fascinating and dangerous. I was so glad to see that Peterson's quick thinking was rewarded with a position at Oxford."

Edward balled his fists. "You have been misinformed—"

Livingstone cut across him. "I do not believe so. I heard the story from Peterson himself, how he saved your party. It is a wonder how a woman could walk with such a reckless man. But there you have it." He tipped his hat and then stopped. "Briggs, you say. I used to know a John Briggs. He dealt in imports."

Catherine stood straight. "Yes. He is my father."

He searched her face. "You look like her. Terrible what happened. Tell me, where is your sister now?"

Her eyes grew wide for the briefest of moments. "Excuse us, but I must return to my father now." She took Edward's elbow and began walking.

Edward looked back to see Livingstone smiling before turning away from them. "As much as I appreciate being away from him, that was a bit of a hasty retreat."

"It was clear that man was intent on causing strife. I chose not to allow him more opportunity to do so."

He was silent for a moment. "I was unaware that you have a sister."

She straightened. "He was mistaken."

Her hand trembled on his arm, and he was thankful that his own hand did not quake. Memories of the Zanzibar expedition still shook him in the wee hours of the morning. Having the specter of it held up in broad daylight in front of Catherine was too much. His heart raced and his face flushed at his own shame. He only hoped she would ask no more about it. They continued walking, lost in their own thoughts, engulfed in silence.

Chapter Twenty Four

A short walk later, Edward slowed his pace and said, "Oh no."

"What now? Is he back?"

"No. It is my Aunt Inez." Edward sighed as she waved to him across the crowded market. He waved back.

"You have an aunt who lives in Greece?"

"No, she is here visiting. I apologize in advance for anything she might say."

"Do not be ridiculous. A woman who speaks her mind is sure to be a friend of mine. Besides, she can only be an improvement from our last conversation."

He leaned in to whisper, "I hope you are right."

Inez was wearing a violet dress that was as impractical for shopping in a crowded market as he could imagine. The skirt was full and wide, more for a formal event than a walking dress. The bodice probably fit her ten years ago, but now it was a graphic reminder of her love of food. She looked pinched, but her demeanor did not betray discomfort though surely she was uncomfortable. Francine wore the most serviceable of walking dresses, in a light taupe. They were a study in the contrasts of austerity and excess.

As they strode up, Inez said, "Edward, it is so good to see you out in the fresh air and sunshine and not choking on dust in some hole in the ground."

Edward introduced Inez and Francine to Catherine. A small smile broke on Francine's face that made Edward smile too.

Aunt Inez focused on Catherine as a magpie focuses on a shiny object. "Edward, you did not mention your acquaintance with Miss Briggs."

"I would be hard-pressed to share all my acquaintances in Santorini in the short time we have spent together, Aunt Inez."

She grinned and held out her hand. "No matter. It is a pleasure to meet you now. May we join you?"

Edward bowed slightly. "Of course, it would be my pleasure."

They walked through the alley together, remarking on the shops. Catherine stopped to look at a display of handsewn reticules, and Aunt Inez stopped with her. "Oh yes, I do need a new reticule. Edward, you should escort Francine to the hatter up ahead. A woman can never have too many hats."

Francine's eyes widened as Inez made the suggestion.

He offered his arm. "I would be delighted to."

As they walked away, Francine said, "I apologize if Aunt Inez has made a muddle of your plans for the afternoon. She means well, but can be quite trying."

Edward gently shook his head. "There is no need to apologize, and I am happy to escort you shopping. Aunt Inez has been a widow for far longer than she was married, and with no children, she has had the time and money to become an independent and eccentric woman. But that makes her rather refreshing, in a way. But what of you? How did you come to be in Santorini with her?"

She sighed. "Inez would be appalled to know I shared this with you, but it was my father's idea. After my first season, I was courted by a young man of whom father did not approve. Father tried to forbid our communication, but we move in the same circles and saw each other quite a bit. He felt a trip might change our minds about each other."

"And how do you feel about that?"

She tilted her head, her gaze tunneling into his own. "You do ask a lot of questions. But in some ways, you remind me of Robert, my beau. He asks me a lot of questions about my feelings as well."

"Your beau should be concerned with your feelings."

"To answer your question, my father could not be more wrong about us."

He sighed.

Francine stared at the ground in front of her. "You disapprove."

Edward stopped and faced her. "No, I do not. However, you may recall my brother Thaddeus. Among other transgressions, he fell in love with a woman that my father did not approve of and left our family for her. The whole country mourned my father's passing, yet he did not come. I can only wonder if he is still alive or if I will ever see him again. It is a heartache I would not wish on anyone, I can assure you. I would never deign to tell you what to do, but I will say that great care and thought should be given to any course of action, as it will likely affect a much greater circle of people, and cut more deeply, than you realize."

She gaped at him. "That... that is what has been preying on my mind. That any breach may be unrecoverable and what that would do to some members of my family." Her voice dropped to a low whisper. "And to me."

"Then you have already heeded my advice." He gave her a brief smile and resumed walking.

They perused the hats, and Francine purchased a pretty blue spoon bonnet. Elena found them as they were completing the purchase, and they soon collected Aunt Inez and Catherine.

"It is getting late," Edward said. "May I escort you ladies home?"

They chatted about the wares they saw at the market as they walked. They stopped at Elena's home first. After saying goodbye, Edward steered them toward Aunt Inez's lodgings.

Inez said, "We should walk Miss Briggs home first. You look a bit tired, my dear."

There was a hint of fire in Catherine's eyes. "Oh, on the contrary, I find the evening air invigorating. I would be content to walk to your hotel before mine."

"As you see fit. I was only looking after your health. These Mediterranean climes can be so hard for an Englishwoman."

"All the more reason to go to your hotel first. I am far more used to the Mediterranean air after all my travels with my father."

Edward's eyes sparkled at Catherine. The fact that she managed to cow Inez was impressive. Somewhat trenchant in her idea as more of a world traveler than Catherine, Inez gave a grand soliloquy on her travels to India as they walked. After leaving Aunt Inez and Francine at their lodgings, he and Catherine walked to her inn.

Edward leaned in toward her. "As I said, I apologize for my aunt."

"No apology is necessary. I understand. And she is charming in her own shrewd way, even if she is a bit obvious in her intentions. I admire her tenacity."

He chuckled. "I appreciate the effort you took to find the silver lining after how she accosted you today."

Catherine nodded and said nothing more. When they arrived at the inn, she turned and smiled at him. "Thank you for the brooch."

Edward frowned, and his eyebrows knitted together as he looked at the brooch. Then his eyes flew wide. "That is it!"

She shrank back, frowning.

"I am sorry. Of course you are welcome, Miss Briggs. It was my pleasure. I was distracted. You see, something has been bothering me all afternoon, and only now did I figure out what it was. Do you mind if we go inside for a moment? I would like you to hear what I have to say."

They entered the small salon at the front of the hotel and sat on a small floral sofa in the corner. Edward said, "Since we saw the jeweler in the market, it has bothered me. Something about the process he used to melt the silver for his jewelry kept distracting me. Dupont's murderer took his wallet but did not take his watch. The authorities told us that the watch was left because it would be traceable by the engraving. This would be a problem if the murderer would want to sell it for money..."

Catherine jumped in. "But as we saw today, at least some locals know how to melt metal and make other jewelry. My goodness, do you think my brooch is from a stolen article?"

He shook his head. "No, I do not. I am sure that jeweler was an honest man. But what just struck me is I remember seeing forges like the one he used in the work camp at the canal. And it would not surprise me if many people there know how to melt metal. More to the point, there are many of them whose job is melting metal to repair the machinery. Since there may have been two people who murdered Dupont, if the worker I caught was one of them, there is still one man missing."

"But the majority of workers are not there to work with the machinery. Most dig by hand. They may or may not have this skill or the equipment."

Edward leaned back. "True. But that leads to the other assumption the canal authorities made—that the watch was traceable. Of course, we know that it is customary to have one's name or initials engraved on a watch, but how many Egyptian peasants know that? And if one did not know that, why would he hesitate to take a gold watch? He would not know it was traceable, and there are at least even odds that he could melt the metal down himself."

"So that would mean the killer was English, or at least European, and would know the custom of engraving the watch, thus making it possible to identify the original owner; or the killer was interrupted and did not have time to take the watch, in which case it could have been anyone."

"Perfect deduction, Miss Briggs."

She blushed under the compliment. "But where does that leave us?"

Edward stood and walked toward the window. “Silence brings answers.”

“Excuse me?”

“I apologize. It is a quote to help me focus.”

He paced around the room for a few minutes, then sat and searched her eyes. “No clear path is coming to me now. First and foremost, I need to interview Monsieur Broussard. And I need to review the possible motives again. Who would want him dead? So far, only Reginald Broussard has a possible motive, or a disgruntled worker, of course. I will need to think on this more, as there is more complexity than we realized.”

Edward thanked Catherine for her help. When he returned home, he visited with Asim. He had improved and was sitting up comfortably in bed. The speed of his recovery under Davis’s care surprised him. Edward smiled to see Asim able to chew food, as opposed to sipping beef broth, and able to walk around. He still held his ribs, which had taken the brunt of the beating, and had difficulty walking for an extended period of time, but the fact that he could walk again seemed a miracle.

CHAPTER TWENTY FIVE

The wind did not flag the next morning, which made work at the site miserable. The small bits of ash flew at everyone's eyes and mouths, and the workers moved around to keep the shifting wind out of their faces. It was a constant battle. The gray weather matched his mood: unsettled and snatching at anything.

As they worked together in the cramped space, Edward drew pictures of his discoveries. He was making precise measurements of a pot when a tall, muscular, bearded man approached his desk. There was a sinewy menace in his movements, as if given the proper motivation, he could injure someone with no trouble at all. He introduced himself with a voice of a man who had worked hard to erase his rolling r's and wet vowels common to the rural areas of France. After so many summers in the South of France at his mother's family estate, it sounded like home to Edward.

"I am Rubeaux, sir. Baba told me to report to you."

"To me?"

"He said you were missing some men and could use the help. Baba also told me to tell you that I can only help today and tomorrow. After that, I am needed elsewhere."

"Ah. Yes, well, any help is appreciated." Edward introduced him to Gahiji and had him show Rubeaux the process of excavating and what was expected of the crews.

Later that afternoon, the wind settled down to brief gusts, and the work was far more agreeable. As they excavated across the floor from Edward, Gahiji came to him.

"I'm not sure, but I think we found something." He brought Edward to a place where a small hole revealed an empty space underneath. Edward stopped all the workers for them to see and asked Gahiji to translate.

"This is something you all need to see," he began, "something easily missed and yet of vital importance. When the ash fell, there was something here to create this space where there is no ash. That thing is now long gone. It could be a person, like in Pompeii, or it could be a chair or a bed or who knows what." He turned to two of the workers. "Get two sacks of plaster of paris and a wheelbarrow full of water."

They did as he requested, and soon he was mixing the plaster by hand in the wheelbarrow. When it was ready, he poured it through a pipe into the hole to fill the void. He needed to make a second batch to finish the job, then he instructed everyone to return to work while the plaster cured.

Later, he called the men over to watch as he and Gahiji excavated the ash from around the now-hardened plaster. After what seemed like an eternity, they uncovered a three-legged table. It was small, with carved legs that were wider at the top and curved to the floor.

Edward stared, his breath coming in shallow gasps. The table was below the fresco of the woman, whom Edward thought was a goddess, and the monkey. "This appears to be an offering table for the goddess."

Gahiji and Edward's eyes locked across the table. A thousand years ago or more, others had placed offerings on this table in worship. The magnitude of that thought and the history between then and now enveloped them both.

Edward spent the next several hours measuring and drawing a precise rendering of the table for his catalogue. As he finished, he stood and stretched his shoulders. He could see a man walking down the path toward the work site. The sun behind the man hid his identity, but his gait seemed familiar. When Edward finally recognized the Earl of Mar, he hastened out to greet him.

"James, what an unexpected pleasure."

"Your excavation is perfectly located between Constantinople and Athens."

"Excuse me?"

"I am on my way from the meeting with the Ottomans to the coronation of King George in Athens. Your placement here in the middle of my journey is fortuitous."

"I am glad you had the time to visit. I am sorry you had to walk here. Were there no carriages in town?"

James smiled. "I chose to walk. It is a glorious afternoon, and after all the time I have spent on my ship of late, I appreciate the opportunity to see the countryside. I stopped here to see if you could spare a few days to join me at the coronation."

"As much as I appreciate the invitation, I will have to decline. There is much work to do before the ball de Lesseps has planned."

The earl strode into the excavation area and across the triangular plaza. "I say, this is extraordinary—and of obvious historical significance. This will make you a name in archaeology and secure a position at Oxford or another fine seat of learning."

"I hope so, but we have much yet to do. Will you stay for a day or two, or leave straight away for Athens?"

"Unfortunately, I am on a rather difficult schedule. England is ceding the Ionian Islands to King George as a coronation present, and there is a devilish amount of work to put things in proper order. I will leave in the morning."

"Then let me show you more of what I have found before you go."

They walked through the excavation as Edward explained the purpose of the various rooms they had found and showed him the frescoes they had uncovered. As they strolled between excavations, the wind blew in earnest again, and all the workers covered their faces. Edward directed James to a room they'd excavated to shelter from the gusts.

"By the way, there are some things waiting for you when you arrive home." James inspected the wall with his back to Edward. "I saw several items I knew to be yours at auction and purchased them to return them to you. I am sure Tynes has them by now."

The thoughtfulness of the gesture stunned Edward, but pride grasped his tongue first. "I do not need your charity."

James turned and waved Edward's protest away. "It is not charity. Think of it more as enlightened interest. I know of no one else who should have those books or the Stradivarius harp or the other instruments you sold. They represent everything you love. After all you have lost, you should not have to lose them as well. Besides, your father would be spinning if he knew you had sold them."

"He did not leave me much choice. But how did you know I had sold them?"

"I have a man who watches the auctions for interesting items. He informed me they were up for auction. It was not difficult to guess their provenance."

"Thank you, James. It was a thoughtful gesture." Edward's discomfort at receiving a gift of this magnitude, even from a well-meaning friend, seeped into the room as he changed the subject. "What is the latest news from the House of Lords?"

James sighed. "There is increased resistance to our expanding presence in China, but despite that, we have opened more consulates and established our presence in the Kowloon Peninsula."

A frisson of cold sped up Edward's spine. "Any further investigation into the espionage surrounding naval information?"

"The official investigation yielded no conclusive evidence. You know that."

"Yes, but we know the information was given to the French. The investigation should continue. When I was in Damietta, I attempted to track down the last lead I found from my father regarding a Mr. Dupont."

James stared at Edward and he drummed his fingers on his crossed arms. "And what did you find?"

"Nothing." Edward looked at the ground. "I did confirm that an Englishman lived on the street but was told by one person that he moved away and by another person that he died."

"Stop this foolishness." James closed the distance between them, his voice smooth as silk at first but with an increasing growl as he continued. "Your father bankrupted your family chasing this ghost, to no avail. As your father's friend, and now yours, it is my duty to advise you. Must I remind you of the precarious nature of your situation? Your circumstances are reduced to the point of selling your most valued possessions. The only thing you should be thinking about now is how to right that wrong and return to your proper position in society. Leave the past behind. Your efforts there are wasted."

The wind had halted, and silence engulfed them. Rebuked, Edward chose his words with care. "You are right, of course. There is no profit for me there."

James stepped back. "I should return to town. I have work to do before I am on my way." James brushed the dust from his hat. As they walked to the edge of the dig site, he chuckled. "It is very like you though. Regardless of the incredible success that lies beneath your feet here, you focus on the impossible."

"The impossible is only so until someone carves a path for its probability." Edward shook James's hand. "By the way, my Aunt Inez decided to visit and is staying at the Lionshead Inn. She would appreciate seeing you again."

"Ah, Aunt Inez. Is she as eccentric as ever?"

Edward gave a small laugh. "She would not be Aunt Inez otherwise."

"I will see if I have time. If not, I will send my regrets."

That evening, after the other workers left for dinner, Edward walked to the western edge of the sea cliff. *James is right. Am I holding onto the investigation as some remnant of my father?* He sighed and looked up. *Regardless, it is done. There is nowhere to go with it now.*

The sun had slipped behind a cloud, painting it with a golden ribbon across the top and a cauldron of fire below as it dipped into the sea. The sight took his breath, and as he let go of his thoughts of murder and espionage, a peaceful gladness saturated his entire being.

As he returned home, Edward passed Patros's house. It remained dark and empty, and he wondered why he was not home. He had assumed Patros would arrive that evening and visit him to tell him what happened. Dinner came and went while Edward pushed his food around his plate, and still Patros did not return. As the night wore on, thoughts of all the ways their plan could go wrong gnawed on his mind. He tried to push them aside, but they became more insistent and the weight of his responsibility for Patros became more crushing. He tried to distract himself with conversation with Asim, but this only increased his feelings of guilt.

The night deepened, and a carriage arrived. Officers Fortier and Girard entered his house demanding, yet again, to take Asim to the jail. As Edward argued about his condition and his need for continued medical attention, Asim came out of the bedroom.

The officers saw how much better he looked. Girard said, "He appears to be fine. We will take him now."

Asim said, "I am better." He turned to Edward. "And I thank you for all you have done, but you can't keep me here forever."

"Even he sees the sense in it," Girard said. "Very good. Let's bring him in."

Fortier went to tie his hands behind his back, and Edward tried to block him. Fortier stepped back and said, "This is not the time for heroics. Let us take him without trouble. We have waited long enough. Your man can attend to him at the jail."

"If anything happens to him at the jail, I will hold you both personally responsible for the lost time on my project, and I will not rest until you are held fully accountable for harming an innocent man."

Girard put his hand on Asim's shoulder to direct him out the door. "It is not up to you to decide his guilt or innocence. It is out of your hands."

Davis opened the door for the officers, and there stood Baba, a young woman, and an older man that Edward had never seen before. The older man shoved the woman through the door, and she fell inside the entryway.

Chapter Twenty Six

Edward scowled at Baba and the pair he'd brought to his doorstep. "I do not know who you have brought—"

Baba cut across him. "I was told I would find the officers here. I will be quick about this. This is Sada and her father, Bari. Asim could not have murdered anyone because he was with Sada that night."

Officer Girard looked at Fortier then at the people before him. "You expect me to believe that it took her three days to come forward?"

Baba translated the question into Arabic. Sada sobbed, trying to speak, but her father shouted over her and pointed his finger repeatedly at Asim. The room shook from his bellowing, and all in attendance stood in stunned silence.

Asim stared straight into Bari's eyes, as stoic as any marble statue Edward had ever seen. Baba finally shouted at the older man, and he stopped yelling mid-sentence.

Baba continued, "She was forbidden from seeing Asim and went against her father's wishes."

"Was she with him the whole night?" Girard asked.

"Yes, that night her father was out on an errand and did not return home until right before work began. She was with Asim the entire time."

Edward turned to Asim. "Why did you not tell us this before?"

Asim closed his eyes and inhaled. As he looked upon her again, his eyes softened, and he seemed to struggle with the emotions of the moment. "Because I was afraid of her father's wrath. Not toward me, but toward her. I had hoped there would be another way to prove my innocence so that I could work to gain his approval."

Sada heard the softness of his words, and although she did not understand them, she understood the look in his eyes. She ran to him, and he caught her in his arms, grimacing as she crashed into his bruised ribs. Her father yelled again, and Baba argued with him. Bari stormed out, spitting on the ground outside the door. Sada's face turned to marble as she witnessed her father's rant, and when he left, she crumpled to the ground again. Asim knelt next to her, whispering in her ear.

Everyone in the room, besides Asim and Sada, looked at Baba. "Her father has disowned her. She belongs to Asim now, if he will have her. Otherwise, she is an orphan."

Edward turned to the couple. "What are your plans?"

"I do not know, sir. But I know they include Sada."

"Baba, is there a place she can stay for the night?"

Baba looked around at Edward's well-appointed home.

Edward took his meaning. "A place other than here."

"Arrangements can be made. I will take her with me. I know someone who will take her in for now." Baba and Asim spoke together and then coaxed Sada to leave. Davis took one look at Asim's haggard features and ordered him straight back to bed.

Edward turned to the officers. "Since Asim was otherwise occupied the night of the murder, you will have to look elsewhere for the killer."

The officers looked at each other. "How do we know that Baba didn't find two people to lie about Asim's whereabouts?"

"Did you not witness what happened?"

"All we have is Baba's translation that he disowned her. It could have been a well-rehearsed play we watched."

Edward slammed his fist on the table. "You have more evidence against him being the murderer than you do supporting that accusation. He is clearly still unwell. Now, if you will excuse me, I have a letter to write to Monsieur de Lesseps."

Girard's eyes widened at the implied threat. "What makes you so sure he is innocent?""He has no motive. If you knew anything about murder, you would know there should be a reason for it. Asim has no reason to kill a man unknown to him. Have you even discovered the victim's identity yet?"

Girard admitted they had not. "All right. He can stay here while we sort out the details of Sada's story. In the meantime, we have a few more questions for you, Mister Tyrington. Tell me, why were you chosen to check on the body at the bottom of the cliff?"

"We already covered this. I was not chosen. I simply went. I am trained in a variety of disciplines that are vital to an investigation such as this. Oh, and that reminds me..." He went to his bedroom, returned with the button he had found with the dead man, and handed it to Officer Girard. "I found this with the body. I forgot to give it to you the other day. It was about six feet from the body on his right side, near his hand."

Officer Girard looked at him sideways. "It's a curious thing we have here. We've worked on the canal for years and have never had a murder that was not witnessed or easily solved. You arrive, and we have two murders in a few days. And you are not only present for both of them, but the first man on the scene for each. Now Asim apparently has an alibi, and we find you've been withholding evidence."

Edward stood. "See here, I will not have you insinuate my involvement in these crimes in my own house. I had nothing to do with this."

Fortier approached him. "I understand that you also have a habit of wandering around the excavation site at night."

Edward walked to the door and opened it. "As head of this excavation project, my habits are my business, and walking does not equate to murdering. So unless you find motive and means, you will need to look elsewhere."

They donned their hats, and Girard said, "We already have means and will doubtless find motive."

After they left, Edward sat at the table and thought about the possibility of his arrest. Even if he was released from the company under suspicion, his hope for a career was over, and if he could not pay his debts, he would be hunted by the person who had loaned him money. *Blast it! How did my life become so twisted? Unless the real killer is found, everything ends for me here.*

There was a small snick as Davis removed the stopper from the newly purchased whiskey decanter.

"No, Davis. That will not be necessary. I have a long night ahead of me. I need to keep a clear head as I wait for Patros to return."

Chapter Twenty Seven

Edward paced the house, his head full of horrible possibilities that he would prefer to not consider. Thoughts of Patros, as bloody and beaten as Asim, filled his mind, and self-recrimination filled his heart. He should have known this was too dangerous, yet he blithely let Patros run off to get hurt, or worse.

He went to his bedroom and retrieved his violin to try to settle his mind on something other than Patros's fate——or his own.

Opening the hard, black leather case, he pulled the instrument from the yellow silk lining. The small dent at the bottom of the violin grazed his thumb, and he was transported back in time over a year ago. He had been in the music room playing Paganini's Caprice no. 24, an arduous piece as technically challenging as had ever been written. It was beyond his ability, but he kept at it, stopping and starting and stopping again to his increasing frustration.

As he was nearing the finale, Tynes burst into the room. "A messenger came. Your father is dying. We must go now!"

Edward had dropped the violin and run headlong into his future as a fatherless son.

He shook off the cobwebs of the memory, picked up his bow, and stood. After tuning the instrument and warming up his fingers, he played Brahms, but it felt wrong. His mind rattled about, and he knew only one piece would suit him: Bach's "Chaconne." The precision that caged the raw emotion of the music was the only balm for moments like this. The violin responded fluidly to the repeated harmonics, and his mind was devoid of thought, as passion carried the moment. Once he began, he played with abandon, wandering about the room and losing himself to the music.

Not long after he'd finished, someone rapped on the front door. Edward hurried to open it, and Patros came in, looking worse for wear. His right eye was black, there was a scrape on his cheekbone, and Edward thought he saw the shadow of a bruise on his neck. Edward bade him to sit and poured them whiskey. As Edward passed him a glass, he noticed the scrape marks on his knuckles. His clothes were torn, and Edward thought he saw a bandage through one of the tears. Patros took the whiskey and drank it in one choking gulp, then held out his glass again. Edward refilled it.

After he drank, Patros said, "They're a rough bunch, that's for sure, but once one of them says you're all right, they start to warm up. Unfortunately, them warming up to you is only a bit better than when they think you'll turn them in. I've had to bribe, drink, fight, and play cards to get anyone to even consider looking at a photograph. They were all 'upstanding citizens,' you see. You have to prove you're as 'upstanding' as they are, if you take my meaning. Eventually, a few started to look at it. One man decided I was trustworthy, and he showed it to some others. Before I left their company this afternoon, another man came to me and said that it might be that this man came from Crete. And it might be that he never gave a name. And it might be that he disembarked at a dock somewhere east of Akrotiri a few days ago."

Edward leaned back. "That would be right before he was killed. Well, that is more than we knew, albeit not much."

"Well, I'm saving the best for last. The final tidbit was it might be that he had an English accent and, in every way, appeared to be an Englishman."

"So, we have an Englishman who lived a life of ease, judging from his hands, and who came from Crete via a smuggler's boat to a dock east of Akrotiri before he died at the dig site, indicating he was here on nefarious business that may include the theft and sale of antiquities." Edward pondered and then, looking at Patros, said, "Thank you. Now go and get some rest. You will need to be at the worksite tomorrow morning, or Baba will murder us both. But if you happen to fall asleep in some dark corner for part of the day, I shall never tell."

The next morning, Edward found Patros in the cafeteria at breakfast. He carried two cups of coffee and looked almost as bad as he had the previous night.

Edward smiled. "Good to see you this morning. I will see Baba at lunch and tell him what you found. In the meantime, tend to your wounds before work starts. You look terrible."

Patros looked incredulous. "These are only scratches. You've looked worse than I do. I am fine. I have the crews prepared to work on the south wall today, and I sent Martin back to Baba."

"Who?"

"Martin. The helper Baba sent."

"Oh yes. Very good." Edward sipped his coffee

They were excavating a series of smaller rooms with rough stone walls along the main road that ran through the village and led into the triangular courtyard. There was little to find in these small rooms, and although the rooms themselves were worthy discoveries in their own right, Edward hoped for more stunning finds like the frescoes, or perhaps jewelry. As they had found no bodies and few personal effects, it seemed likely that these people had some warning of the eruption and had fled.

It was late in the morning when the workers alerted him that they had found another smooth stone wall. He instructed them to space themselves along the wall and dig. He even helped dig to move as much ash as fast as they could. They sang a song in cadence as they worked, and he too was singing along, forgetting his troubles, his heart light with the possibility of discovery.

Soon he saw what he had hoped was there: the bright colors and swirling shapes of another fresco. The top band was red, with blue curls that looked like waves lapping the bottom of it. As they dug deeper, they revealed a portion of a fresco with large boats carrying many men using oars. Over the morning it became clear this was a fresco of the fleet leaving port. The men had uncovered enough of the room that they had to brace the walls to keep them stable. While they erected the proper braces, he catalogued what they had found thus far.

At lunchtime, Edward went to Baba's office. Baba scowled. "Did Patros find anything?"

"We do not know who he is yet, but we know he came over on a boat a few days before his death. He was an Englishman. But that is all we know."

Baba grunted. "The police found out more than you. They identified him as Mr. Allen of Scheffield. They are trying to locate his next of kin, although they haven't found anyone yet."

Edward sat. "How did they find out who he was?"

"They asked at the local inns. One of the workers at the Dendrosa east of town recognized his picture, and that is the name on the registry."

Edward's mind raced. Mr. Allen of Scheffield. Not a name he recognized from his archaeological acquaintances. Of course, if he traded in black market antiquities, Edward would not know him.

"Thank you, Baba. This is helpful. By the way, how did you find Sada?"

Baba smiled, a broad, fat-cat smile and raised his eyebrows. "I have my ways." Turning his back, he said, "And that is all I will say about it. Except that Asim will need to take responsibility for her soon, if he is going to."

Edward agreed and left, glad that Baba had his secret ways of discovery. He walked without thinking about where he was going, but his feet knew the way.

Entering the inn, Edward startled himself from his reverie and asked at the desk, “Is Mr. Briggs in?”

Catherine called, “Mister Tyrington?”

He turned to see her standing in the front window of the parlor and went to her.

“Mister Tyrington, my father is indisposed at the moment. Is there something I can assist you with?”

The room was cozy, packed with sofas upholstered in floral patterns and dark wood furniture, but light streamed in from the south-facing windows and bathed the room in warmth that only the Mediterranean sun could give.

He kissed her hand. “I am sorry to come unannounced, but some information has come my way, and I was hoping to share it with your father.”

“What information?” She sat on the sofa and invited him to sit in the chair opposite.

Edward fidgeted then sat. He would rather not involve her, but she may know the man since she managed her father’s affairs. “The company police have identified the body we found at the excavation site. His name is Mr. Allen from Scheffield. Is that name familiar to you?”

“No, but...” She rose and moved to leave the room. “Wait one moment.” When she returned, she had a copy of Debrett’s book of peerage.

“You travel with a copy of Debrett’s?”

"You would be surprised how helpful it is when traveling abroad. Let us see who Mr. Allen of Scheffield is." She leafed through the pages for several moments. "He must not be anyone important, because he is not in here."

"His hands tell another story. Whoever he was, his hands were soft and well cared for, not hands that had done any type of labor. And he remains a mystery."

"It seems so. What will you do now?"

"I planned to visit the Dendrosa Inn to see if any one there can shed more light on Mr. Allen. It occurs to me that if there are women working there, they would never speak freely with me, but they would speak to you. May I impose on you to accompany me?"

Chapter Twenty Eight

Edward asked for directions to the Dendrosa Inn, and he and Catherine walked to the east side of town. The road east was rather deserted for a weekday afternoon. Edward noted that Catherine brought her parasol and kept it dutifully over her head as they strolled to the inn, much to his own disappointment. He enjoyed watching her bask in the sun, but he supposed after his comment, she would refuse him that honor again.

He introduced himself to the person at the front desk as an investigator from the Suez Canal Company. They were brought to the laundry room to meet a young man named Davidos who cleaned rooms at the hotel.

As they entered, Edward introduced himself and Catherine and stated the purpose of their visit.

"I've told everything I remember to the other officers," Davidos said.

"Yes. Please tell me again. I would like to make sure their report is as thorough as possible."

Davidos sighed as he hung up linens he had washed. "He seemed a nice man. English but not mean like other Englishmen—no offense, sir. He kept to himself. He rarely left, but when he did, it was nighttime. There's nothing else to tell."

"When you say he was nice, what do you mean?"

"Well, for one, he looked me in the eye and spoke to me. Most Englishmen ignore me or order me about. That gentleman *spoke* to me. Asked me what life was like for a boy who worked at an inn in Greece. He asked me about school, where I learned English, what I planned to do with my life, things like that."

Edward meandered through the room, trying to be as unintimidating as possible to Davidos. "Where *did* you learn English?"

"I apprenticed with a silversmith in Athens for a time. He was English. I left after my accident and came here to live with family."

"Accident?"

He stopped hanging linens and held up his hand. The ring and pinky fingers on his right hand were misshapen.

Catherine bowed her head and said, "I am sorry you were hurt."

Davidos ignored her comment. "And he was different in another way. He gave me money each day. Not much, but he always gave me something when I finished cleaning his room."

Edward smiled. "He does sound like a nice man, which makes it all the more puzzling that he was murdered. Did you notice anything odd about his room or his habits? Did he have any visitors?"

Davidos brought another bundle of linen to the clothesline. "As I told the other officers, he only went out at night. He did have a runner give him a message that last day."

"Do you know what the message said?"

"Of course not. I could lose my job if I read other people's messages."

Edward walked to the clothesline and whispered, "I would say it was simply being curious." He opened his hand, which held a rather substantial bribe.

Davidos stared for a moment and then swiped Edward's hand with his own. "Seems like you're a nice Englishman as well, sir. I don't know what the note said. It wasn't written in Greek. But it had numbers like a time."

"What time?"

"Two o'clock."

"Did he ever leave at two o'clock in the afternoon?"

"I told you he only went out at night. I wouldn't know if he left at two o'clock in the morning."

Edward stepped away. "Did you tell this to the other officers?"

"No, sir. They threatened me and were rough. I told them some things, only enough to make them go away. You seem nicer, so I told you everything."

"Thank you for telling me this. I will deal with them accordingly. Would it be possible for us to see the room?"

"There's nothing to see. The other men took all his things, and the room has been cleaned. You can talk to my uncle at the desk. He has the key."

Edward did so, and soon he and Catherine were in the room. As Davidos had said, the room was clean, with fresh linens, freshly mopped floors, and little dust on the few pieces of furniture. They looked under the mattress, in the night table, under the drawers, everywhere they could think of where someone might hide something, but with no luck. They ended their search, thanked Davidos and his uncle for their help, and left.

As they walked back to the inn, Catherine summed up what they knew. "Based on this, we can assume that one, he did not want his presence here known; two, he knew someone locally who wrote to him in English; and three, they arranged a meeting for two o'clock, which was either in the afternoon and he did not go, or it was at two in the morning, in which case the note came from the killer."

He agreed with her summary. They walked the remainder of the way in silence, mulling over what they knew. When they neared the inn, Edward stopped.

"Martin!"

Catherine stopped too, her mouth open in surprise.

Edward took her hands. "Martin Rubeaux! M. R. Services!"

"I am quite at a loss."

"Oh, what a dullard I am. I am sorry, Miss Briggs. There were several mysterious entries in Dupont's personal ledger of equal payments to M. R. Services. There is a man who works for the company named Martin Rubeaux. He may be the recipient of those funds."

"That seems a stretch. There are likely many individuals with the initials M. R. in the company."

He looked a bit crestfallen. "Yes, I suppose you are right. This is starting to unwind me a bit, and I am seeing murderers behind every tree. But he did seem a bit...I do not know how to describe it. While he worked at the site, it was as if he was always watching me, trying to calculate who I am."

"An attentive employee is nothing to be suspicious of and quite possibly should be given greater responsibility."

Edward scowled. "It was more than that. It was more of a feeling that there is something suspicious about him. You are right though. He is one of a hundred men with those initials, and I am grasping at straws. I apologize for my outburst, Miss Briggs."

They arrived at her doorstep, and he thanked her for her assistance. Then he left to return to the work site.

That evening Edward ate a hasty meal, got the necessary address from Patros, and returned home. "Davis, I will require dark clothing for this evening."

"Of course, sir. Dress attire or..."

"No. Plain clothes."

Davis laid out some clothing, and Edward requested different pants.

"If I knew what you would be attending, I could better assist in making clothing selections."

"Unnecessary. These will do." Edward's look conveyed that he would brook no additional questions on the matter.

He left the house, pulled his hat down on his head, and headed to the worker village between the center of town and the sea. This arrangement minimized the number of laborers wandering into town while granting management, who were located at the heart of town, easy access to its amenities.

Edward stopped at the corner of a small alley to get his bearings and noted that the building a short distance away was where Rubeaux lived. He found a secluded spot from which to watch and leaned against the darkened corner of a wall. He had waited less than an hour when a man walked out, and he recognized Rubeaux's loping walk. He watched him travel the length of the block and turn the corner.

As he looked back toward the door, a woman exited a nearby alley and entered the building. She looked like a cleaning woman, but there was something familiar about her. Something that made him sure he knew exactly who it was.

Chapter Twenty Nine

The door closed behind the woman who entered Rubeaux's building, and Edward was frozen in his incredulity. *Blast it, what reckless thing is she up to now?*

He had no choice but to follow her into the boardinghouse, despite his own deep misgivings about the prospect. He stormed across the street, venting his anger at her stupidity with each step. The building before him was a rather run-down two-story boarding house with a sign in French that read, "Rooms Available."

Edward opened the front door and stepped into a dingy hallway that smelled of lamp oil and pungent laborers' laundry left undone. He looked about, but Catherine was nowhere to be seen. He knew Rubeaux's room was number five, so he headed down the hall. He scratched on the door. With no answer, he twisted the handle, which was unlocked, and went inside.

Even with only a bed, a nightstand, and chair, the room felt crowded. There was a faded tapestry from at least fifty years ago on the wall over the bed and little else to indicate someone lived here.

As he crossed to the nightstand, the closet opened, and Catherine said, "Thank goodness it is only you."

He stifled the urge to cry out, caught his breath, and whispered, "What are you doing here?"

"The same thing you are."

"Have you lost your senses? Do you know what could happen to you hiding in a man's closet?"

"I had only planned to check his room. I hid when you arrived."

Edward drew a breath and took in her outfit. "What are you wearing?"

"My servant's clothes."

"And your hair..."

"Has ash from the fire grate to make it gray."

Despite his anger at her, her costume was impressive. "We need to get you out of here now."

"We are here; we should look around."

"There is nothing to see here," Edward said.

Catherine opened the drawer of the nightstand, which had a few French francs on it. "There is a trunk in the cupboard."

His curiosity bowled over his hesitation. He opened the door and lifted the lid of the trunk. Edward riffled through the top portion where letters and stationary were kept. He found letters from Rubeaux's mother asking after his health and work. The postmark was from the small town of Auvergne. Edward had never traveled there, but it was not far from his grandpère's estate, where he summered as a child. There were other letters from a lady friend asking when Rubeaux would return to France and complaining about her mother. He checked between the layers of clothes and along the bottom of the trunk, but found nothing.

As he was about to give up, his finger brushed a small loop on the bottom of the trunk. He pulled it, and the bottom right corner lifted. He pulled it farther and slipped his hand underneath. It was a small space that only took a portion of the bottom. Edward slid his hand around and felt a soft leather folio. Opening it he found one hundred French francs.

He showed it to Catherine. "A tidy sum for a man of his station, and the same amount noted as payment in the ledger."

The front door of the building slammed, and he scrambled to put the money back and restore the trunk as it was. They ran into the cupboard and closed the door. The cupboard was small, and Catherine stood on top of the trunk with her hand on Edward's shoulder as he stood in front of her. There was no room to move, and between the heat of her breath on his neck and the wool of her skirt pushing against his legs, his temperature skyrocketed.

The door to Rubeaux's room opened, and Edward squinted to see between the slats of the closet door. Neither he nor Catherine dared to breathe as Rubeaux and another man entered the room.

"Thought you weren't going to come back to work with the rest of us. Thought you'd got too good overseeing that special crew."

"Not likely." Rubeaux crossed the room and sat on the bed. "Besides, that Tyrington is a queer one."

A bead of sweat formed on Edward's brow, but he dared not wipe it for fear of making any noise. *Now is not the time to be discussing me, Rubeaux.*

"How d'you mean?" Rubeaux's compatriot was a rough-looking man, lean and wiry with a small scar that deformed his lip on the left side.

"I don't know. He's jumpy. Nervous. Always thinking about the damn pots we dig up and how to not damage them. The drawings he made of them were exact. I can't imagine why anyone would care enough about a few old pots and rooms. And he has no leadership. He's bribing the men with extra rations to get them to dig right. It was easy, and I haven't eaten that well in years. But he's odd, and I'd rather work with those I know than some odd Englishman."

Edward was covered in sweat by now, his embarrassment seeping out of his pores by heat and circumstance.

The other man nodded and handed Rubeaux a bottle from his coat as he sat in the chair.

"To free whiskey." Rubeaux raised the bottle and took a healthy swallow. "Where'd you get it, anyway, Louis?"

"I'm not saying. Drink up. The night is early yet, and I need to find a woman."

Rubeaux took another swallow, then handed the bottle back. "Do you smell perfume?"

Edward's heart froze, and Catherine's grip dug deeper into his shoulder.

"No."

"That damn Yvette was probably in here again. And I don't mean cleaning. She's always snooping around trying to catch me alone."

Louis took a choking swig. "She's wanting the attention of a strapping man instead of her sad sack of a husband."

Rubeaux gave a threatening laugh that bordered on a growl, which caused a frisson to go up Edward's spine. "She couldn't handle my attention, and that's trouble I don't need. Let's go."

They both drank until the bottle was empty. Rubeaux told his friend to wait outside then pulled out the money that Catherine had found in the night stand and left. The front door slammed again, and Edward exhaled.

Chapter Thirty

It was several minutes before Edward felt it was safe to move. He and Catherine unfolded themselves from Rubeaux's cupboard and made sure everything was as they'd found it. Edward listened at the door and then peeked into the hall. The hallway was clear, and they left the building.

They sneaked down a side alley. It was a safer option than happening across Rubeaux in the street. They skirted the edge of the village in silence and only spoke again when they were in town.

Edward stopped and turned to her. "What in the world were you thinking? You could have been killed—or worse—in there!"

Catherine stammered, "I... I... I wanted to know if he was tied to the ledger entries."

He paced in front of her. "Of all the harebrained, stupid——yes, I said it——stupid ideas that you could have had, this was by far the worst! Two people have been murdered. It is not safe for you to be involved in this, Miss Briggs."

She appeared on the edge of tears but rallied and shot back, "I am involved, whether you like it or not. I will not now, nor ever, acquiesce to your demands that I remove myself simply because you believe me to be incapable due to the fact that I am a woman."

His voice dropped to a hoarse, threatening whisper, as if the words had to claw their way out of his throat. "See here. I do not need your help investigating. I do not want your help investigating, and it is not safe for you to do so. Do you know how to defend yourself in a fight?"

Catherine failed to heed the warning in Edward's voice and locked her eyes with his. "No, and by the black eye you had the other evening, neither do you."

Edward saw red. He grabbed her left arm and pulled her along the street to her lodgings. When they arrived, he flung her at the door and spat, "Good night."

The night held little sleep for Edward, and he tossed and turned in his anger. He awoke before dawn and, in the darkness, thrust himself into his clothes without waiting for Davis. His thoughts turned to Catherine and her apparent need to prove herself as his equal.

The thought caught him up short. *Similar to how I used to be with Henri.*

He thrust his arms into his shirt and searched for his buttons. He was always trying to prove himself better than Henri to his father. Better at ciphers, better at puzzles, better at any game his father gave them, but Henri always won. And it was clear Father took more joy in that than Edward's abilities.

Adding the buttons to close his shirt helped refocus him on the present and his issue with Catherine. Once dressed, he took a bread roll from the kitchen and left before Davis awoke. He stormed down the trail to the dig, unaware of the lightening sky or the beauty of the early morning that surrounded him.

He could not investigate a murder with Miss Briggs getting herself into trouble at every turn. *Small wonder her father wanted to marry her off. I feel sorry for the gentleman that gets roped into that.*

At midmorning, John Briggs arrived by carriage. Edward's affection for John outweighed his anger at his daughter, and he was genuinely glad to see him. He shook his hand. "What brings you here, John?"

John doffed his hat and indicated that they sit. "I came to inform you that Monsieur Broussard arrived last night, but will only be here a day or possibly two. He is on his way to another meeting in Cairo. Would you help me interview him this afternoon at my lodgings?"

"Yes. What time do you suggest?"

"Would two o'clock be possible?"

"Yes, I will be there."

"Thank you." John turned to leave and stopped, his back to Edward. "Also, do you know of any reason Catherine might be upset?"

Edward's breath caught in his throat. "None whatsoever." He did his best to ensure his tone was as smooth as possible. "But women are such fragile creatures."

"Yes, I suppose that is it. I will see you later then."

Edward spent the remainder of the morning scouting new locations to excavate to gain a better understanding of the extent of the village. As he worked, John's question needled at him. Was John accusing him of upsetting Catherine? His forcefulness was for her own good; she was reckless, impetuous, and foolhardy with her own safety. It was a wonder nothing horrid had happened to her already, and at some point her luck would run out.

He identified several low spots and wall sections that held promise before leaving Patros in charge and heading into town to interview Broussard. As he walked, he brooded over the upcoming fete of politicians and the ramifications of the announcement of his discovery. It was a boon to have his name as the lead archaeologist for the site, and that would pave the path back to solvency. But he was also uncomfortable with the fame this project would bring.

As he got closer to town, he forced himself to think about the interrogation of Broussard. He mentally reviewed the questions he wanted to ask and how best to phrase them to extract the truth.

When he arrived at John's lodging, he found the Briggses with Broussard in the parlor. They seemed to be reminiscing about happy times, as evidenced by their smiles. Edward greeted John and was introduced to Broussard. He greeted Catherine only as cordially as decorum dictated, and she made no attempt to hide her displeasure with him as she excused herself from the room.

Andre Broussard was an old gentleman with white hair and a stooped stature. His lack of energy and the slowness with which he moved, or responded, was unexpected for a man in the import-export business. Typically, men in that business were energetic, and Edward had always been impressed by their quickness of mind and a feeling that they were running against the clock. Even at his age, Mr. Briggs conveyed an urgency in his dealings that Monsieur Broussard obviously lacked. Monsieur Broussard's movements took time, as did his words, and Edward mentally recalibrated his plan on how the interview would go.

Edward closed the door so the men could speak more freely. The interview started on pleasant terms with John and Broussard discussing stories from their long history together, including meetings in dangerous ports and balls with heads of state.

At length, John brought the conversation closer to the point. "Did you hear that Monsieur Dupont was murdered a few weeks ago?"

Broussard looked startled. "Who?"

"Monsieur Dupont. He used to work for you."

"No, I had not heard that. But it was a long time ago that he worked for me. Few people maintain contact once they leave my employ."

"It was not long ago, only two years, correct?"

"Hmm. It seems longer."

Silence hung in the air. Edward let the silence work on Broussard's conscience, waiting for him to rush to fill it. Broussard seemed familiar with this tactic because he remained quiet, content to let the silence fill the room for days if necessary.

At length, Edward spoke. "You have not asked what happened, Monsieur Broussard. When people are murdered, that is the first question on everyone's lips."

Broussard started. "Of course. What happened?"

"He was shot at close range." Edward leaned in toward Broussard, hoping the grim violence of the image would loosen his tongue. "Struggling for the gun that killed him."

Broussard's mouth hung open for a moment before he recovered enough to say, "He must have associated with a rough crowd to meet that end."

"Did he associate with ruffians while in your employ?"

Brightening visibly, Broussard said, "Why, yes he did, a crowd of thieves that stole shipments from my company. You remember, John, when your shipment was lost? It was Dupont's fault. I caught him and dismissed him."

"Yes, I do remember that," John said. "And I appreciate how you made that right."

He beamed at John. "It was my duty to do so."

Edward leaned back. He had made that a bit too easy for him. "What do you know about how your son accosted Dupont and his wife in Egypt six months ago?"

Broussard began coughing. It was clear the question had thrown him, and it was also clear by the way his eyes glanced between John and Edward that he was buying time to think of an answer. His coughing fit subsided only after John brought him a glass of water.

When he'd finally recovered enough to speak, he said, "I do not know where you have received your information from, but it appears to be in error. My son has stayed in Algeria for the past two years."

Alarm bells rang in Edward's head as he recognized the lie for what it was. John saw it too and interjected, "Since your mother died, God rest her soul."

Broussard looked shaken by the comment. "Yes."

So that was the key to this man. He mentally applauded John for so surreptitiously presenting it. Edward sat forward. "I understand your mother was a good and righteous woman. I am sure you and your son miss her dearly, but we can all be comforted that she has gone to her heavenly reward and continues to protect and watch over you both."

"Y... Yes," Broussard stammered.

Edward stood to pace the room. "I must say, though, the veracity of the claim against your son is unimpeachable. Several people witnessed him at the scene in Egypt, and Monsieur Dupont identified him to another. There can be no doubt that it was he who accosted them six months ago."

"I... He... He was not there." Broussard broke into a feverish sweat.

"Would your mother approve of your lies about poor deceased Monsieur Dupont?" Edward stopped in front of Broussard and gave his most imperious look before he continued. "I believe she would have held a higher standard than that."

Broussard mopped his brow. "Leave my mother out of this."

"All I ask for is the truth about your son's whereabouts and motives. We know he was in Egypt six months ago, and there was animosity between him and Monsieur Dupont, and that he threatened him. We could have the Algerian authorities bring him in for questioning. I have no doubt Monsieur de Lesseps could arrange it."

The color blanched from Broussard's face as he held his breath. Then, in a great sob, he broke down, reached for his handkerchief, and covered his face. "All right, all right. Yes, my son traveled to Egypt six months ago. He fled in the night, and it took me days to track him down. I thought his escape might have something to do with Dupont, but I did not know where he was. My son is not well. Not well at all. He is a compulsive gambler and an angry, explosive young man. I never knew until I left him in charge of my business when my mother died, God rest her soul. When those shipments were lost, it was not Dupont's fault, although my son tried to blame him. My son had scrapes with moneylenders before. I knew the truth, yet I was too distraught to face it. I had just lost my dear mother, and I could not stand to lose my son, too. So I pretended to believe him. Dear God. I almost ruined poor Dupont. I treated him so unfairly to try to keep my son and keep what little family I have left whole."

Broussard hung his head and tried to compose himself. After some minutes, he was able to continue. "Realizing how I had dealt with Dupont, I tried to make it right and got him the job with de Lesseps through some of my contacts. I thought that made up for my duplicity and my son's wickedness. But my son had other plans. Six months ago, he found out through a friend that Dupont was quite well in Port Said. I was not even sure where Dupont had gone, whether he was in the offices in France or in Egypt, or which city in Egypt. When my son left, it took me several days to discover Dupont's location and retrieve my son."

Edward looked at John and then asked, "What did your son plan to do?"

Broussard drew a deep breath. "He would never say. I know he accosted the Duponts and visited their home, but I never heard details of what he said or did beyond that."

"Has he traveled at all since then?" John asked.

"I know what you are driving at, and the answer is no. I hired a man to watch him. A guard, so to speak. The doctors told me he should be in an institution, but I cannot bear to do it. Those places are horrid, and I can afford to keep him comfortable in my own home."

"You are sure he has not left?" Edward said.

"I am positive. I will not go into the details of how he is kept, but I will say his leaving unnoticed is impossible."

Edward sat next to him. "I am sorry this interview has been so difficult for you, and you should know that what has been said here will stay between the three of us. But I hope you understand that it was necessary to help determine who may have murdered Dupont. Your son was the only enemy we could find."

Broussard composed himself. "Yes. I understand, and I appreciate your discretion. If his deeds became common knowledge, I would be ruined and would have no means to keep him safe."

John leaned forward. "We will tell no one. And I appreciate your candor."

"I am sorry to have distressed you." Edward stood. "Please accept my apologies and my gratitude for your information. I must return to my work now."

As he neared the door, Edward heard a rustle on the other side, but when he opened the door, the hall was empty.

Chapter Thirty One

As Edward walked back through the center of town toward the work site, he was stopped by a familiar voice.

"Edward, is that you?"

He turned. "Aunt Inez. Francine. How nice to see you both."

Inez asked, "Why are you not at the dig site?"

"I am returning there now. I would love to stay, but I am already behind hand."

She looked a bit crestfallen. "Will you be available for dinner this evening?"

Edward felt a pang of guilt at the concern on Inez's face. He smiled "Yes. I will come to your lodgings at eight o'clock."

"Oh, that would be wonderful."

Edward left them and walked back to the site, reviewing the interview with Broussard. He believed Broussard's story and reconsidered the possibility that the worker he himself had captured was indeed the murderer. He concluded that he had done what he could to investigate Dupont's death and there was nothing more he could do to help Henri in that matter. He spent the remainder of the afternoon focused on cataloguing the day's finds and turning the murders over in his mind, searching for something overlooked.

When he returned home to prepare for dinner, Davis informed him that Asim had left.

"Girard visited and informed him that they had corroborated his story and that he was free to leave. Asim felt he had already overstayed your hospitality, asked me to convey his thanks to you, and went back to the tent city. I told him he could not return to work at the dig site until sometime next week."

"Well, I am glad we could clear his name and he is in much better health than when he arrived. Thank you for all you did for him."

Davis presented a silver salver holding an envelope. "This was delivered for you today."

Edward did not recognize the handwriting, but it was a woman's, and the thought of its writer clenched his stomach. He was half of a mind to toss it into the fire. Instead, he sighed and opened it.

Mister Tyrington,

I do not deserve this indulgence, but I ask with my whole heart that you please visit me this evening after dinner. There are things that cannot be written, and I would like the opportunity to speak with you.

Thank you in advance,

Miss Briggs

Edward replaced the note in the envelope and stuffed it into his pants pocket. "I will need to dress for dinner, Davis. I will dine in town with Aunt Inez."

As Davis prepared his clothing, Edward sipped whiskey and ruminated until he finally had a plan. It was a long shot that she would agree but worth the effort if it paid off. His mood improved, and he whistled while he reviewed the black pants; crisp, white shirt;

luxuriously embroidered waistcoat; and black top coat Davis had laid out for him. Edward remarked that he had taken extra care in his choices this evening.

"Well, sir, how you look reflects on me. I would hate to be the talk of any below-stairs gossip because I failed to help you look your best."

"I am glad to see you protect your spotless reputation, Davis."

"Well, someone has to, sir."

Edward smirked. "Quite."

After dressing, Edward walked toward town. At the highest point in the path, the sun descended into the sea, turning the whole whitewashed village a warm, reddish orange. As he reached the edge of town, he walked through the olive orchards. The trees were beginning to bloom, and their scent was perfection.

That's it. Miss Briggs' perfume was based in olive blossoms, *Eleagnus angustifolia.* He inhaled deeply, and he relaxed. *Careful, Edward. That perfume has always undone you a bit.*

During dinner Inez was solicitous of his health and his mental state, reaffirming that it was his efforts that had cleared Asim and that he would soon be recognized for his archaeological discoveries. He dismissed these comments as quickly as they came up and changed the subject often to avoid dwelling on them. Despite his efforts to direct the conversation, Inez and Francine repeatedly returned the conversation to a Frenchman named Fontaine that they had met in town. He was beyond charming, by Aunt Inez's depiction, and it was clear she thought he might be a good match for

Francine. Despite Francine's earlier assertions regarding her beau, she affirmed his charms and the witty conversations they had.

He finally asked, "Where did you meet Monsieur Fontaine?"

"We were shopping, and he was looking for a scarf for his mother, who has, by his words, the same 'liquid brown' eyes that Francine does. So he asked her to try it on so he could see how the color worked with her eyes. He was so engaging, we had lunch with him."

"Does he live here, or is he visiting?"

Inez looked at Francine, who smiled in a secret sort of way. "I do not think he mentioned that, do you remember, Francine?"

"No. I asked, but I cannot recall his answer."

Edward smirked. "He must have been charming indeed if neither of you can remember the conversation."

Throughout the remainder of the meal, he tried to be as convivial as possible, telling stories of the better times in Zanzibar and some of his other adventures to stretch the evening and arrive at Catherine's lodgings later. If she thought he was not coming, her relief at finally seeing him may put her in a more pliable frame of mind. Or it might bend her toward a volatility that he would rather avoid, but that was a chance he was willing to take.

It was half-past nine when he arrived at Catherine's inn. He was shown to the parlor, where Catherine waited. Unlike his daytime visit, the room now seemed cluttered and uncomfortable without the sunlight through the windows.

She swallowed hard when she saw him. "Thank you so much for coming."

No amount of beeswax or blush could hide the fact that she had been crying. Her eyes were puffy beneath, and she had a general waterlogged look that was juxtaposed by the dashing figure he endeavored to present. He noted her dress was a dark gunmetal gray bordering on a lilac shade. The bodice was more revealing than he had previously seen her wear and, combined with the look of her face, it gave an odd and unfortunate impression. But rather than engender pity from him, he saw the manipulation in it and focused on his plan.

He barely kissed her hand. "Not at all, Miss Briggs. What is it you wish to speak to me about?"

"May I offer you a whiskey?" She went to the spirits table.

"Yes, thank you."

Catherine poured herself a healthy glass of sherry as well. They sat, and he waited, unwilling to be the first to speak.

She swallowed a sip of her sherry. "I asked you here this evening——"

There was a knock on the door, and Catherine started and leapt toward it. She spoke in hushed tones with her lady's maid there. "If you will excuse me, my father has requested my presence. I shall only be a moment."

Edward nodded. "Of course."

She hurried out of the room, closing the door behind her. He stood and wandered around the somewhat cramped quarters. The few furnishings in the room were of average craftsmanship, as one would expect in this type of inn. There were no books, and there was little to keep his mind occupied while he waited. Soon after, he heard Catherine using terse but hushed words outside the door before she re-entered the room and closed the door.

She smiled as if all was well, but he knew better. "I apologize for the delay."

"Not at all." He glanced at his watch. "Now what were you saying, Miss Briggs?"

Catherine perched on the edge of a chair like a nervous cat, her hands wringing a handkerchief between them. Edward sat on the sofa and leaned back, knowing his apparent ease of the situation would unnerve her.

"I asked you here to apologize."

"Apologize for what?"

Her lips thinned as she apparently realized he was going to make her say all of it. "I apologize for not taking more care of my own safety last night. I apologize for endangering both of us with my impulsive behavior." Her tone turned from contrite to sour. "I apologize for ridiculing your black eye. Is there anything I missed?"

"You do not need to apologize to me. I was mistaken to think our relationship could only improve, given the circumstances of our first meeting, but that assumption was my fault. Your lack of care is none of my concern, although I daresay it would impact your father's business greatly if something were to happen to you."

"That was cruel."

"On the contrary, Miss Briggs, it was accurate. Your safety is your and your father's concern. I am a bystander in the whole affair."

"But I want to help you investigate the murders to clear your name."

Edward sat forward. "Ah, well, I will have to advise you against that, and I will no longer share information and request assistance from you. So, if that is all..." He rose from his chair.

"No, wait!"

The corner of his mouth twitched for a split second, but she seized on the expression and stood in front of him. "Oh, I see. My apology is a game to you, is that it? You have been playing the unconcerned bystander? Pushing me to eat more crow, and bow and scrape before you? Well, you had best forget it, Mister Tyrington. I will not be made a fool of. Not by you, not by anyone."

Edward held up his hands before him. "Miss Briggs, I admit I did not sleep much last night. You caused me great worry. I am in this beyond my depth, and I would hate to see you hurt on account of trying to help me."

"But anything that happens to me would not be your fault, and I want to help."

"Do you believe that I could forgive myself if something happened to you during this investigation? That I would not blame myself for the rest of my days? Because I would, and I am afraid it is a burden I could not live with."

She walked to the fireplace to warm her hands. "I am sorry. I promise I will not be so reckless again."

"Miss Briggs, your very nature is reckless."

"That is entirely unfair." She turned to glare at him, lips pursed.

He joined her before the fireplace. "You have provided assistance in the investigation, and you have a keen and deductive mind. But your safety must be paramount, and we both need to have that as a primary concern."

"As I said, I would like to assist in finding the perpetrator of these terrible crimes. Arresting random workers and blaming them does not serve justice, and that is not something I can abide."

Edward sighed. "If you would be willing to promise to only investigate with me and not on your own, and to follow my instructions during this investigation, your help would be valuable."

Catherine crossed her arms. "I promise."

"I am not finished yet. In exchange for that promise, I will do something for you. You have told me that your father has been...'parading you before every eligible bachelor,' and that it is not your wish to marry. Therefore, in exchange for your tempered assistance, I will play the role of interested bachelor to keep your father from pestering you. However, should you break your promise and put yourself in danger again, I will tell your father the entire story and let him deal with you."

She placed her hands on her hips, incredulity on her face. "Oh, that *is* cruel."

"Not cruel, per se, more like an insurance policy. You see, I do not doubt that you mean to keep your promise, but I doubt your ability to keep your impetuosity in check, which would endanger your promise. I am hopeful that the threat of exposure will help keep you to your word."

Catherine's face contorted in anger...and something else. Respect? Admiration? Understanding? It was hard to read.

She settled into her chair and brooded for several minutes, drinking sherry and turning the prospect over in her mind before asking, "You will keep me informed of all developments and allow me to investigate with you?"

"As long as that does not threaten your safety, yes."

She stood and faced him, her tone clipped. "How do I know you will not decide that everything threatens my safety?" She turned and walked to the window.

Edward waited a moment, then stood beside her, his tone gentle. "Because I do need your help, and I believe I have shown myself to be fair-minded regarding your escapades. Otherwise, I would not make this offer."

He saw her reflection in the window snicker before she spoke. "And there is the added benefit that this arrangement also serves to cow your aunt's designs for you and Francine?" She faced him and crossed her arms.

He bowed his head. "Touché. I admit that may also be a motivating factor here. Regardless, this is the deal that is being offered. Agree or not; it is up to you."

After a few more minutes of contemplation, she offered him her hand. "Then I accept your terms."

"Excellent." Edward pulled a sheet of paper from his breast pocket. "Sign here."

Her jaw dropped. "What?"

"Come, Miss Briggs. You know as well as I do that any verbal contract is only worth the paper on which it is written. Otherwise my exposure will be a case of my story versus your denial."

She snatched the paper from his hand, walked to the desk, and signed it. "This is nothing short of extortion."

"If you do not wish to participate in this investigation, there is no need to sign. We can part ways here and now." She looked down, and he walked to her. "But you do have a brilliant mind, and I admit I am concerned about my future here. But I am also concerned about yours."

Catherine handed him the paper. "You have bested me."

He pocketed it. "Please, call me Edward. As we are 'courting,' that is appropriate."

"All right, Edward, please call me Catherine."

"I look forward to working with you, Catherine. I do apologize for this, but I must have some surety about your safety going forward."

"I hope to not regret this, Mister—Edward."

Edward kissed her hand and left. He whistled as he walked through the olive groves, and when he returned home, he avoided questions from Davis regarding his excellent mood. That night, he slept better than any other since his return to Santorini.

Chapter Thirty Two

The next morning, after he set his crews to their various tasks, he wrote a note to Mr. Briggs requesting a lunch meeting, alone, and sent it to him by a runner who was instructed to wait for a response. The response was positive, suggesting a time and location at a restaurant near his hotel.

The morning wore on with delay after delay at the work site. Edward checked his watch repeatedly and asked others the time as well since it appeared his watch was moving too slowly, but it was the dread of what was coming that made the day seem to crawl along. When it was time to go, he could not leave fast enough. He arrived a few minutes early and waited for John at the table closest to the door. His nerves were shot in anticipation and hatred of the deception in which he was about to engage. He jiggled his match safe in his pocket as he watched the street for John.

When he arrived, Edward made small talk about his discoveries, the current relationship between France and Egypt, the place of the Ottomans over the pasha, and any other topic through the meal until he could no longer delay the purpose of his visit.

"Sir, I am sure you are wondering at my unexpected invitation to lunch, so I will not delay any longer. I have enjoyed getting to know you and Miss Briggs these past few days." Edward looked out the window, unwilling to look John in the eye as he spoke the next words. "There are some things in life one seems to know instantly, regardless of whether one is ready, or was even seeking it. What I am trying to say is, I enjoy your daughter's company and would like to ask your permission to court her." His stomach dropped, waiting for the blow that he dreaded, and assumed, would come.

But as Catherine had warned him, John was only too pleased at the prospect. "This is a bit unexpected but welcome. Welcome indeed. I understand about instantly knowing. That was how I felt about Catherine's mother. An extraordinary woman she was, and I knew I wanted to spend the rest of my life with her as soon as we met. I only wish our time together had been longer." He lifted his glass. "To a successful courtship, Mister Tyrington. Catherine is a talented helpmeet who will bring value to any enterprise she joins."

Edward raised his glass for the toast, smiling while he winced inwardly at what he had done. He had grown to consider John a friend. Deceiving him in this manner—in any manner, really—was something he had not thoroughly considered when he devised this plan and something he wished he could retract. John was genuinely happy, and Edward was genuinely miserable, although he made every effort to appear delighted.

That evening after a small dinner at home, Edward donned his darkest cloak and left the house. He watched to make sure he was not followed as he made his way to Rubeaux's lodgings. There were a few people on the streets, alone and in pairs. In Rubeaux's window, a lamp was lit, and there was evidence of movement inside. He waited for the street to clear, then settled into the darkness beneath the stairs across the alley and waited.

After some time, he flexed his knees to ease their aching when a man in a galabia walked down the opposite side of the street. Edward clung to the shadows in the hopes of remaining hidden. Several minutes later, an old cleaning woman carrying a large bag came down the street toward him. He pulled his hat down a bit further.

"You are terrible at blending in," Catherine whispered as she passed.

He grabbed her arm and hissed, "What are you doing here?"

"Blending in, which is more than I can say for you. You did not even notice me pass a few minutes ago."

"The only one who passed was an Egyptian man in a galabia."

"Wrong. An English woman passed, dressed as a man in a galabia. And it has been me following you since you left your lodgings at 8:52 p.m., but I am sure you were unaware of that." She followed with, "Close your mouth, it is rather unbecoming."

"Skulking around in the dark is not in the terms of our agreement."

"You leaving me out of the investigation is prohibited by our agreement."

The lamp went out in Rubeaux's room, and Edward pulled her deeper into the shadows. "We will argue later."

Rubeaux exited the building and turned right. Edward clasped Catherine's hand, and they stalked through the dark abandoned alleys far enough behind him to keep from being noticed. They followed him for several blocks, moving closer to town and the homes of the canal project managers.

Here the buildings were farther apart, with small gardens between. Rubeaux's pace slackened, and they slowed, moving from one dark area of cover to another. Rubeaux stopped near a door that Edward knew, and Edward pulled Catherine into the nearest side alley, where they crouched next to a stairwell that had a small pile of refuse beside it. Conditions were worse further along the alley and they decided this was the best spot despite the odor. They remained silent as they waited, and every once in a while, he peered over the stairs and around the corner. The cramped conditions were bad, but the smell was worse, and it seemed an interminable amount of time that they waited.

Edward wondered what this must be like for Catherine. Why was she so insistent on being a part of this when it was filled with uncomfortable waiting?

Edward heard a door close. He peeked out and saw Baba locking his door. He turned their way, and Edward motioned to Catherine to crouch further. Baba passed, and then Rubeaux followed him at a distance, much as they were doing to Rubeaux.

After a minute, they emerged from the alley to catch sight of Rubeaux rounding a corner. They hastened to catch up when a couple came around the bend. Edward and Catherine slowed their pace to not appear to be rushing, and looked down as they passed. After the couple had moved on to the next street, Edward leaned around the corner and saw Rubeaux much farther along. They followed two more blocks, where the homes became more spacious and the gardens larger.

He chanced a whisper, "Whoever he is seeing is someone important."

Catherine nodded, and they continued on as Baba approached a house. They were still a block away and ducked into a landscaped area where there were shrubs tall enough to hide them. Edward peeked out at Baba talking to someone. He did not see Rubeaux and surmised he was hidden as well.

Baba's conference with the person who answered the door took only a moment. He was handed something before he turned back in their direction. Edward hustled Catherine farther from the street, and they waited to see Baba, and then Rubeaux, pass again. Coming out of their concealment, they followed like the line of creeping ducklings that they had unknowingly formed.

It was a short walk this time before Baba stopped under a street lamp. He seemed to be reading from a paper he had pulled from his pocket. He walked farther on, then stopped in front of a home and knocked. A man came to the door. They spoke, and the man donned his coat and left with a leather bag. Baba and his new compatriot walked toward the worker area of the village.

Catherine squeezed Edward's hand and pointed down a side street. They stepped into the dimly lit alley and stopped in a dark doorway. She handed him a lump of gray fabric. "Quick, put this on."

He looked incredulous, but she donned her own. "It is a galabia. We will fit in better in this area if we are seen."

Edward donned it as fast as he could. Since it was a loose shift with ties, it was easy to wear over his street clothes. They placed cloth on their heads with sturdy rope to hold them in place and walked back onto the street. Rubeaux was farther away, and Edward regretted the unnecessary step of donning the galabia.

However, when they reached the end of the street and rounded the corner, he saw the wisdom of it. Baba and Rubeaux were down the hill at the edge of the tent city where the Egyptian workers lived. Catherine gave him a sideways glance, obviously quite pleased with herself. He ignored her silent gloating and hurried down the hill so as to not lose their quarry.

It was clear Baba knew where he was going as they entered the rabbit warren of tents. There were a few people about, but not many, as it was growing late and the morning's work would come early. Some fires still smoldered, and a few men sat around them passing pipes.

They moved toward the sound of a woman groaning. As they neared, it was clear she was in pain. Edward and Catherine turned to hide in the darkness of the other tents.

Baba went to a tent, said something, and entered. There were several figures rendered in shadow on the walls, including the image of a pregnant woman lying on a cot. She let out a scream, and there was hurried discussion before Baba emerged, leaving the doctor he's brought to assist in the birth. Baba left, and soon thereafter, Rubeaux scuttled from his hiding place to follow Baba again.

They returned the way they came, with Edward and Catherine following behind. As they left the tent city, Edward pulled her down another alley. "It is late, and they are probably returning to their lodgings. We should do the same."

Catherine collected the galabias they wore and, as she packed them in her satchel, knocked a plant off a step. The container crashed to the ground. They locked eyes and ran to the farthest darkened doorway they could reach.

It was moments later when Rubeaux's head looked down the end of the alley. Edward held his breath as Rubeaux started toward them. They squeezed against the doorway as he approached.

Seeing the broken pot, Rubeaux looked one more time down the alley and, satisfied, headed off.

As he rounded the corner, Catherine looked at Edward and opened her mouth to speak. Edward clapped a hand over it and shook his head. A moment later, Rubeaux peeked down the alley again.

They stayed hidden for several minutes before daring to emerge from the doorway. Edward motioned to Catherine to stay put. He sneaked down the alley and looked around the corner. Rubeaux was at the far end of the block and turning toward his own home.

Edward returned to Catherine. "It is safe now, at least from Rubeaux. We need to get you home."

They took a shortcut through the village, and it was late when they arrived at Catherine's door. He said, "I will contact you tomorrow."

She nodded, walked around the garden path toward the back of the inn, and went inside.

Chapter Thirty Three

The next morning Edward went from breakfast straight to Baba's office. As he entered the cramped space, Baba raised one eyebrow and regarded him coolly. "What do you want?"

Edward smiled and dove right in. There was no point in pretending he was there for Baba's company. "Two things. First, have you had any word from the police on the investigation?"

"No. Have you discovered anything?"

"Not yet."

"What else?" Baba pursed his lips.

"Would it be possible to send Rubeaux back to my excavation?"

"Why do you want him?"

"With preparing for the ball and locating new rooms to excavate, we require as much assistance as we can manage, and he is now familiar with our operation."

Baba sighed. "I'll send him over later today."

Edward returned to the excavation and organized his best workers to clean everything in the fresco rooms. The rest of the crew surveyed and excavated areas to the west. He found a quiet corner to work alongside Patros for a time. They spoke about the upcoming ball and the preparations needed, and then Edward homed in on his quarry.

"Patros, do you trust Baba?"

Patros faced away from him so he could not see his expression. He was silent for a time. "The ocean has many currents."

"What is that supposed to mean?"

"I thought it was obvious."

Edward shifted position to look Patros in the face. "I am being serious. I would like to know how trustworthy he is."

Patros stopped working and thought for a moment before answering. "In part, that depends on how trusting *you* are. You asked if I trust him. Yes, I do, with my life. Does that mean I understand or trust everything he does? No. Does that make him trustworthy to you? No."

Edward laughed. "You are a cryptogram of contradictions, but if I take your meaning, it depends on the situation."

"That is one way to look at it. The other is whether he feels you are trustworthy to him. If so, he will keep faith with that. If not, he will not be so motivated."

"Thank you. You have been almost no help whatsoever."

Patros laughed. "My pleasure."

During the lunch hour, as Baba sat to eat with his compatriots in the cafeteria. Edward took a roll and fruit and ate them as he walked to Baba's office. *This is ill-advised, but I must know more about Rubeaux.*

He skirted around the building and found the area deserted, so he worked the lock on the office door with a pick.

Memories of sneaking around the Essex estate with Henri flooded his mind. Henri had been intent to learn all the secrets the estate held, including those in rooms that were locked. He had worked the entire summer on lockpicking after hearing of Alfred Hobbs and his great lock controversy, wherein he picked some of the most impenetrable locks at Westminster Abbey to show his skill. After months of practice, Henri had perfected his technique. He taught Edward how to feel the action of the lock and how to provide the proper encouragement for it to disengage. They had spent the last two weeks of that summer visiting every forbidden room on the estate.

The lock yielded smoothly, and he slipped into Baba's office like a ghost. The room was cool, and there were files and papers in stacks on the floor around the desk. Edward hastened to the cabinet behind the desk and worked the lock on the top drawer. He was careful to leave no scratches from the pick, and soon he had the drawer open. The files were well organized and neat, but they were labeled in Arabic, leaving him in the dark about what they contained.

Edward thumbed through receipts and orders, and finally found what he sought: the personnel files. There were dozens of files in this section, and it took him a few minutes to find Rubeaux's. He learned Rubeaux was twenty-two years old and had one incident with the police for fighting about six months ago. As he returned the file, Dupont's name on a folder caught his eye. Looking more closely, he discovered that Rubeaux had been assigned to Dupont until a few days after his death, at which time he was reassigned to the quarry on Santorini.

He returned the file to the cabinet and went to the door. Through the window, he heard: "Baba, I am glad you are back. We need to discuss the work at the south end of the quarry."

Edward's heart skipped a beat, and he watched through the blinds as he held his breath. Baba spoke to the person, then moved away from the door and around the corner of the building. Edward sneaked out, locking the door behind him, and hastened around the other corner, past several smaller buildings, and back to the excavation.

After lunch, the sun was scorching hot, and he moved the men to work in the shaded areas of the site. Edward saw Rubeaux lope toward the excavation site. *Interesting that there is no sense of urgency in his stride like there was last night.* Edward gave no indication that he'd noticed him walking up and managed to ignore him until Rubeaux was nearly on top of him. "I am sorry to have missed my extra rations today, but I am here as you requested."

Edward felt the sting of rebuke for his leadership all over again. "Never mind that and get to work overseeing the group hauling ash."

He knew he should not be petty and snappish, but giving Rubeaux the hardest, least interesting job on the project was something he relished. Besides, if he decided to lighten Rubeaux's load later, he may be more forthcoming with information. At least that seemed like justification enough.

Through the remainder of the day, Edward put Rubeaux through his paces, and Rubeaux performed every task he was asked to do with focus and ease. His final task was to assist Edward in completing the catalogue for the day. The remainder of the crew had left, and it was only Edward and Rubeaux at the site. Edward remarked on his work and asked what field his previous employment had been.

"Many things, sir. I come from a farm in southern France. You learn a lot about hard work on a farm."

"What brought you all the way to Santorini?"

"Looking for a bit of adventure. Farm life will teach a man a lot, but there are many things in this world you'll know nothing about if you don't get out every once in a while."

"True enough. Do you still have family in...what town did you say you were from?"

"Yes, I still have family in France, along with goats and cows, who sometimes feel like family."

Edward noted that he did not reveal his hometown, and Edward gave his most winsome smile in response. "That sounds beautiful. These types of projects can be rewarding in their own right, but being homesick can wear on your soul. I hope you are faring well. We are finished here for this evening. Thank you. I will see you tomorrow."

Before going home, Edward went to the botanical garden in town. He scanned the rows of flowers until he found what he was seeking. He picked eight nutmeg geraniums, which were meant to request a meeting at eight o'clock and one goldenrod to suggest caution. He tied the bouquet together with a string and found a runner to deliver it to Catherine. He hoped she carried her floriography book on her travels, along with her Debrett's.

He returned home and ate a quick supper. At eight o'clock, he informed Davis he was going out and would likely return late. He stepped outside and walked down the path toward the village. Minutes later, he stopped and waited. Catherine appeared from the darkness and strode up beside him. She was again dressed as a maid on her night off, in a rather worn dark-gray walking dress, serviceable boots, and a small hat with a veil to help conceal her face.

He nodded and walked off the path and into a copse of wind-worn trees. "Thank you for being prompt. Now, let us clear the air a bit, shall we? Do you think following me last night is in keeping with our agreement?"

"I was never more than thirty-five feet from you and spent part of the evening holding your hand, so yes, I do believe it was in keeping with our agreement. You would have never made it ten feet into the tent city if it had not been for my costumes, and you know it."

"I am willing to concede that point. I do commend you on your ability in that arena. But back to the matter at hand. I share my information with you, and you must do the same for me, including telling me when and where you are planning on sleuthing."

"I will do so in the future."

"Good. I looked into Rubeaux's employment record today. I discovered that, until a week ago, he worked for Monsieur Dupont as a courier. He has only been on the island of Santorini for a short time, which makes him a prime suspect—if the police would look at anyone other than me or Asim." He informed her of his day with Rubeaux, none of which surprised her.

"You will not get far questioning him. For one thing, he has no respect for you. You heard what he said while we hid in his cupboard."

Edward's jaw clenched.

She continued, "And he is up to something, following Baba around. People who are up to something are never forthcoming with information."

"True enough."

"Who are we following tonight?"

"Lord Livingstone. I do not know why he is on Santorini, and my father harbored many suspicions about him. I would like to know if he goes anywhere to see if I can glean his purpose here. Besides, we have had two close calls with Rubeaux, and I do not want him to suspect we are following him."

They arrived at Livingstone's lodgings at the hotel Athinios, not far from the sea cliff near the center of town. They hid across the alley in the doorway of an old church. The night had begun balmy enough, but the clouds came soon after they settled in, and the weather turned threatening. Edward suggested leaving, but Catherine would have none of it.

"Whatever is afoot will not wait for fairer weather."

They waited, huddled in the doorway as the first rain drops fell. She shivered next to him. He removed his cloak and placed it across her shoulders. She nodded in thanks. The wind blew some trash down the lane before the rain came in earnest. As Edward regretted his decision to come out this evening, the rain slackened and stopped. That was one nice thing about Santorini: when the rains came, they never lasted long.

Soon after the sky cleared, Livingstone's door opened, and he stepped out. Edward nudged Catherine, who nodded. They followed him at a distance for several blocks until they entered the central part of the village, with its winding streets and impressive gardens.

The water still ran through the gutters, and walking was sloppy. They both stepped carefully where they could but did not always manage to keep clear of the water, mud and waste. In his effort to step around the puddles, Edward did not pay close enough attention to where they were going until Catherine nudged him and whispered, "Look."

Livingstone slowed his stride near a man who leaned against a wall about a block from them. Edward and Catherine turned down a nearby alley to stake out a better viewing position. They moved into a stairwell that led underground and watched through the wrought iron railing beside it.

The interaction was brief, but an envelope changed hands before both men moved away. Livingstone continued walking, and the person he had met stayed against the wall for a moment before following Livingstone. A few blocks up, Livingstone turned right. At that intersection, the other man turned left.

Edward pulled Catherine to follow him. "I swear that is Rubeaux. He has the same loping gait. Livingstone may have paid him to do something. I would like to know what it is."

They followed Rubeaux as he turned north, toward the wealthiest part of the village. He strode up to a home, and Edward noted the address. The name Fontaine was on the mailbox. They skulked in some nearby shrubs, and Edward chanced to whisper to Catherine, "This is the house Baba visited last night."

She nodded, and they waited in the darkness.

From nowhere, a hand clapped on Edward's shoulder and a voice growled in his ear, "Come with me."

Edward froze, and Catherine's eyes were huge as another man came up behind and grabbed her.

CHAPTER THIRTY FOUR

Catherine stood and, in her farmer's French, said, "You frightened me! We are just leaving work and going home!"

Her voice was reedy and thin, and her eyes were big as saucers. But she held her own against the man who had grabbed her. The part of Edward's heart that was not constricted by fear beamed with pride at her quick thinking.

The light was dim, and Edward could not make out either of their faces as the second man said, "I don't think so. You're going to see Mr. Fontaine."

The men escorted them up to the house, holding Edward's and Catherine's hands behind their backs. They were pushed into a luxurious living room with a fire blazing in the grate. When Edward turned to look at them, one man holstered his weapon and stood by the door while the other exited. Catherine warmed herself by the fire.

Edward strolled over to her. "If asked, your name is Marie Blanc. Let me do the talking."

A rather stocky gentleman with light hair and wearing a deep-green velvet smoking jacket entered the room. He clucked at the guard by the door. "Leave us." Edward guessed he was in his mid-thirties.

The man poured glasses of whiskey and sherry. "Mister Tyrington, Miss Briggs, what an unexpected surprise for you to come visiting. Especially in such...colorful attire."

Catherine burst forth. "Why have we been brought here against our wills?"

Edward raised a hand to stop her, but the words were already out. She froze, and Fontaine chuckled. "I have heard about your brashness, Miss Briggs. Frankly, I was not sure I believed it until now."

"How do you know who we are?" Edward asked.

"As the chief of police, it is my business to know. It is also my business to know who is lurking on my property."

"Monsieur Fontaine," Edward said. "We do apologize. We were a bit lost and attempting to get our bearings."

Fontaine's well-practiced smile slid across his mouth. "Of course you were. But the question remains of your rather intriguing mode of dress. Does Miss Briggs work for her father by day and as a cleaning woman by night?"

Catherine's mouth opened and closed several times, but no words came out.

He handed around the glasses. "Let us be honest with one another. Why were you hiding in my bushes?"

Knowing he was trumped, Edward sipped his whiskey. "I followed someone here."

Fontaine leaned back in his chair. "Why were you following him?"

"I was investigating Dupont's and Mr. Allen's murders."

"Some say the murderer is you, Mister Tyrington."

Catherine gasped.

"Only based on the flimsiest of circumstantial evidence," Edward said.

Fontaine leaned forward, steepling his fingers in front of his face. "I, too, am interested in finding the real murderer. Do you have any suspicion as to the culprit?"

Edward relaxed and shared his interview with Monsieur Broussard and the ledger entries for M. R. Services. "If the police were interested in the real murderer, they might have already uncovered these things."

"You are a good investigator. If you determine anything else of consequence, you must inform me as soon as possible. I would like to catch the murderers, and my men are, shall we say, not trained in deduction to your caliber. It is too bad sleuthing is not your vocation, because I could use a good man such as yourself. Monsieur LeMarchal hired you, is that correct? How long have you known him?"

"We went to university together."

"Ah, yes, during his family's exile from France for opposing Louis Napoleon. What did his family do in England?"

"As I said, he went to university. His father worked."

"For whom? It must have been difficult for them being in England those years."

Edward stood and walked to the fire. "Why the sudden interest in the history of the LeMarchal family?"

Fontaine pivoted to face Catherine. "Forgive me, Miss Briggs. I have all but ignored you. How is your father?"

She removed Edward's cloak and smoothed her hair. Despite the ash she had added to make it appear gray, her hair glowed in the firelight. She forced a calm smile. "My father is fine, Monsieur Fontaine. You seem to know quite a bit about us. Did you also know that I am friends with the LeMarchal family?"

Edward clenched his jaw, and his eyes widened as she began to speak about Henri. It was as if a demon possessed her, and she spoke clear and fast. But as he listened, it became obvious that prattling was all she was doing. Filling the room with fluff and great vacuous stories about the antics of Henri's cousin's hunting dogs, the winter it was so cold they lost two horses, and the baby his second cousin had the previous spring. On and on and on she spoke, scarcely taking a breath, until an hour had gone by and both men looked as though they were bored into a stupor.

At great length, she said, "Oh my word, I have taken up all the conversation. My father warns me of that, you know. I sometimes get so excited I cannot contain myself."

Monsieur Fontaine stood. "It is rather late, Miss Briggs. You should be on your way. Mister Tyrington, I hope you will share any other information you find with me and my men. It is important that we solve these murders as soon as possible."

"Of course, Monsieur Fontaine."

Once outside, they walked three blocks before Edward pulled her aside. "What was all that talk about Henri's family?"

She smirked. "He wanted information, so I gave it."

He looked in her eyes, and her smirk slipped into something far more serious. Her lips parted as her eyes searched his.

Edward leaned in and kissed her. The warmth of her lips belied her shivering as his tongue found hers. She responded in kind, and he pulled her closer and placed a hand on her cheek. It was a soft kiss, passionate but respectful, a kiss that lingered in its own pleasure, neither hurried nor staid.

When she pulled away, he kept his eyes closed for fear of looking at her and breaking the spell. He finally opened his eyes to see her smile, along with something else, something almost wistful in the gray of her eyes.

She looked at her feet. "We should go."

He linked his arm in hers and walked her home.

The next morning was Sunday, and Edward worked on his archaeological notes through the morning. After lunch, he heard a noise in the olive orchard behind the house. Then it came again. Both he and Davis stood by the edge of the windows that faced the rear of the property so they could peer out but remained hidden. A boy hid under one of the shrubs at the edge of the orchard. He looked to be about twelve years old, and he was apparently trying to be stealthy, but the dried leaves on the forest floor gave him away.

Edward motioned to Davis to join him by the front door. "Have you ever seen that boy before, Davis?"

"No, sir."

Then it struck him. "I met the chief of police last night in a rather less than satisfying manner. I suspect he has sent this boy to keep an eye on me."

"Were you arrested, sir?"

"No, nothing so dramatic, but it was a visit that I would not wish to repeat." *At least not the part that included Fontaine...* The corner of his mouth twitched as he remembered the taste of Catherine's lips. "Davis, in case this boy is here to spy on me, I need you to go to the botanical garden after I leave, pick a bouquet of flowers, and have a runner deliver it to Miss Briggs." He wrote a note that read, "Market Jeweler," and told Davis where the botanical gardens were. "Make a bouquet of two nutmeg geraniums and one goldenrod and place this note in the middle."

Before Davis left to complete the errand, Edward donned his coat and hat and began the most circuitous route to the market that he could think of. He made sure to whistle as he left to alert anyone nearby of his departure. He strolled toward the worker village, and after a few blocks, he made a sharp turn toward a small church and stopped. His vantage point on the steps of the church allowed him to see the boy, who slowed and then looked for a way to stop without appearing obvious. It was clear he had never shadowed anyone before, and Edward wondered who was paying him.

He almost felt sorry for him, but not quite, as he entered the church and sat in the light filtered by the stained-glass windows. He tried to remember who Saint Neophytos was as he sat under his statue's watchful gaze. The services had ended, but the scent of incense still lingered. For a few moments he was lost in the wonder and adoration of his childhood view of religion, until he realized that the smell had invoked darker ghosts. Memories of him and Thaddeus thumb wrestling in church as his parents ignored them, the time Thaddeus picked a flower from the church garden for Edward because he was his favorite brother. The guilt of his happy memories pressed on him. He was grateful when the door of the church opened, and he spun around to see a woman entering, back-lit by the sunlight outside. As the door closed behind, he saw she was dressed as a maid and had a small bottle in her hand. She pulled the stopper and thrust the bottle into the holy water font in the narthex of the church. Edward remained still so as not to startle her. When the bottle was filled, he saw her drink from it before replacing the stopper and leaving. As she opened the door, he saw the boy outside across the street waiting for him. *At least I know where he is.*

His own bitterness gnawed at him as he rose and crossed the room. He listened at the door at the back of the church that likely led to the priest's private area. Hearing nothing, he opened the door a crack and peered down a long hallway with two doors on the right, a door at the left, and a door at the far end of the hall that appeared to be the rear exit of the church. He walked down the hall, and as he passed the first door, a voice said "Have you come to confess your sins, my son?"

Edward stopped in his tracks. The grillwork on the confessional doors was thin wrought iron in a very ornate pattern. Although he could not see the priest well through the grille, he could tell he was older by his white hair. The priest did not look up at him but kept his head bowed and said, "You are welcome to rest here, my son."

Edward thought of his childhood priest and reached for the doorknob. Perhaps it was his guilt that stopped him, or his lack of faith, but rest was not something he deserved. He turned and ran from the building.

Edward ran his fingers through his hair and donned his hat as he jogged down a side alley away from the church. He stopped and looked at his watch; it was almost quarter past one. He ran through a few alleys to make sure he was not followed on the way to the market.

Edward tried to clear his mind, but it was impossible. The best he could do was focus on his surroundings, each fruit seller, each kiosk of scarves sold by women sewing in the shadows, the animals that hung skinned and dried for sale, they were his salvation in this moment. He walked to their meeting spot, but the jewelry seller was not in the space Edward recalled. He looked around to see if Catherine was also lost, but she was not there. Asking the person in the adjacent booth, he was told the jeweler was in the next alley over. He walked away and, from a nearby doorway, heard what he knew to be Catherine's scream.

Chapter Thirty Five

A man with closely cropped hair and a grizzled beard burst from the doorway and ran into the crowd. Edward decided to forgo chasing him and raced to the door to find Catherine, steeling himself for what he might find.

Catherine lay on the ground, somewhat dazed. Her eyes were open, and she rubbed her head. Edward knelt next to her. A lump was forming near her temple.

He took her hand. "Catherine, are you all right?"

"Thank God it is you. Yes, I am all right." She sat up and propped herself against the wall. Several people came to see what the fuss was about, but none offered any assistance.

"Do you need a doctor? Are you cut anywhere?"

"No, he did not have a knife." She became more aware of her surroundings. "Do you have a flask?"

Edward nodded and pulled a flask from his pocket. "It is whiskey."

"Good." She took a slug. When she had caught her breath, she rubbed her head and said, "Do you know who accosted me? Reginald Broussard. For all the assurance his father gave that he could not escape from his home, he has, and I would wager has done so several times."

"Good God. It is a miracle you were not killed. What did he want?" He sat next to her and took a slug of whiskey himself.

"For me to leave him and his father alone, and to stop dredging up the past. He said he saw my letter and knew his father was here, and that I was meddling where I ought not be. Then he said some rather despicable things, so I bit the hand he had over my mouth and stomped on his foot. That's when he threw me down, and I hit my head on the floor."

Edward inspected her injury again. "You will need something for that lump. Are you sure you are not hurt anywhere else?"

"I do not believe so."

He helped her to stand and continued to check her head. He then inspected her eyes to ensure there was no indication of head trauma. As he stared into her eyes, he thought of their kiss and his mind flew from physician inspecting her to man in throws of emotions he was not prepared to address. Catherine seemed to sense his shift, because she pushed at him and said, "I am fine. You do not need to hover over me."

He stepped back from her, and she walked into the alleyway. "A spot of tea will go a long way toward settling my nerves. There is a tea shop nearby. We can sit and discuss whatever you wanted to see me about."

He offered his arm. "I wanted to strategize about our next move. However, Broussard on the loose changes things, as he is now the prime suspect. We should report that to the police. Speaking of which, Fontaine is having me shadowed by some local boy now."

"Is he still following you?"

"I lost him. I took over an hour's long stroll getting here. I left him in the village."

Edward directed her to a small café at the back of the market. They stepped into the cool shade and sat at a secluded table by a persimmon tree. Catherine ordered a chamomile tea, and Edward ordered coffee and a plate of pastries.

"I wanted to discuss what we have learned and what we should do going forward," he said. "Despite our efforts, we have not removed anyone from the list of suspects, and Broussard has now added himself back onto it."

She sipped her tea. "Indeed. So, what do we know? Broussard is the prime suspect for Dupont, but so far there is no connection to Mr. Allen. Rubeaux is up to something by following Baba, but we do not know what. Baba is up to something with Fontaine, but again, we do not know what."

Edward leaned forward. "I have a theory about that. The first night, Baba met someone at Fontaine's house and received a slip of paper. It was probably the address of the doctor, since he checked it outside the doctor's door and then brought the doctor to the tent city to assist with the birth of a child. This leads me to the conclusion that the child may be Fontaine's."

"A good theory, but it does not relate to the murders, so it does not help us."

He gazed at her for a moment. The azure of her dress made her eyes appear even bluer, and her hair was tousled in a most pleasing way after her encounter with Broussard. "True. We have too many possibilities for Dupont's murder and none for Mr. Allen's, and we do not know if the murders are connected in any way. I still like Rubeaux as the main suspect. It is quite possible he was blackmailing Dupont, or Dupont was using him in some way that required payment. Since he was in both places during the murders, he is at the top of my list. I plan on following him again tonight, but I would ask that you allow me to do this alone. You have already been attacked today, and I would like to know that you are safe at home."

Catherine nodded. "I will acquiesce to your request. But you must inform me of what happens as soon as you can tomorrow."

"Agreed. We need to report the incident with Broussard to Officer Girard. They should look for him."

She agreed and then hesitated.

"Edward, there is one more thing to discuss." She twisted a kerchief between her fingers. "I meant it when I said I had no intention to get involved with anyone. What happened last night was...was...an aberration. As such, it was not anything that you should ever consider repeating. Quite frankly, I should have slapped you."

Edward's heart froze, and his face masked the blow those words delivered. Somehow he managed to offer, "I apologize for attempting to modify the terms of our agreement. It will not happen again."

She continued fiddling with her kerchief and changed the subject. "By the way, did you see the flowers by the window at Fontaine's home? Begonias and a yellow chrysanthemum."

Edward nodded. "Beware slighted love. He may be in a bit of a fix with his wife or possibly some other woman."

"Which demonstrates that he, too, may be a student of floriography."

"Good point. To make this easier, let us develop our own flower language. Since buttercups are blooming, let us use those to arrange meetings. The number of buttercups will be the hour of meeting. Daisies and asters are beginning to bloom. A daisy will suggest a meeting at the jeweler in the market. An aster will suggest a meeting near my home. Does that suit you?"

"Yes, those combinations will only mean childish innocence or childish undying love by any dictionary interpretation. Very good. Now if you will excuse me, I would like to go home and rest. Please escort me to the police and then home. I am a bit wary with Broussard on the loose."

Edward was reticent to visit another police station with Catherine, but this one was far less menacing than the last one they visited together. Still, Catherine's cool demeanor at the tea house slipped away, and her tone became more agitated. Officer Girard was not in, and she was determined to give her report to the most senior person below him. After they found that man, she sat twisting the strings on her chatelaine nearly to ruin as she gave her account of Broussard's attack. When they finally were able to leave, her pace outstripped his. It was clear she was intent on getting home as quickly as possible in silence. Walking back to his house alone, his mind was awash in recriminations.

Damn, damn, damn. I should have never kissed her. What made me think she would be interested in me? A smile betrayed his thoughts. *Well, her mouth certainly was.*

He stopped, took a deep breath, and tried to refocus on clearing his name. His entire future was in a precarious position. If he could not clear his name, there was no point in pursuing her. An impossible romance was an unnecessary distraction.

Before he descended the hill toward his house, he stopped. The sun was low in the sky, and his elevated position was the perfect vantage point to survey the property around his house. He thought he could see a man in a small copse of trees to the east of his house and another figure farther away.

As he surveyed the situation, a cat rubbed between his ankles and around his feet. He tried to discourage its attention, but the cat cried as he walked away. Edward stopped, and it crawled between his feet again. He walked again, and again the cat chased his feet and cried. He reached down and scooped her into his arms to keep her from alerting everyone to his presence. Her purring was almost as loud as the crying, but there was nothing to be done about that.

Skirting the far edge of the orchard, he opened the gate to the adjacent sheep meadow. He walked into the meadow looking for the sheep and found them near the watering trough. Slapping a few on their rumps, he chased them toward the gate. Others followed, and soon most of the herd charged through the orchard, bleating and scrambling in his yard. He dropped the cat outside the sheep pen and raced back to his house. In the ensuing mayhem, Edward sneaked around to the kitchen door and crept in.

Edward bellowed, “Blast those damned sheep!” and charged out the front door. “I am going to have a word with Farmer Markos about this.” He slammed the front door and ran through the orchard. There was no sign of either man he had spied from the hill. He went to talk with the farmer, and several boys and three dogs came to chase the sheep in the orchard. He re-entered his house and avoided a discussion with Davis by heading straight to his bedroom.

As he crossed the threshold, a man was climbing out his bedroom window.

Chapter Thirty Six

"Stop! Thief!" Edward leapt out the bedroom window after the mysterious man. "Davis, help! Stop!"

The person had a head start. Edward chased him through the shrubs and into the orchard.

"Oof." Edward found Rubeaux lying on the ground with a dog growling and tugging on the hem of his pants and a teenage farm boy with a shepherd's crook holding him down.

Edward thanked the boy and took control of Rubeaux, lashing his hands behind his back with a small length of rope that the boy provided. Davis arrived and asked one of the boys to run into town and get the first police officer he saw. It was a scant few minutes before the boy returned with an officer in tow. Edward realized the officer must have been the other man lurking here a short while ago.

"Officer, I saw this man climbing out of my bedroom window as I returned from notifying the farmer to get his sheep out of the orchard," Edward said. "One of the farm boys was good enough to detain him for me."

"Who are you, and what were you doing inside this man's house?" the officer asked.

"Martin Rubeaux, and I wasn't inside his house. He's a liar."

The officer looked him up and down. "Don't accuse your betters." He reached into Rubeaux's pocket and came up with something of interest. "Oh, and what is this?" He opened his hand, and there were Edward's father's cufflinks.

He gasped. "Those are my father's. They have a T engraved on them."

The policeman dipped into his other pocket and pulled out another plain, onyx cufflink engraved with a T.

"That is mine as well."

Rubeaux struggled. "He put those in my pocket before you arrived."

The policeman asked, "Who carries three cufflinks in their pocket? Why in the world would he do that? You'll have to come with me." Turning to Edward, he said, "Sir, we will need you to make a written statement as well."

Edward had Davis retrieve Patros's carriage to bring himself, the officer, and Rubeaux to the police headquarters, where he made an official complaint. When that was done, he walked to the Athinios hotel.

The walkway outside had a beautiful view of the sea from the top of the bluff, with low, white walls on either side. He looked in each well-lit window to see if his Livingstone was there, and indeed, he sat at the table drinking from a teacup. The butler answered his knock.

Edward said, "Mister Tyrington to see Lord Livingstone."

He was shown into the front room to wait. It was ten minutes before Lord Livingstone arrived. When he entered, he walked past Edward's outstretched hand and sat. "We may pretend at civility in public, but there is no one to put on a show here. What is it you want?"

Edward's breath caught in his throat for a moment. "If you want direct discourse, I will get to the point. What is your link to Rubeaux?"

"Poor Edward. I see you suffer under the same lack of intelligence your father exhibited. I should have refused you entry to my house, but I admit I was curious as to what might bring you here. And the reward for my curiosity is the question of a dullard. How disappointing you are. I had hoped for a bit more entertainment from you."

"I am not here to entertain you. I am here to get answers."

"And you are deluded enough to think I will provide them?" Livingstone laughed. "You are even duller than your father, if that is possible."

"Leave my father out of this."

Livingstone went to the spirits table and poured himself a drink without offering one to Edward or even facing him. "That is impossible. Your father served me injustice after injustice and took valued positions from me on nothing but a whiff of suspicion. Now you expect that I will answer to you?" He took a large swig of whiskey, put his glass on the table, and turned toward Edward. "No, I do not think so. I am happy to see you spiral inexorably into debt and ruin, and I will not raise my smallest finger to give you information or assistance of any kind."

"Why are you in Santorini?"

Livingston laughed. "Not because I got a job scrabbling in the dirt from my university friend Henri. You should take care. Not everyone here is as they appear on the surface. Poor boy, you are so far out of your league, so unprepared for the circumstance that surrounds you. Go back to London, little Edward. Go back to university and your little sandbox. The world is a large place, and you are a small, small man."

Edward straightened his cuffs with care and surveyed Livingstone before smiling. "I understand now. You came to Greece because you are tired of following my brother around the House of Lords trying to curry favor with the Crown. Poor, bitter Livingstone."

"Leave!" Livingstone marched to the door and opened it.

"Do not in any way think this is finished." Edward strolled from the room and walked straight to Monsieur Fontaine's home.

The same guard that had held him at gunpoint previously met him at the door, and he placed his card on the silver salver to be presented to Monsieur Fontaine. A few minutes later, he was escorted into the library.

"I did not expect that you would return to my home so soon, although I am glad you are no longer skulking about. What brings you here this evening?"

"The arrest of Martin Rubeaux. I caught him stealing my cufflinks. What do you know about him?"

"I have had no reason to know much about him at all, although I am sorry to hear he tried to steal something from you. He will be punished, of course."

"What have the police found in regard to the murders?"

"I am not in the habit of divulging information from ongoing investigations to men who are suspects. I am sure you understand."

Edward stood and went to the spirits table. The move was an unprecedented breach of protocol, but he was past caring. He poured them both a drink and handed one to Fontaine, who took the glass and appeared rather nonplussed.

"Let me share what I have found, then." Edward sat by the fireplace and told him about how Rubeaux worked for Dupont right up until Dupont's murder and had requested a transfer to Santorini, which made him a more likely suspect for both murders, since he was also in both places at the proper times and had ties to Dupont.

"One's work assignment does not make one a suspect for murder," Fontaine said.

"That is the only criterion that has been used to place me under suspicion."

"That is where you are wrong. You were the first man on the scene with both bodies. You admit to frequent nighttime trips to your work site. One victim was British and could have been known to you. And although Miss Briggs has claimed you had nothing to do with the murders, being that you are courting her, her word is, shall we say, less than reliable. Furthermore, no one can corroborate your whereabouts during the fireworks display at the canal when Dupont was killed. That is far more than your work assignment casting suspicion on you."

"You cannot be serious. You are actually considering accusing me? I figured that to be some harebrained idea of Girard's, not a real path of action. It is preposterous that you would consider me a murderer." Edward dared not pick up his glass for fear of giving away that his hands shook from a combination of fear and rage. Instead, he straightened his shoulders. "Then why have you not arrested me?"

Fontaine smiled. "You know the answer as well as I. Your diplomatic stature as the brother of a lord would make that a difficult option without more concrete evidence that places you at the scene of the murders. However, unless someone else is found to be a more credible murderer, you are our prime suspect for now."

Edward's mind reeled. Without Rubeaux under consideration as the murderer, he was in far more trouble than he had reckoned. "What about Lord Livingstone? Why is he in Santorini? He was also in Egypt at the time of Dupont's murder. And it would not surprise me if he was acquainted with Dupont."

"Your lack of surprise notwithstanding, we have found no implication of Lord Livingstone in either death." Fontaine stood. "Thank you for visiting, but I believe this interview is over."

Livingstone burst in the door as Fontaine reached it to show Edward out.

"What do you mean by arresting—Mister Tyrington, what are you doing here?"

Edward stood. "Fontaine, you did not mention that you know Lord Livingstone."

"I do not believe he was a topic of discussion during your last visit."

The three of them eyed each other for a half a minute before Edward said, "I must go."

Monsieur Fontaine escorted him to the door and ensured that one of the guards walked him to the street. Even outside, Edward could hear the faint shouting between Fontaine and Livingstone.

Chapter Thirty Seven

Edward walked away from Fontaine's house with a frozen heart, the words of their conversation haunting him: "Without more concrete evidence that places you at the scene of the murders..."

Like cufflinks. Of course.

Since there was only one onyx cufflink and its mate was in his drawer, it would be a perfect way to frame him. The gold cufflinks were likely for Rubeaux's personal enrichment.

He jogged to Livingstone's lodgings and circled once to see who might be there and better understand the layout of the building. Night had fallen, and the suite was dark, except for one light in the upstairs corner room, which was likely for his man. The door was locked, so he took a pick from his pocket and worked on it.

His hand shook slightly as he recalled his father catching him and Henri sneaking into locked rooms that summer. He and Henri had picked many locks as they explored most of the Essex estate that summer. A small outbuilding was one of the last places undiscovered. It had been Edward's turn to pick the lock that day, and he did so deftly, but he was unprepared for what lay beyond the door. At first it was dark, but as they uncovered the windows, he knew immediately he should not be there. Everything of his mother's was in this room—set up beautifully, as if she would come through the door laughing about something at any moment. Edward and Henri stood in the center of the room, mouths open. Edward's heart clenched as he willed himself to not cry, his voice locked and his body unwilling to move. They stood frozen in shock and grief. His father was supposed to be at the House of Lords that day but had returned early. As he and Henri stood absorbing the sanctuary they had violated, his father walked in. Edward knew he had desecrated something precious to his father, crossed the threshold on a deeply held secret. He knew his relationship with his father would never be the same, and although this gave Edward a glimpse into his father's heart, it was a glimpse he stole, a view he was never supposed to have. The guilt of it weighed on his heart still.

The lock's action yielded to his efforts, and he tiptoed into the main room of Livingstone's lodgings, relocking the door behind him. He stood for a few moments to allow his eyes to adjust to the darkness, and the shapes of the room revealed themselves: the long sofa to the left, the chairs by the fireplace that held a small bank of embers still visible, the desk by the far window.

He avoided knocking his leg on the coffee table, and made his way to the desk. The rolltop cover was locked, as were the drawers. Edward used his pick again and rolled the top of the desk back.

Everything was in perfect order. The envelopes were in their slot, the inkwell was stowed. Edward rifled through the two drawers and central cabinet but only found writing paper, postage stamps, and other sundries one would expect to find in a desk. He closed the lid and picked the lock on the first drawer.

There he found a revolver and a pair of gloves. He sniffed the muzzle of the gun. It smelled of gun oil, as if it had been recently cleaned. Replacing it, he moved on to the next drawer. The lock on this drawer was more stubborn. He spent several minutes prying and shifting what little play there was in the drawer's position, trying to find the right location for the tumblers to move, but nothing worked.

Skipping to the next drawer, he worked the lock, and it opened. Inside was a stack of letters with an illegible return address except for the city: London. Edward opened one and skimmed past the pleasantries of weather and travel. Two-thirds of the way through the first page, he found what he had come for:

He continues to provide stubborn opposition to our plans in China, and something must be done. I remain unsure how such a junior lord has managed as much consolidation of power as Charles has, but he must be stopped. I understand you have business in Egypt soon. A short journey to Greece may be in order to see what you can do from there.

Edward stopped reading. There were six letters with the same handwriting on the front, so he stuffed them into his jacket pocket and closed the drawer. Hearing the key in the front door, he bolted into the next room, which was the dining room. It was too spare to hide in, so he moved into the next room.

As someone entered the house, Edward closed the kitchen door behind him. The fire was cold in here as well, and it was black as pitch. Footsteps climbed the stairs, and he heard Livingstone's voice above him.

"Stop fussing over me. I will undress myself. If you must do something, make me a cup of tea."

Edward had only a few moments before he would be discovered. Finding the rear kitchen door, he ran into the back alley and, from there, ran home.

He scouted out the area around his house for a half hour before deciding the police had not returned to watch him. As he watched and waited, the same cat came to visit him, twisting about his ankles and purring as he petted it. "Out and about again, eh, little cat? Although I suppose you could say the same about me."

He walked to his door, and the cat ran up to rub against his ankle. He went inside, and as Davis helped him remove his coat, the cat meowed outside. "Davis, do you know whose cat that is?"

"I have asked several people, and I believe she is a stray."

"She is not the farmer's?"

"No, sir."

The cat meowed again in a more plaintive tone. "Davis, please put a bowl of milk out for it. I will dress myself for bed."

Davis did as he was requested, and Edward retreated to his bedroom.

He was still anxious over his theft of the letters as he read them in his room. But the contents were far more of a shock. Although Lord Blankenship, the author of the letters, was careful to never state it outright, it was clear that Edward's brother Charles had pitted himself against some powerful foes and had assembled a bulwark of staunch supporters of his resistance to further intervention in China.

It appeared Blankenship and Livingstone blamed Charles for a sudden shift in political sentiments in the House of Lords and had made attempts to discredit him. Their most recent effort was to discredit Edward as a way to sully his brother's reputation. It would be disastrous for both Edward and Charles if Edward were found in possession of the letters.

Although it was late, he left for the dig site and set to work as soon as he arrived. Edward dug a small, deep hole in the ash below his work table. He removed a well-preserved amphora jar from the collection of those he had already catalogued, stuffed the letters into it, and stretched a parchment wrapper around the jar and over its top. He placed it in the hole and buried it.

When he arrived home, the cat was outside, and she snaked around his feet again. He sighed, picked her up, and brought her into his bedroom. He prepared for bed and what little sleep he might find. Dislodging the cat from his pillow and putting her on the floor, he lay down, only to have her return to lay by his feet, purring. Edward looked at her, her bright green eyes surveying him from her odd brindle coat. It was clear that someone had taken care of her, as she had a relatively clean coat and did not appear to be starving. The hour and his exhaustion being what they were, he turned off the light and let the cat settle where she would.

When he awoke, he stroked the cat, which had nestled next to his hip, and watched the sun rise higher over the horizon.

Davis came to dress him and remarked, "How did the cat get into your room, sir?"

"I let her in. He was outside creating quite a racket."

"Is it your intention that we adopt a cat and that I care for it?"

Edward sighed. "I doubt, at this point, we could rid ourselves of it. She is quite persistent."

Davis smiled and pet her. "She does worm her way into the heart, doesn't she? Per your wishes, I shall care for little Kako."

"The Greek word for mischief. How fitting." Edward chortled. *He probably named her weeks ago.*

Edward said, "It occurs to me that Rubeaux may have stolen my cufflinks for their value, or someone may have wanted them to implicate me in a murder. All our personal effects should be kept locked in the safe, and the house should remain locked as well."

"Good thinking, sir. One cannot be too careful. I will secure our personal effects after breakfast."

Chapter Thirty Eight

Asim returned to work that morning with little sign of his injuries. He approached Edward with a quiet reverence, and Edward said, "You would have done the same for me, Asim, I have no doubt."

"Regardless, sir. Thank you."

"But if we look at the whole picture, I would say that you helped save my life during the knife fight, so let us call it even, shall we?" Asim opened his mouth to speak, but Edward continued. "Now, we should get back to work. I still have exhibits to prepare before tomorrow's ball. I hope you will assist me with the tours that are planned."

"It would be an honor, sir."

At lunch, Edward went to visit Catherine. It was a perfect morning, and the buds of wildflowers were almost ready to burst along the path into town. Some were familiar, but others were a mystery to him, and he looked forward to their unfolding. He arrived to find Catherine sipping tea in the parlor. She reported the knot on her head was improved and suggested they go for a stroll so they could speak away from other people.

Linking his arm in hers, they walked to the square at the top of the bluffs. Looking down the ashen bluff to the sea, Edward noted the various shades from turquoise to azure as the ocean deepened away from the shore. It always amazed him how inadequate the English language was to name all the shades of blue, but today his heart was not held by the poetry of it as he worried what his future might bring.

Once Edward made sure they were alone, he told Catherine of his adventures the night before, his visits with Livingstone and Fontaine, and his conclusion that they were trying to frame him for murder.

She looked incredulous.

He held up a hand. "Before you protest against that theory, there is proof in the letters I took that Livingstone is here to see what mischief he can make for me in order to discredit my brother."

"You think he murdered people so he could frame you? As distasteful as that man is, I find that hard to believe."

"No, he came here to see what trouble he could create, and once Dupont was murdered, he surmised there might be an opportunity to frame me. The murder of Mr. Allen provided him even more opportunity to turn suspicion toward me and thus discredit my brother in the House of Lords. There is a long history of animosity between my family and Livingstone. It is not a terrible stretch to imagine that he would do this."

Catherine nodded. "Assuming you are correct, we must find the murderer as soon as possible. So far, both Rubeaux and Reginald Broussard have means and motive for murdering Dupont. They both have means for murdering Mr. Allen, but no motive can be found. Could Livingstone have a reason to murder him?"

"I do not know. And although I would assume a lord would distance himself from such an act, the letters relate a desperation to stop my brother that may have forced him to seize the opportunity. I must find out more about Mr. Allen to understand how all this fits together." He searched her gaze and took her hands in his. "Catherine, I am concerned that I am in grave danger. Should something happen to me, I buried the evidence of Livingstone's intent at the archaeological site in a jar underneath my work table. I am sorry to bring you into this further, but I have no one to turn to, and I do not know how long it will be before they find—or create—the evidence they need to arrest me."

She held his gaze and gripped his hands. "I understand. I will do all I can to help."

Edward nodded. "Thank you. You should return to your hotel. The less you are seen with me now, the better. And please, I beg you, do not investigate this alone. The stakes are too high, and it is clear someone is capable of murder."

As they headed back to her inn, a face peeked briefly out of a doorway. He slowed and squeezed her arm. "Broussard is up ahead of us, lurking in a doorway near the flower seller."

Catherine unhooked her arm from his. "I will walk alone. When he comes after me, grab him."

"Are you sure?"

"Yes. There is no time to argue."

Catherine walked away from Edward, and he crossed to the side of the street closest to Broussard's hiding spot. When he was in place, Catherine passed by Broussard, appearing to be engrossed in her shopping. He grabbed her from behind and clapped a hand over her mouth, then he picked her up and carried her toward the nearest doorway.

As she struggled, Edward raced forward, snatched a pot from the flower seller, and brought it down on Broussard's head. He dropped, unconscious, spread on the street like a spilled bag of oats.

Edward removed Broussard's shoes and took the laces to tie his hands behind his back. "In case he tries to run again, that should slow him down a bit."

A crowd had gathered, and Edward instructed a street boy to get the company police.

The police arrived, along with Baba, who said, "I should have known it was you."

Edward pointed to Broussard. "This is the man who accosted Miss Briggs on a previous occasion and is known to have threatened Monsieur Dupont and his wife six months ago."

Baba's eyes opened wide before he schooled his expression. The police officers grabbed Broussard, who was just waking. They took Monsieur Broussard away, and Edward and Baba escorted Catherine to her inn.

After she was safely inside, Edward said, "Baba, it is time for truth between us."

"Let us speak in my office."

They walked to his office in silence, and when they were alone there, Edward continued. "I have spent the last several nights following people to see how they might fit into the two murders. First I followed Rubeaux, only to discover that he was following you."

"Me? Why?"

"I do not know why. But we saw you go to the doctor's house and then to the tent with the pregnant woman."

Baba's eyes grew huge. "You cannot tell anyone of that. No one. Ever. Do you understand?"

"As it happens, I refrained from telling Fontaine the other night."

"What? When did you meet Fontaine?" A vein in Baba's forehead pulsed as he stood. He tried to pace around the office, but it was too cramped.

"The other night. His men caught Miss Briggs and me following someone else to his house."

"You were caught outside his house?" he hissed. "He is a powerful man. You must not cross him, and you must not trust him. What else have you told him?"

"Most of what I know about the two murders and who might be responsible."

"Did you tell him about Patros's investigation?"

"No, I left that part out."

Baba pulled a bottle of Retsina from his drawer and poured two glasses. "At least there's that."

They sat, and as they drank, Edward shared the whole story of his night with Fontaine, his adventure arresting Rubeaux, and his suspicion about the cufflinks. Then he questioned Baba regarding everything he knew about Fontaine and Rubeaux.

Baba fidgeted with papers on his desk. "As I said, Fontaine is powerful—and ruthless as well. You are right to be suspicious of him. Everyone who works here knows that when he asks you to do something, it is in your interest to do it fast. He began asking favors of me a year ago, involving various Egyptian women he saw—smuggling them into his house and back out. It was important that his wife be ignorant of the truth. With her in the same house, that took a bit of work, but those of us in his employ made it happen. Besides, it was harmless enough. What Frenchman doesn't have a mistress or two? But he has forced us to do other things as well. Rubeaux has been here on and off, on loan to this operation from Dupont's. He may also be doing 'favors' for Fontaine. I do not know."

"Why would he work here on Santorini when he was Dupont's employee?"

"If he were blackmailing Dupont, as you suspect, don't you think Dupont would want to be rid of him? He only happened to be here twice, and it was clear Rubeaux was not happy about it. After that, he stayed in Egypt with Dupont, until last week."

Edward ruminated on this for a bit. "I thought Dupont might have been involved in another issue that my father had investigated, which involved a Dupont who lived in Damietta on Hadad Street. I have found no other possible evidence of what Rubeaux might be blackmailing him about."

Baba's eyes grew wide. "Did you say Hadad Street?"

"Yes. Henri and I went there to look for this Dupont, but the people there said he had left and become a sailor." He tried to say the word in Arabic. "That is what they said."

"Taking up Arabic now? That word can mean either shipping or sailing. There was one evening years ago when we were setting up the quarry operation. Dupont was here. I collected him from the ship and brought him to his lodgings. His trunk had an address on Hadad Street in Damietta on it. I tried to ask him where he lived, since I have family there, but he was unwilling to talk about it."

Edward's jaw hung open as his mind processed all that Baba had said. "If it was the same Dupont, it is quite possible he was involved in something of far-reaching ramifications that entailed great danger. I cannot say more than that, but it sheds a whole new light on motive for his murder. Thank you. Your help has been invaluable."

Chapter Thirty Nine

Later that afternoon, as Edward cleaned amphora for display during the ball, a carriage creaked to a halt, and he heard a heated discussion over a donkey braying without end. Recognizing one of the voices, he hurried to the road.

Henri was arguing with the driver that he needed to attend to the donkey's hoof, which had taken a stone. The driver removed the stone, much to everyone's relief, as the donkey quieted down. Henri paid the driver and told him to wait for his return.

Running his fingers through his hair, he hugged Edward. "I am sorry that I am later visiting you than I had planned. De Lesseps decided we should travel together in a flotilla, and I have been working almost without break on preparations since. It is good to see you."

Edward stopped. "De Lesseps is here?"

"Yes. He is at Monsieur Papadopoulos's house, overseeing the final arrangements for the ball tomorrow. The Earl of Mar is with him as well. We saw his ship as we were docking. De Lesseps invited him to stay in one of the bungalows there since the representative from the Duchy of Savoy canceled at the last minute. I am sure de Lesseps will be here to see the site tomorrow during the tours."

Panic rolled through Edward's gut like an avalanche. "I am unprepared for this."

"Relax." Looking around, Henri said, "The site looks very well organized. Show me some of your discoveries. I am anxious to see them."

Edward gave Henri a thorough tour of the site, moving out from the main area to the farthest extents while explaining each item and room they found and the techniques used to recover them.

By the end, Henri beamed. "I knew you were the right choice for this project. You have outdone yourself. Your efforts here are remarkable, and I know de Lesseps will be astonished with your discoveries."

"Thank you." Edward's tone turned serious. "There is something else I must tell you." His words came fast as he explained the situation with Livingstone, Rubeaux, and Fontaine, and his suspicion and proof that they were likely trying to frame him.

Henri held up his hands. "Slow down. You say you have proof of Livingstone trying to frame you?"

Edward told him of the buried letters and that, according to Baba, Dupont used to live on Hadad Street. Again the story came forth in a gush, and again Henri slowed him down. He pulled a flask from his pocket and handed it to Edward. "Drink and tell me the story from the beginning."

He did as he was told. When he finished, they sat on a black lava ledge near the edge of the bluff.

"I do not know what to say," Henri said. "You are in danger, but we still do not know who the murderer is or if both men were murdered by the same hand. Try to keep someone with you as much as possible—and not Miss Briggs. You have exposed her to enough danger. Edward, how could you? She is a just a woman."

"She is by far the cleverest and most competent woman I have ever met."

Henri gave him a sideward glance. "I must return to my preparations for the ball. Please make sure you stay with others as much as possible. And do not follow anyone. I am concerned for your safety." As he left, he turned back. "Where was Mr. Allen staying?"

"The Dendrosa Inn."

Henri nodded, and Edward returned to work.

Edward was bone tired when he returned home after dinner. He asked Davis to bring him coffee to help him stay awake for the task of finishing the map for the tours. He was focused on his work as Davis placed the cup on the table, but something caught his eye.

Edward grabbed Davis's wrist. "Where did you get that?"

"Get what, sir?"

"That scar on your left forefinger." He released Davis's wrist and looked in his eyes. "What burned you there?"

"A ship's engine, sir. I have had that scar for almost as long as I can remember. I am surprised you only now noticed it."

"As am I. And you got it from a ship's engine?"

"When I was young, I joined the Navy for a period of time. I was initially assigned to the engine room. It was a grueling occupation, and after I had done my service to the Crown, I decided to find another type of work. Through some connections I had further up the command chain, I was offered a job as footman for your family. I worked my way up from there."

Edward stood and paced. "How have I never noticed it before?"

"I am sure I don't know. Why does it concern you so now?"

"Because that is the same kind of scar I saw on Mr. Allen's hand. Otherwise, his hands were soft and well cared for. A gentleman's hands in every respect, except for that scar. I suppose it could have come from anything that might have burned him, but it looked quite like your scar."

Davis gave a short laugh. "Yes, but my hands are not a gentleman's hands. Laundry, cleaning, sewing, and my other duties leave my hands rough, although I do try to care for them."

"I was not disparaging your hands, Davis. But how did Mr. Allen, who is not listed in Debrett's book of peerage, receive a scar so similar to yours?" Edward shook his head. "I am sorry to frighten you. It was the shock of seeing a scar so similar. It may be coincidence. And right now, I need to finish my map. You should get some rest. I will get myself ready for bed."

Edward completed his map after midnight, undressed himself, and dropped into bed next to Kako, who snored lightly and treated Edward's bed as her own.

Chapter Forty

Davis woke Edward before dawn. A sliver of the setting moon cast feeble shadows through his windowpane as he rose. There were the remnants of dreams haunting his awakening with fear, but the inevitability of the events of the day brought him a fatalistic sense of peace. The tours and visitors were set, the ball would follow. The rest was a fait accompli.

He dressed, ate a light breakfast, and arrived early to ensure all was ready. Although he doubted anyone would arrive as soon as the tours were scheduled to start, he wanted to be prepared should some insomniac lord decide to be the first one to arrive at eight o'clock.

Edward had arranged with Baba that all the workers would be at the quarry that day, except Asim, who would assist Edward by demonstrating various techniques and instruments during the tour.

As if conjured from his premonition, a French count and his wife arrived at eight o'clock, along with Aunt Inez and Francine. Edward gave them the tour of two of the rooms and the triangular village plaza. He had displays of the map and photographs of other impressive finds at the site, and he discussed the process of using plaster of paris to make casts of items that had long since decayed. Julian took a group picture with the fresco of the goddess as a backdrop to be given out as souvenirs at the ball. It was clear the Suez Canal Company would spare no expense to drum up more financial and political support.

As the group left, Julian handed Edward a photograph. "Henri asked me to give this to you. It is a coded message of some sort that he found at the Dendrosa Inn. He hoped you could work on deciphering it. He says he is too busy with de Lesseps to look at it."

Edward took the photograph from Julian and sat at the desk. "Where did he find this? Miss Briggs and I searched his room."

"He said something about a flower pot. I did not understand what he meant."

Edward scrutinized the photograph. It was a jumble of letters. He scanned it for single letter words, such as *I* or *a*, and then for frequently used letters that might represent vowels. The next half hour only brought one other couple to tour the site. Edward worked on the cipher, which was more difficult than any that his father had given. He had deciphered the words "Grayson" and "Navy." Edward wondered who Grayson was and whether Henri had intercepted someone else's communiqué, but the reference to the Navy intrigued him, and he kept deciphering the note.

He was working on the code when it seemed as if the floodgates opened at the site, and there were groups of people ten at a time to visit the archaeological dig. Edward started the tour by asking everyone to introduce themselves so he could better tailor his information for various interests the dignitaries might have and present the information in the proper language. He gave the tour in French, German, and English, as needed, and for the Egyptian dignitaries who came, Asim translated. Julian took photographs as fast as he could of each group, and soon his assistant was running plates back to his rooms for others to develop.

It was hectic, but Edward found he enjoyed it far more than he had anticipated. He felt very comfortable explaining the complicated processes used in a way that even the most unscientific lord could understand. At midday, there were no visitors, as a special luncheon event was being held elsewhere. One of Julian's assistants brought Edward and his group lunch, and Edward continued his work on the cipher.

"Espionage against the British Crown." A lump formed in Edward's throat. They had continued the investigation. How had his father convinced the Navy Office to investigate when he could not convince the House of Lords?

The knowledge that somehow Mr. Grayson had died investigating his father's concerns weighed on him. Soon the creak of carriage wheels on the road told him the next group had arrived. He put the photograph under others on the desk and rose to greet the visitors. This group included the pasha, three courtiers, de Lesseps, Empress Eugenia, and several high-level officials from the company.

Edward was ready, having had the morning to refine his presentation. Asim was quite nervous before the pasha, but managed to get through the demonstrations. De Lesseps seemed pleased and discussed with the pasha how they could capitalize on the find. He mentioned sending some of the pottery as gifts to influential people.

Edward held his tongue at the suggestion. Despite his strong conviction that the best place for the antiquities was in a museum, that was not a common view among the political elite, and discretion was the best course in this situation.

He conducted several more tours throughout the afternoon, and the last tour finished at six o'clock. After the last people left, Edward lit a lantern, organized the room, and returned the items he had shown to their storage area. With another hour before he needed to leave to get dressed for the ball, he pulled out the cipher and what he had managed to decode up to that point, and settled back in to work. After a while, he had the next segment: "I have intercepted the transfer of documents to Monsieur Dupont and need to arrange a secure drop of intelligence."

Focused on his work, he did not notice someone enter until they cleared their throat. He turned to see the Earl of Mar standing at the edge of the darkness.

"James!" Edward rose. "I was not expecting to see you here. How was Athens?"

"It was wonderful. King George, who is far more agreeable than I had imagined, is ensconced on his throne, and England has provided him more land to rule. What could be better? I am sorry to have missed the tours here. I see you have made even more progress since my last visit."

Edward crossed to the main table and rolled his map. "I promise to give you a tour in the morning. I understand you are staying with Mr. Papadopoulos. I am surprised you are not there dressing for the ball. I should leave to dress as well."

James had crossed to the desk with his back to Edward and seemed to freeze there. His shoulders sagged a bit.

Edward said, “James?” but received no response.

James straightened his back. His elbows separated, his jacket shifted, and although it was well done, Edward recognized the motion for what it was.

“I can assure you there are at least four copies of the photograph you pocketed.”

“I had wondered if this day would ever come.” James sighed and looked to the ceiling.

“What day?”

The earl turned and pointed a gun at Edward’s chest. “The day it becomes necessary to deal with you.”

Chapter Forty One

Edward's mind slowed to a crawl. The gun held by his friend James, Earl of Mar, was a Lefaucheux revolver, a French gun. *James hates the French.*

"Wh...what are you talking about?" Edward said.

The muscles in James's jaw twitched as he ground his teeth. He seemed agitated yet deadly calm. He was the eye of the hurricane, where calmness supersedes the chaos but one senses the destruction coming.

"You have always been a curious lad. I wondered if your curiosity would be your undoing, and it seems the answer is yes."

Edward stared at the smooth barrel. The earl was sweating, but his hand was steady; his strong, gentle grasp on the gun showed his comfort with it. Edward wondered how many other men had faced the barrel of this gun for James to be so calm. *How many had begged for their lives? How many never had the opportunity? Was Grayson one of them?* He followed the hunch.

"That cipher implicates you in Mr. Grayson's death, does it not?"

"Curious, yes, but rather slow, I should say."

Edward was shocked to take offense at that and his mind raced through his conversations with James. As he tried to think, the oddity that one of his dearest friends stood pointing a gun at him slowed him down. His mind flew to the conversations of comfort he'd had with the earl at the funeral: James telling him his father was at peace in heaven, the conversations about Edward's scientific interests, the paths he might choose, and his budding career. One phrase in particular struck him.

"*As your father's friend, and now yours, it is my duty to advise you.*"

He was Father's closest friend. Someone he trusted deeply, as I do—rather, did. "Father told you of the clues he uncovered. And you made sure he never found anything substantial."

James seemed impatient. "Of course. Have you never heard the adage 'Keep your friends close and your enemies closer'?"

Edward thought through their interactions since his father died for more clues. "*I purchased some items from auction to return them to you...*"

Edward's mind stopped, and he stared into James's eyes. "You purchased my belongings from auction to make sure there were no remaining clues within them that might implicate you in any way."

"One must be thorough." James poked the air before him with the gun.

"And you have always dissuaded me from taking up the investigation. It was you all along. You have been selling naval secrets to the French."

James broke into a beaming smile. "I knew you had it in you. I would clap for you, but my right hand is rather busy at the moment."

Edward could not comprehend James's beaming reaction. None of this made sense. James had been a loyal servant to the Crown his entire career.

"But why?" Edward leaned against the table as he played for time and his mind tried but failed to understand how his friend could point a gun at him.

"I am the same as you. I fell on a bit of hard luck with the shift in the opium trade in China several years back. The market was flooded, and my fortune dwindled. Had you been more politically savvy, you would have realized that selling political secrets is far more lucrative than selling books and instruments."

Edward was defiant. "But that is treason."

James dismissed his protest with a laugh. "Oh, Edward, you are so passionate about right and wrong, but you lack the proper vision. How you persevere under the weight of all that moral fabric is beyond me. By selling only certain secrets, the Crown was never in any real danger."

Edward was determined to know the truth now and desperate to keep James distracted so he could try to think of a way out of this. "Why did you kill Dupont?"

"I did not kill Dupont. That was your man Grayson. Dupont was far too valuable to me. I was genuinely distraught when he was murdered."

Edward's mind spun hard. *Grayson had determined that Dupont was the contact and intercepted him with the information.* He took a gamble. "You met Dupont that night to deliver whatever secret information you sold him. Grayson caught him after your meeting, and in a struggle for the documents, he shot Dupont."

James leaned against the table, seeming to take great pleasure in watching Edward piece the story together.

Edward continued, "How did you find Grayson here on Santorini?"

"Suffice it to say, I did a bit of investigating of my own. There were several ways in which 'Mr. Allen' stood out from the normal pack of politicians and sycophants that follow de Lesseps around."

"You followed him to Santorini when he left Egypt and lured him here to the archaeological site."

"It seemed fitting to implicate you if I needed to keep you from meddling further."

"You killed Grayson, but where are the documents?"

James smiled, and his free hand almost imperceptibly touched his coat pocket. "Do not worry about those." He continued, "You are a bit smarter than your father; I will grant you that. I thought his dogged persistence far outstripped yours, although it turns out that you are just as tenacious and even more trouble."

"My father had found Dupont. It was his last clue. He knew who your contact was."

James's eyes narrowed, and his jaw clenched and released, clenched and released, almost as if he were chewing this thoughts. "My small crimes would have gone unnoticed if your father had not continually hounded me. And he still kept investigating, using his own money, until he bankrupted your family."

Edward balled his fists. "He knew you were behind it."

"That is where you are wrong." James smirked, and his grip tightened on the gun. "He knew someone in the House of Lords was behind it, but he never considered me a suspect. He was quite convinced it was Livingstone, whose life he made a living hell. No, he would share his clues with me, and I would tie up the loose ends before he could get to them. As he got close to discovering the truth, I took more drastic measures and poisoned him in the House of Lords dining room to put the matter to rest."

Edward heard a shocked gasp from the darkness in the adjacent room. James turned to look, and Edward leaped toward him, grappling for the gun. As they struggled, the gun discharged into the darkness, and Catherine screamed.

Chapter Forty Two

Edward pushed James up against the wall. As they struggled for the gun, James's knee slammed into Edward's groin, and he fell to the ground in agony. James pointed his gun at Edward.

A voice said, "Drop your weapon!" A bullet flew from the dark, and James turned and fled toward the bluffs into the night.

Edward called to Henri and stumbled over to him. Henri held a blood-soaked handkerchief to Catherine's head above her right ear. Edward sank to his knees and took her head into his hands.

"Henri, get my knife, some cloth, and a glass of water from my desk."

Henri tore across the room while Edward removed his jacket and placed it under Catherine's head. When Henri returned with the items and one of the lanterns, Edward said, "Get help. And have someone tell Davis what has happened. He will know how to treat her."

"In case he returns." Henri handed Edward his gun and ran out as Edward sank into a mental paralysis of prayers for Catherine's life.

"Stay with me, Catherine."

He used the water to rinse the wound. His hands shook as he took his and Henri's handkerchiefs and made a bandage over it. Then he tied a muslin cloth used to wrap artifacts around her head to keep the bandage in place. It was not enough to stanch the flow of blood, so he made a second bandage on top and wrapped her head again.

Edward dabbed some water on her face to see if he could wake her. Her eyes fluttered open, and she reached for her head.

He took her hand. "You have been injured. Help is coming. I will take care of you."

She groaned and closed her eyes. "It hurts."

"Do you remember what happened?"

"That awful man said he killed your father." Her eyes widened, and she tried to rise.

Her words seared his heart again.

"Shh." He eased her back down. "I am glad you are able to speak and remember so much; that is a good sign."

"Bloody hell, my head hurts."

"It will be all right. Davis will know what to do."

His mind spun. He needed to keep her engaged and focused on something, but the only subjects he could think of—her injury and his father's death—were the two he knew he could not talk about. They sat in silence for a minute.

Then Catherine said, "Tell me a story to keep my mind off the pain. Tell me about the iguana."

"What iguana?"

"Henri told me there was a story about an iguana at Oxford."

Edward's mind was in freefall, and then it clicked. "Ah, yes. It was before Christmas break, our first year. I helped to take care of the iguanas in the biology lab for the autumn semester." He stroked her hand and placed it on her stomach, then used both of his hands to hold the bandages in place. "Some of the boys felt I was the teacher's favorite, and they had no love for me or the reptiles. The night before we were to leave for break, it was well past midnight before our trunks were packed and lined up in the hallway to be loaded by the porters. Sometime after I had finished packing, one of the boys stole an iguana from the lab and put it into my trunk."

Catherine's eyes fluttered, and she reached for her head again. Edward caught her hand and placed it back in his on her stomach. "It is best if you leave the injury to me, Catherine."

Her breath came in short gasps "Hurts. Stop the pain."

Edward changed his hand position on the bandage, and she relaxed a bit.

"That is better. What happened next?"

Edward shifted his position to better hold her head and continued. "The next morning, our trunks were brought to the curb to be loaded onto the carriages. As Henri and I awaited our carriage to return to London, I remembered a book that I wanted to read during the journey, and thank goodness I did. I found the iguana half frozen to death in my trunk. I removed my scarf from my neck and wrapped him in it, then I made a nest of a sweater and placed him inside my coat. The carriage arrived, and we had to leave, so there was no choice but to carry it in my coat for the journey. Henri and I became fast friends after that."

Catherine gripped his hand, as if speaking was a great trial. "What did your father think?"

Edward stroked her hand again. "Shhh. Do not try to speak. Save your strength." He continued. "Needless to say, my father was more than a little surprised to see my traveling companion. We fashioned a place for him to live by a fireplace over the holiday and fed him winter vegetables and mice, when our cat killed one. Near the end of the break, we fashioned a more reasonable way for me to transport him back to school. I returned the iguana to the biology lab and explained to the professor what had happened. He was grateful for my efforts. The boys who had done the prank spread the word far and wide of my love of reptiles, and from then on, I had few friends at school. Henri always stood by me though."

Her eyes fluttered open again, and she whispered. "He said he knew you had great compassion and cared for things that normal society would discard."

A carriage rumbled toward them. "Help is coming, Catherine. You will be in good hands now."

"I have been in good hands, Edward. I have always known that."

Henri entered the room. "We need to get her into the carriage."

Edward handed Henri his gun, carried her to the carriage, and laid her on the seat. He placed a pillow under her head and sat on the seat opposite. Henri joined him and yelled out to the Egyptian driver to go.

As soon as the door closed, Henri asked, "What happened?"

"This is not the best time to explain," Edward said.

Catherine opened her eyes. "If you think I will wait for an explanation... "

"All right, all right." Edward continued, "It started when Julian brought me photographs of the coded letter you found, Henri. By the way, where did you find it? We searched his room."

"I decided to move my lodgings to the Dendrosa Inn once you told me Mr. Allen was staying there before he died. I searched the inn as best I could without alarming the guests and staff. I kept looking for an effective place to hide something and found it in the garden by a large flower pot. I looked beneath, and voilà, the cipher was there. Did you decode it?"

"Partially. It indicated Mr. Allen's true identity was Mr. Grayson from the British Royal Navy office, who was here to investigate the sale of British secrets to the French."

"Your father's investigation?"

Edward sat forward. "Indeed. Dupont was James's contact to sell secret information, and Grayson had intercepted him and gotten the secrets back. I had deciphered that much when James arrived."

"Were you expecting him?"

"No. We spoke, and then I saw him take the photograph and put it in his jacket. That is why he threatened me with his gun. You heard our conversation. Why were you there?"

Henri said, "I had planned to come to the site for a brief visit at the end of the tours. I saw Miss Briggs in town, and she asked if she could accompany me. Of course I accepted, and we walked to the site because there were no carriages to be had. As we neared, I heard voices and decided to play a joke on you by hiding in the next room."

"That was the best joke you have ever played." Edward gave a deep sigh of relief. He looked from Henri to Catherine and back again, a lump rising in his throat. “Thank you both for saving my life.” He swallowed hard. “I doubt I would have survived the night but for your distraction.”

“After we had hidden, we soon realized it was no ordinary conversation. I did not know he had a gun. We both heard him admit to murdering your father, you both heard Miss Briggs gasp, and then the gun went off.”

Catherine said, “Gun? I have been shot?”

Edward took her hand before she could place it on her bandages, and he looked in her eyes. “Yes, you have, but the bullet only grazed you. Otherwise, you would not be able to talk now. Davis will know how to care for you.”

The look of fear that had distorted her features smoothed to one of trust, and Edward wanted to hold her. She had almost lost her life saving his. He owed her far more than he would ever be able to repay. He turned toward the window and closed his eyes against the emotions that pushed him, drawing a deep breath.

“We will need to notify the police and search for James,” he said.

Henri shook his head. “I thought your father died of a heart condition. How could James have poisoned him? And why admit to it now?”

“I can only imagine he told me to cause me great pain, and he assumed he would kill me shortly so his confession would have no consequence. I have spoiled his plans with my investigation, and he wanted to hurt me.” Edward rested his chin in his hands. “There are some venoms and poisons that cause heart problems. If he had administered something like that, it could have gone unnoticed.

And it is unlikely that anyone would suspect foul play since Father died in the House of Lords dining room."

As they approached town, there was quite a bit of activity on the road. Edward opened the window to talk to the driver as the carriage stopped.

A policeman opened the door. "Here they are!"

Henri said, "We have an injured woman who needs immediate medical attention."

"We know. We will join you."

Two police officers took control of the carriage, and several other officers ran behind them. They drove to Catherine's hotel, where Davis stood out front awaiting their arrival. They moved Catherine into her room, where Davis and Catherine's lady's maid attended to her while John stayed by her side. The owner of the hotel ushered everyone else into the hotel parlor and closed the doors, trying to minimize the already significant disturbance to the other guests.

Officer Girard looked rather smug. "I am placing you under arrest."

"For what?" Edward said.

"For your attempt to murder the Earl of Mar."

Chapter Forty Three

"What?" Edward was incredulous. Officer Girard could not seriously be considering arresting him for murder. "James was about to murder me when he shot Miss Briggs!"

"In self-defense, according to the earl," Girard said. "He claims you threatened him with a gun after he confronted you with evidence that proved Mr. Allen blackmailed you to cover up your murder of Mr. Dupont."

"That is a lie. I never murdered anyone, nor did I attack the Earl of Mar. He admitted to murder—the murders of Mr. Allen and my father. Then he tried to kill me, but he missed and shot Miss Briggs instead. Both Monsieur LeMarchal and Miss Briggs can attest to it."

Officer Girard laughed. "They are your friends and quite possibly accomplices. Their word will not carry much weight. With the evidence we have for the murders of Dupont and Mr. Allen, coupled with the earl's testimony, we should be able to prosecute you for all three incidents. You will hang for your crimes."

Edward was crazed with anger. "What does the cipher from Mr. Allen's room say?"

"It doesn't matter now. The word of an English lord is sufficient to hang you."

Henri interjected, "The cipher must be an important clue."

Girard turned to Henri. "Your involvement in this is minimal, and it is likely you will not be charged," he continued with an ominous tone, "unless you continue to involve yourself."

"But you did not answer the question: What does the cipher say?" Edward asked.

Girard threw up his hands. "It does not matter. The fact is we know who Mr. Allen was, and the earl's testimony will take care of everything else. You will both remain here under police guard until we can find a proper place to hold you. Or, if you prefer, we can put you in the custody of the Greek police. However, I'd prefer this didn't escalate into even more of an international incident." The officers left and locked the door behind them.

Edward flung himself into a chair. His mind reeled. James had set the perfect trap. *How could I have failed so completely?*

Throbbing below the surface was the dull pain of his father having been murdered, taken from him far too early by a man he thought was his friend. Edward placed his head in his hands and tried to think.

Henri's sigh brought Edward out of his thoughts just as they were turning toward a possibility. Henri stopped pacing. "Whatever you are thinking, stop. I know that look."

"No, no, hear me out. James is guilty of treason. He was selling naval secrets to the French through Dupont. He gave the information to Dupont at the ball. During the fireworks, Grayson confronted Dupont and shot him while trying to either arrest him or get whatever James had given him. James figured out that it was

Grayson, who was posing as a Mr. Allen, and followed him here. He lured him to the archaeological site to implicate me since I was being persistent about the investigation. He then searched Grayson's room and found the secrets he had sold. That means he is still in possession of the evidence of his treason."

"Unless he burned it."

"Yes. But why burn it when he can sell it? The French paid him well for that information. Why not hold onto it and wait for another opportunity to supply it? There may even be a reward for such a thing."

The door to the parlor was unlocked from the outside, and Davis stepped inside. "Miss Briggs will recover as long as we can keep any infection away. The bullet only grazed her head."

"Thank God." Edward gave a great sigh.

"I gather I will not need to lay out your clothes for the event this evening, given the police outside the door."

Edward motioned to a chair. "Davis, please sit. We are in a bit of a situation, but you may be able to help." He went to the spirits table, poured a whiskey, and handed it to Davis.

"That was unnecessary, but thank you, sir."

Edward and Henri sat and explained the events of the day to Davis. At the end of the story, Davis stared at one then the other.

"First, we need to know which room the earl is staying in. He may have the information hidden there, and we need to get the naval secrets back if we can," Edward said.

Davis said, "I should be able to find out where he's staying from Beaumont, Monsieur de Lesseps's valet." He stood to go.

Edward and Henri paced past each other for over an hour before they received any word. When Davis returned, he was let in by the guards at the door under the pretense of attending to Edward's knife wound. He crossed the room with Edward and Henri in tow and bade Edward to sit in the chair farthest from the door while he pretended to inspect his wound before the officer left them.

He spoke in a whisper. "I did as you requested, and James is in Papadopoulos's northwest guest house. Given the situation, I also asked Beaumont if there were any other changes to the guest list. He said they received a letter this morning that the French Foreign Minister Monsieur Thouvenel would also be attending."

Edward snapped his fingers. "Thouvenel, yes. He was there after Catherine discovered Dupont's body. He...he searched him. He must have known Dupont was to get information."

Henri broke in. "Which means he may come tonight to meet James and complete the delivery that was interrupted by Grayson."

"Exactly. Which means it is imperative we get into the ball."

Davis continued. "I also spoke to Patros, sir. He ran me to ground and asked what was afoot. I told him everything. Given the circumstances, I hope that was all right. It seemed that he could help, and already he has helped quite a bit." He leaned in further and whispered, "He arranged to have your guarding officers changed before the ball starts. They will open the door and let you know that you have new guards, and the new guards will be distracted by something to allow you to escape."

Henri laughed. "If Patros were here, I would kiss him."

"Shh," Davis warned, "This is dangerous, and I do not want to get anyone in trouble."

"Of course. So all we need now is a plan," Henri whispered.

Davis stood. "Patros is working on that. And I should go now to assist him."

A half hour later, a guard stuck his head in the door. "We were instructed to inform you of our shift change for the night."

Five minutes later, Henri poked his head out the door to find the hallway empty. He motioned for Edward to come with him.

Chapter Forty Four

Edward and Henri crept into the corridor and out the back door of the inn where the Briggses were staying, which led to a small alley. Having been here before with Catherine, he ran to the right, which led to a larger side street. As they approached the intersection, Henri motioned that Edward should hide in a stairwell below street level, which Edward did, while Henri checked around the corner. Henri motioned for Edward to join him, and Edward saw halfway down the street that the front of the inn had several police officers. He and Henri looked left, where the road ascended the hill into darkness.

Henri said "You go first. Stop just after the crest of the hill and wait for me there. I will keep watch, and if they come this way, I will create a diversion."

Edward nodded and walked up the darker side of the street at a normal pace so as to not arouse any suspicion. He crested the hill and saw a small copse of olive trees to the left. He waited there, and Henri soon joined him. Out of sight of the police—or anyone else, for that matter—they sprinted through the darkness out of town and toward Patros's home.

When they arrived, Patros rushed them inside, closed the door, and crossed himself. "Thank God Baba got you out. There may be hell to pay in the morning, but tonight there's other mischief afoot. I understand you will both need entry to the ball."

Edward answered, "Yes"

Patros held up a tuxedo. "Henri, this is yours."

"Excellent."

"We know that Pierre Chambery took ill this afternoon and will not be attending. You will be masquerading as him."

"Will that work?" Henri asked.

"It had better. It is the only option we have."

"Then who will I be?" Edward asked.

Patros turned to him. "You will be Pierre's wife, of course."

Henri and Patros burst into laughter.

Indignation flushed Edward's face. "Now see here, I will not wear a dress. There must be someone else I can be. Who else is not coming? What about the Duke of Savoy?

"He sent his regrets earlier, and many people know he will not be there."

"There must be another option. I could be a server."

"I've tried to devise another way, but if you are a server, you would have to serve," Patros said. "Have you ever served at a ball?"

"Well, no, but how difficult could it be?"

"Harder than you think. Also, none of the other servers are English, making it quite obvious that you don't belong there. If you are a musician, you would be stuck with the orchestra and not free to move about, which given the circumstances seems to be required for the evening. And there have been no other cancelations that we've been informed of. Either go as Pierre's wife or don't go at all."

"Then I should go as Pierre, and Henri shall be the wife."

"Everyone at the ball has seen your face today. You will be recognizable. A disguise as a woman should work, but anything closer to your normal appearance will be detected."

Edward rubbed the back of his neck. "What in the world would I wear?"

"Go in the bedroom. I have made arrangements for you."

"Patros, this is too far. I will not wear a dress. That is final."

"Then you will not be at the ball, and you can leave it to Henri alone to collect the information you need to clear your name while you remain under arrest. It is your choice where you spend your evening."

Edward sighed and walked into the bedroom. It had only one lantern, with a bed, chair, washstand, small chest of drawers, and privacy screen. Catherine sat in the chair on the far side of the room.

He ran to her and knelt before her. "Are you all right?" He reached for the bandage around her head. "You should be resting in bed. How did you get here?"

"And miss this? You must be joking. Besides, the bandage looks far worse than the wound. It was a scratch. Davis came to borrow one of my dresses for you while you were still at the hotel, and I informed him that he could only have it if I could do the alterations and present it to you. After some...discussion, he relented and brought me here."

Edward beamed. If she was able to cow Davis, she was all right. "I am so glad you are feeling up to 'discussing' things with Davis. I understand tonight is to be the most embarrassing night of my life."

"It is a good thing nobody will know who you are then." She pointed to a beautiful, bottle-green gown hanging on the closet door.

He cleared his throat. "All right, let us get on with this masquerade."

"First, you need to shave. Patros's shaving things are on the washstand. Your face needs to be as smooth as possible."

After he'd shaved, she bade him to stand behind the privacy screen to dress then instructed him to remove his clothes but keep on his own undergarments. First she handed him a chemise over the privacy screen, informing him that this would go over his normal undergarments. His jaw dropped at the shapeless garment while she explained how he was supposed to put it on. Then she passed over the corset.

"You cannot be serious," Edward said. "I have nothing to corset, nothing to…to…"

Catherine gave a small smile on her side of the screen. "A good woman diminishes her… assets. You will be a very good woman. But the corset will give you some shape, and I made pillows of discarded material. They will, um, help fill out the corset."

"Pillows?" He sighed. "You are enjoying this far too much." He put the corset on and, grumbling to himself, added the pillows, then declared he was ready to be laced. Catherine came around the screen behind him, arranged the laces, and instructed him to brace himself against the chair in front of him. He held on, and her foot dug into his back as she pulled the laces as hard as she could. His breath left him as she tied the corset into place.

He whispered, "I cannot breathe."

"Welcome to a woman's world, Mister Tyrington."

"This cannot be how they are worn."

"Oh, but it is. Take shallow breaths. You will get used to it, and the corset will loosen a bit on its own."

Edward added the corset cover and under-petticoat. She helped him secure the hoop, then handed him the over-petticoat and helped him secure it. Finally, she took down the dress and helped him into it. She assisted in draping the velvet over the hoop and had him turn several times to make sure the length was right. When she looked up, she chortled.

"Please, this is mortifying enough without your laughter."

"You need this." She placed a dark wig on his head and pinned it in place. The pins scratched his scalp, and the wig was hot and uncomfortable. She covered the wig with a bonnet and tied the string at his chin, then handed him his own pair of formal white gloves. "You will have to wear your own gloves because there are no woman's gloves that will fit you. Since this is a long-sleeved dress, the shortness of the gloves will not be an issue."

"Yes, heaven forbid I wear the wrong length gloves."

She ignored the comment. "A woman's shoe will not fit, but nobody will be able to see your feet, so it does not matter. Not with you taking tiny steps because you cannot breathe." Catherine reached around him and tied a chatelaine around his waist.

"Now there is something useful." He pulled his handkerchief and a pocket knife from his trousers and placed them in the small purse.

"Since you have been out in the sun, your skin is like a Greek fisherman's. Let me powder you up a bit." She applied some powder to his face and then handed him a fan. "Use this and keep it close to your face. It will make you look more comely. And now one final item." She pulled a sheet of paper from her own chatelaine. "This is an agreement that you will bring me my previously signed contract regarding our courtship, and all copies thereof, or I may tell all, far and wide, of your masquerade tonight."

Edward was aghast. "You would not."

Catherine sat back in her chair. "Do you truly want to test that assertion? Besides, as opposed to our previous agreement, I have witnesses to corroborate my story."

Edward's mouth tried to form words, but none would come. Finally he said, "You have bested me."

She smiled and handed him a pen.

He signed. "If I survive the night, you will have the document, and I will require your promise that no word of tonight's masquerade shall pass your lips."

"It would be nicer if we could trust each other."

Edward took her hand in his. "I do trust you, Catherine."

"Then if all goes well tonight, we can burn both contracts together tomorrow." She squeezed his hand, then stood and opened the door for Edward to rejoin Henri and Patros. "May I present Madame Pierre Chambery."

They both tried to school their reactions, but nothing could stop their laughter. Even Edward, who was fuming, could see the humor.

Catherine asked Edward to walk about the room. He was as graceless as anyone would imagine, pushing the skirt out of the way or holding it up very high in front of him so that he could walk forward without tripping over the fabric. She gave him pointers on how to walk, sit, and curtsy in a ball gown and made him practice several times before she was satisfied. The whole while, Patros and Henri stifled fits of laughter.

After Edward managed a passable curtsy, Henri said, "My beautiful wife, Valentina."

Edward stopped. "Dear God no. Valentina? As if the clothes are not humiliating enough, I have to be called Valentina?" He studied Henri's face. "Although I see I already have the added humiliation of a husband with white hair and more of a mustache than any one person should have. Did some small woodland creature die under your nose, Henri?"

Patros smiled. "Call him Pierre. That is how Monsieur Chambery wears his mustache. Show him the monocle."

Henri placed a monocle in his eye, and Edward laughed. It would be almost impossible for anyone to recognize them.

"You will only need to be the Chamberys long enough to get inside," Patros continued. "Once there, you should keep to yourselves. We don't need to cause an international incident as Monsieur and Madame Chambery."

They used Patros's carriage to travel to the ball. Boarding the carriage was a graceless endeavor for Edward, who almost fell headfirst into his seat. Catherine had explained how to lift his dress and how to bend to get in, but the size of the skirt befuddled him through the narrow carriage door, and he almost tore the dress in the process. The Egyptian driver looked askance.

Henri joked, "Excuse her. My wife has been at the sherry." Turning toward the carriage door, he said, "Dearest, how many times have I told you to stay away from the sherry until after we arrive at the ball?"

The carriage ride was uncomfortable, and between his inability to draw a full breath and his impending masquerade as a woman, Edward was miserable. Henri tried to be quiet, but laughter stalked him until he succumbed to a good laugh to get it out of his system. Edward was less than appreciative and almost glad when they arrived at the ball. Almost.

The driveway to the ball was alight with lanterns on poles, and footmen were stationed to help the passengers disembark from the carriages lined up to discharge the guests. It was clear that the sheer number of guests had required some improvisation on the part of Mr. Papadopoulos in that more than half the "footmen" were Egyptian. As they entered the drive, Edward sank back in his seat. Standing nearest the road was Baba, instructing some of the workers in their new task. As the carriage stopped, Edward whispered "The footmen may know me. Their leader, Baba, certainly does."

Chapter Forty Five

Henri exited the carriage in front of the ball, pointed to the next carriage back, and said to the footman, "Oh, there's Madame de Lucardo. You will need to help with her. I can manage my wife."

The footman nodded and went over to assist his coworker, who appeared to struggle with the notoriously large woman. She swatted the other footman with her fan as he attempted to assist her with a bit too much force, and Baba joined the fray to try to calm her, to limited effect.

Henri handed Edward down out of the carriage and offered Edward his arm. The reflecting pool by the front door mirrored the flaming torches placed on poles along the length of the walkway. Edward sweltered in all the layers of garments, and any movement of air, even from the feeble fan, was a welcome relief. The servant announced them, but his voice was lost to all but the closest observers due to the general hubbub and noise of the entrance hall.

As they strolled through the lobby, Henri patted Edward's hand on his arm. It struck Edward as a touching gesture and reminded him of the depth of their friendship that, even after their arrest, Henri would participate in this insane scheme to try to clear his name. It brought a lump to Edward's throat. Wearing a dress was turning out to be an emotional experience.

The ball was in the central courtyard, which was paved in its entirety in small mosaic tiles of a variety of blues, as if the sea itself washed up to the doors of the house. Three sides of the courtyard were surrounded by a covered loggia with grand columns between each archway. The fourth side of the courtyard was open to the sea cliff and what in daylight would be a spectacular view of the sea and the volcano's caldera, with Faros lighthouse on a point of the sea cliff not far from the house.

As they entered the courtyard, there was an area for mingling, while the far portion of the loggia to the left contained the orchestra, and the area to the right was filled with dining tables. The festivities were already in full swing. The orchestra played, and people danced in the main courtyard. As they moved through the party, Edward heard several snippets of conversation.

"The murals were astounding."

"And to have discovered so much in such a short time."

"De Lesseps will garner more support with these discoveries."

He was unused to hearing praise for his work, and he smiled at their compliments for the tour that afternoon. He was well pleased—until he remembered that in all likelihood his career in archaeology was over and it was quite possible his life would be forfeit as well.

Henri uncoupled his arm from Edward's and took two glasses of champagne from a waiter. He handed one to Edward.

"Salud." He clinked his glass against Edward's.

Toasting was the last thing Edward wanted to do, but Henri was far more comfortable in his role, and Edward found his resilience reassuring.

As Edward drank champagne and fanned himself, Henri led him by the elbow to a far corner of the courtyard where they could converse in relative seclusion and devise a strategy for the night. By the time they stopped, Edward had finished his glass of champagne. "God, I could use a whiskey," he whispered.

"Ladies do not drink whiskey at balls, only in the privacy of their own homes."

"Fantastic. Then get me more champagne."

"Only after we devise a plan for the night."

"We need to find James and follow him. If there is a meeting, we must interrupt it." Edward's voice dropped lower. "I forgot to ask—do you have a gun?"

Henri patted his jacket, and Edward nodded.

"All right," Henri said. "We will start on this side of the courtyard and work our way around until we find him."

He took another glass of champagne for each of them from a passing waiter and again led Edward by the elbow, telling him to drink more slowly. "I do not need a drunken wife to deal with."

Edward pursed his lips. "Very funny."

They strolled across the loggia. Edward avoided eye contact and fanned himself while Henri leaned in to make a comment now and again and to give the general impression that they were interested only in one another. Edward noticed several beautiful women and prayed his actions this night would never become general knowledge. They passed Empress Eugenia, who spoke with the pasha, de Lesseps, and Lord Livingstone.

Henri escorted Edward to a chair in a corner away from the crowd. "I will look in the men's smoking lounge to see if he is there. Stay here."

Chapter Forty Six

As Edward watched Henri leave, the whalebone of the corset dug into his ribs, and a bead of sweat ran down his forehead. He removed a handkerchief from his reticule, dabbed his head, and was shocked at the powder left on the cloth until he remembered he had makeup on his face.

As he stowed his handkerchief, a rather drunk gentleman with many military accolades pinned to his chest approached him and asked him to dance. Edward responded in high-pitched French that he could not dance and that his husband was due to be back any moment. He thought the mention of a husband would send him away.

"If you will not dance, then I will sit with you instead." Sitting seemed more of a necessity for him rather than a choice, given how he wavered on his feet. He dropped into the chair in the most graceless manner possible. "What is your name, dear?"

Edward waved his fan in front of his face. "Priscilla. My husband will be back any moment, and I must warn you he is a jealous man."

"Do you know who I am, child?" He leaned toward Edward to thickly whisper in his ear. "I am General Beauregard Hautpool, and one little jealous man does not frighten me."

Edward frantically waved the fan in front of his face. "Be that as it may, sir, I have no interest in displeasing my husband, so I will leave."

As Edward rose, Henri arrived. "To whom are you speaking, Valentina?"

"Who is Valentina?"

"My wife, of course."

"She said her name was Priscilla."

Henri laughed. "*Mon petite choux*, she is always playing her tricks. Come dear, let us dance."

As Henri steered him to the dance floor, Edward whispered, "Henri, no, I cannot dance with you."

"Of course you can. It is a waltz, so we will not have to dance with other couples. Just let me lead."

Before he could protest further, Henri danced him onto the floor.

"No, this is too much," Edward hissed. "You have no idea what it is like wearing this costume. I have not been able to breathe since I was tied into it, and with all the layers, I am ablaze with heat."

"That gentleman thought you looked like you were ablaze." Henri snickered. "But the fact remains that we need to find James, and this is one of the only places we have not yet looked. He was not in the men's lounge."

"How can you remain so calm?"

"I am focused on our goal, and you would do well to remember it as well. A misstep by our quarry may be the only thing that saves your neck."

They slipped into silence as they danced, Edward focusing on not stepping on Henri's feet. As much as he wanted to hunt for James, being led on the dance floor and managing the multiple layers of dress proved too much for him, until a voice focused him as none other could.

"Yes, Mister Tyrington is my nephew. I can say the family is quite proud of him. I am not sure where he is. I would have expected to see him by now."

Edward squeezed Henri's hand and glared at him, and Henri moved them to a safer distance from Aunt Inez.

"Thank you. She cannot see me. If anyone will recognize me it is... Wait, Henri, did you see that? Fontaine went to a room behind the orchestra with Francine. We should see what they are up to."

Henri held Edward fast. "No. We have only one purpose tonight. What your misguided cousin may be doing at a ball is not our concern."

"But we know Fontaine is a lecherous man who has no real interest in her. Her reputation is at stake."

"Her reputation is not your responsibility. Not tonight. Tomorrow you can take that up with her. Look. The earl is four couples away from us." Henri spun Edward so he faced the other direction, and he could see James dancing a short distance away. Henri spun him back around. "It is best if I face him rather than you."

They danced for the next several minutes. The orchestra finished playing, and James and his partner left the dance floor. Henri and Edward followed at a reasonable distance. James thanked his partner for the dance and walked to the main house.

As they moved through the crowd, they passed a waiter, and Edward grabbed another glass of champagne from his tray.

Henri gave him a look. "You would do well to keep your head about you."

"I am sweltering. And mortified. Besides, it is only champagne."

"Like all French things, it is best not to underestimate it."

Edward rolled his eyes and drank.

James stopped and joined Thouvenel, the pasha, and Empress Eugenia in conversation near the entrance to the villa.

A troop of waiters carried trays past them to the serving tables on the loggia. There was a general rush of guests to the food, and Edward and Henri lost sight of James. The pasha and Empress Eugenia came toward them on their way to eat, and Henri and Edward ducked behind a column to remain hidden from view. When they looked again, the earl and Thouvenel were nowhere to be seen.

"Do you see them?" Edward whispered.

"No, they must have gone the other way. Come on." Henri started to walk away.

Edward grabbed his arm and hooked his own into it. "Do not leave me behind."

They walked as fast as they dared to the foyer and saw Thouvenel and James as they reached the landing at the top of the right-hand staircase.

Henri tugged Edward into an alcove under the stair. "Stay here."

Edward stayed behind the column, and Henri leapt up the steps. When he returned, he said, "They have gone into the second room on the right."

"We should be able to see it from the upper loggia," Edward whispered. "There were steps outside that we can take. It will be easier to see their activity through the windows."

Henri nodded and escorted Edward back outside to the staircase. They waited near the bottom in a darkened corner until they felt sure nobody would see them. Most of the crowd was busy eating and focused on conversation at their tables. The two men moved up the stairs, hunched over so they were hidden behind the low wall and handrail, and moved as fast as that position would allow. It was difficult for Edward not to trip on the front of his skirt, and more than once the lace pulled apart as he stepped on it.

As he watched the front of his dress, Henri whispered, "Get your derriere down."

Henri had turned back in his direction, and Edward looked back to see his posterior higher than the wall. He crouched further, and they climbed again. They made it to the top and crept across the porch to the wall of the house. They moved along the wall, peering in each window before they passed.

James's voice carried from one of the few lit windows they approached. "I was not able to meet him. I am glad we were able to make alternate arrangements." Henri and Edward crept up to the edge of the window and watched James and Thouvenel in a spacious library filled with bookshelves, a large fireplace and comfortable seating.

"As am I," Thouvenel answered. "I had not planned on being so involved, but I do not mind telling you this information is crucial to our current work."

"Then let us toast our successful management of the situation." James poured whiskey for them both, handed Thouvenel a glass, clinked it with his own, and drank. "However, we should reduce our commerce for a time. I had managed suspicions in the House of Lords to almost nothing after the elder Tyrington's death, but there is renewed suspicion, and I have more work to do to ensure our continued safety."

"Understood. What will you do with the younger Tyrington?"

"It is already done. He is under arrest for making an attempt on my life. And there are other things afoot to ensure he will be tried for the murder of Dupont, and Mr. Allen as well. I suspect he will not be much longer on this earth. And of course, his arrest will discredit his brother, who has insisted on maintaining suspicions of espionage in the House. I have several allies who will be more than willing to assist in this endeavor, for reasons unrelated to me or my work."

Livingstone and Blakenship, no doubt. Who else?

James stood and drained his glass. "I should have the situation well in hand within a few months, and by autumn we should be able to resume our normal relationship."

Thouvenel stood and exchanged envelopes with James. "Excellent. When you are ready, make contact in the usual way. I will not be involved in future transactions, but we will send a trustworthy courier."

They each checked the received envelopes and, seeming satisfied, placed them in their respective pockets.

"It is, as always, a pleasure doing business with you." James shook Thouvenel's hand.

James turned toward the window as Henri stood and burst through the door with Edward in tow.

Chapter Forty Seven

James had his gun drawn before Henri could reach for his own and cross the threshold. "Not one more step. Put the gun on the ground," James growled.

Henri and Edward stopped inside the door. "You will not get away with this," Edward said. Henri took out his gun and slowly put it on the ground.

"Kick it toward me," James said.

Henri had put his foot next to it and slid it part of the way between them when a man walked in, saying to his companion, "Here's another party, let's join them." He drunkenly pushed past Henri into the library. As his lady companion staggered in, James and Thouvenel ran past them and down the hallway.

Henri grabbed his gun off the floor as Edward pushed past the drunk couple and into the hall. Henri chased Thouvenel to the right, and Edward chased James to the left. There were screams from the disrupted partygoers as James raced through the crowd on the first floor. As Edward flew down the stairs following James, he heard another disruption from the courtyard and saw Francine running toward the main house, yelling. Aunt Inez hurried toward her, and all was a tumult.

Edward put the women out of his mind and sprinted after James, past the footmen at the front of the house, and into the open fields near the top of the sea cliff, but the corset and dress slowed his pace. When he could no longer see James, he stopped to let his eyes adjust to the surrounding gloom. As he strained to hear over the beating of his own heart, the beam from the lighthouse cut a swath through the darkness as it rotated back toward the sea. He held his breath and searched for any movement, but there was none. The darkness that followed blinded him.

The light was no help at all, and now he was blind again. He removed his pocket knife and cut himself out of his costume. He removed the wig and was left in his own undergarments. It was better that than running around in a dress.

Where would James go from here? In a second, Edward knew. *His ship. He needs to return to his ship and flee.* He scanned the land around him and saw that it dipped to the east.

Edward ran through the scrub grasses to the east, away from the lighthouse. With the next sweep of the light, he raced to the cliff to get a better view. As he neared it, he discovered a path down the cliff face. He ran, and his feet found it before the light swung out of sight.

He walked the path in utter darkness. He slid his hand along the ash and pumice stone of the inside wall as he descended. About a quarter of the way down, he stumbled on something in the path and fell to his knees. Righting himself, he felt the wall and discovered an opening. He felt the crumbled step he'd tripped on with his foot, and he stepped into an old cave. A poor man's beach shack, as it were.

He felt the blood drip from his knee where he had hit the stair. "Blast it. The last thing I need is an injured knee."

"Talking to yourself, Edward? Most unseemly." Edward froze at the sound of James's voice. "Before you do anything rash, I am still armed."

"Why have you not killed me already then?" Edward asked.

"It is hard to get a good shot in the dark, and there is enough rock in these walls that I am as likely to be hit as you."

"Then we are at an impasse." Edward searched the dark to find some hint of whether James still had the gun.

"No, I still have the advantage. It is best not to lose sight of that."

"This must be a new sensation for you, James, hiding in the dark like a common criminal."

"Do not try to rattle me, boy. I have done many things in my life, some of which were far less savory than this moment."

Edward sneered. "I would never deign to try to perturb the great Earl of Mar."

They stood in silence for a few moments, Edward trying to find an advantage. Then the earl asked, "Have you ever gambled?"

Edward's mouth was dry, and it took a second for him to find his voice. "I have played my share of poker, yes."

"Have you ever been convinced of the perfection of your hand, and when you reached for the last card, the entire bet came crashing down?"

"Yes."

"This was to be my last transaction. That was my promise to myself. I no longer need the money, and it was time to end the charade. And then everything went wrong, and there were so many loose ends to be tied to set things to rights. Too many loose ends."

"That is not what you told Thouvenel."

"It is best to end unsavory relationships from a distance."

The waxing moon must have risen to the east, because the light shifted in the sky beyond the cave opening. A strange calm washed over Edward as he crept further into the cave. *Now it is he and I.* Nothing mattered anymore. Only one would leave this cave, and Edward was not sure he cared which. He only knew that the world with both of them in it was too hard to bear.

His heart pounded as if each forceful beat would be his last. "Was my father a loose end?"

"Yes."

"And me?" Edward's ears roared with the sound of his own blood, his own mortality screaming at him to care, to be smart and use his wits to get out of this place. His soul keened in grief at the loss of his friend who had so steadily guided him after his father's death, and for the loss of his father by his friend's hand. He remembered the birthday celebrations James had attended and wished so many returns of. He thought of the Christmas hunt where they would ride together exchanging jokes along the way. He thought of James's counsel about which girl he should ask to dance at a ball. A hundred scenes of happy times with his friend James pressed into his mind. It was too much. He focused his mind away from the noise.

"Although you are the most difficult thus far, yes, you are also a loose end." James stood and moved in front of the opening, his body outlined by the faintest moonlight.

Edward knelt carefully and snatched a rock by his foot. He threw it against the side of the cave closest to James. James pivoted toward the sound, and Edward rushed at him. James fired as Edward pushed him out of the cave entrance.

The gun blast was deafening, and the bullet ricocheted around the cave and sounded like a firework. Edward's fingers dug into the edge of the opening, and the rock scratched his hands as he fell off the stair and onto the path. James stumbled backward, propelled by Edward's push, over the step, past the path, and off the cliff.

Edward's knees took the brunt of his fall, and a rock scratched his cheek as his head hit the ground. The ringing in Edward's ears overpowered all other sensations, and time seemed to slow to a crawl as he curled in agony waiting for the pain of the noise to pass.

He had no idea how long he lay there when he felt a kick in his back. He rolled away from the pain. Livingstone stood over him with a gun pointed at his face, then he kicked Edward's legs. He appeared to be screaming, but Edward could not hear the words. He tried to fend off Livingtone's blows, but he was too slow, and Livingstone seemed to be possessed by a demon's strength as he kept kicking at him.

A thought pierced through the fog that surrounded Edward's mind. *Why does he not shoot me?*

Chapter Forty Eight

Edward laughed at the incongruity of his situation. It seemed as if Death stood over him in the form of an irate Livingstone, yet he failed to use the one tool he had to hand: a pistol. He laughed through the pain, through the ringing in his ears that was deafening, through all that he had lost. *I forgive you.* The thought came unbidden. Perhaps it was the nearness of Death, perhaps he had truly lost his mind, but his laughter quieted although the beating continued, and Edward's only thought was *I forgive you*. It had not been his intention to ever forgive Livingstone. He had hated him for years; through all the trouble between him and his father, through all the implications, through all the suspicions, there was one common thread: hatred. But this night, as Livingstone kicked at his bruised body, there was only forgiveness. Edward was far past trying to figure out why.

At the faint sound of another gun being discharged, he felt nothing until Livingstone's body fell across his. He was heavy, and the smell of whiskey pierced Edward's nose.

He felt himself screaming as he struggled to get out from under Livingstone but heard only the ghost of his own terrified voice. Henri ran to him, holstered his gun, and rolled Livingstone off.

Henri grabbed Edward and held him. The joy at seeing him alive shone in the tears in Henri's eyes.

Still deaf, Edward allowed Henri to help him up and walk him to the top of the cliff, where a small crowd had formed in response to the shots. Henri directed the police who had arrived toward Livingstone's body and then escorted Edward home.

Edward awoke in his own bed, unsure of how much of his memory was accurate and how much he had dreamed. Kako was snuggled in the crook of his arm, and before he opened his eyes, he stroked her. He smacked his lips to wet the dry fuzz that lurked on his tongue. Grogginess crushed his mind as he tried to remember. His right ear still rang, and his head pounded. Then the pain of losing his father and the betrayal of his friend settled around his heart like a snake, crushing all the light his life had ever held.

He opened his eyes to push away the memories. Henri sat in a chair against the far wall, watching him. They stared at one another. The press of everything that had occurred crowded in, and Edward rolled onto his side to hide his pain from his friend.

Henri came to the bed and poured a glass of water, his voice softer and gentler than Edward had ever heard it. "You gave me quite a scare last night. When I heard the shot, I thought I had lost you forever."

Edward covered his eyes and took a deep breath, trying to snuff out the memory of it. "I... I cannot. Not now, Henri."

"I understand." Henri put a hand on his shoulder. "But do not think you can lie about for days. There is still a village to be excavated, and you have work to do."

"I am no longer under arrest?"

"No. I captured Thouvenel, and although de Lesseps's initial response was disbelief, the envelope in his pocket could not be ignored, especially when they recovered James's body and found the corresponding envelope of payment in his pocket. I sent word to Miss Briggs about James's arrest, and she told me where you had put Livingstone's letters. I had Julian photograph them, and I added those to the evidence to Fontaine to dismiss the case against you. However, he was unwilling to drop the charges. Once I debriefed de Lesseps on his collusion with Livingstone, he removed him from his post and wrote the order to drop the charges himself. He plans to make a full report to the British government of Mr. Grayson's death, James's sale of secrets, and Livingstone's and Blankenship's treachery. Of course, he hopes this will somehow redeem his work in the eyes of English. I am astounded how single-minded he is."

Edward exhaled. "Thank God. And James... is dead."

"Yes."

He closed his eyes. *Damn you, James, for I was damned in trusting you.*

Swallowing hard, he put thoughts of James aside and opened his eyes. "But how did you come to be there as Livingstone was beating me?"

"As luck would have it, I chased the far slower quarry and captured Thouvenel early on, so then I came to assist you. When the light from the lighthouse spun around, I saw a person go below the cliff edge and headed in that direction. I saw someone kicking a body, which turned out to be you, but did not know who either of you were at first. I heard Livingstone and determined he was attacking you once I heard you yell. Thank goodness I got there when I did. Davis took it upon himself to be stationed near the ball in case he was needed, and it was quite fortuitous that he did. You may recall him tending to you in the carriage. You were rather delirious, and Davis gave you a sedative. Rest while you can, Edward. Davis and I will be in the other room if you need anything."

As he crossed the threshold, he stopped. "Oh, and one other thing. De Lesseps would prefer to limit the notoriety surrounding the canal project. To that end, he has requested all involved to refrain from sharing the story with anyone other than the police and government officials."

"I understand. However, given the attendance last night, trying to hide this story is a fool's errand."

Henri nodded. "Likely so, but we should still honor the request."

Later that afternoon, the heat drove Edward from his room. As he entered the living room, Aunt Inez rose from her chair and came to him. "You had me worried sick. Monsieur de Lesseps was here, and he and Monsieur LeMarchal refused to allow me to see you. Are you all right?"

"Yes, Aunt Inez. I am as fine as can be expected. I needed rest. Thank you for waiting."

She inspected the wounds to his hands and face. With a thousand questions apparent on her lips, her eyes searched his.

Edward looked away and walked to the window.

"Edward, you should eat. Davis, please fix us something."

Davis bowed and left for the kitchen, and soon he brought them olives, cheeses, and fruits to dine on. Inez insisted on eating with Edward and kept offering him food, as if that would fix all that he had been through.

To distract her from feeding him and to satisfy his own curiosity, he asked, "What happened with Francine at the end of the ball?"

"She discovered what an absolute cad Monsieur Fontaine is."

Edward looked up, his brows knitted. "Is she all right?"

"Yes, she is fine. He tried to coerce her into allowing him some liberties he had no right to take. To her good fortune, she had been trained in the Inez Preparatory School of Defense."

Edward tilted his head. "The what?"

"A few years ago, I taught her some rather obvious ways to defend herself against unwanted advances. There is always at least one overprivileged, under-bred young man at any cotillion who feels he has the right to take...liberties. I showed her how to repel such an attack."

"How did she defend herself?"

"When he pulled her close, she—with great prowess, as I understand it—stomped on his left foot. Then as he bent over, she slapped his face and pushed him into the edge of the stone fireplace." She took a bite of cheese.

Edward stared at her. "And? What happened next?"

"Well, she ran away, of course, and yelled for anyone to assist her lest he pull her back into his clutches. I came running and removed her—after giving him a piece of my mind whilst beating him with my fan and warning several other young women about his poor breeding."

He smiled at the picture of it in his mind. "You know he is the chief of police here."

"I do not care if he is the pasha himself. Bad behavior will be dealt with accordingly."

"Your strength is inspiring." Edward chuckled and shook his head.

Inez asked about the events of the evening, and Edward summarized as briefly as he could while attempting to keep the confidence that de Lesseps had requested. He hated to tell her that his father had been poisoned, as it only reopened old wounds, but she had the right to know the truth of her brother's death. She took the news hard, and after she had a whiskey to calm her, Edward asked Davis to escort her to her inn.

While they were gone, he returned to his room and took more of the sleeping draught Davis had concocted. He needed to float in a carefree sea and to not think for a while.

The next day, Edward told Davis that he planned to visit Miss Briggs.

Davis asked, "May I walk with you when you visit her? I need to check on her and her father as well."

They left together after lunch and walked in silence. Edward's heart and thoughts were too heavy for words, and Davis seemed to be content to forgo conversation. The path into town meandered through what was now a profusion of blooming wildflowers and grasses. It seemed as if the breath the spring had held was exhaled in a torrent of color and release.

The town was far busier than the last time he'd walked here, and an idea took hold of him. "Davis, I have an errand to run. I will join you at the inn in a few minutes."

He detoured to the botanical garden and plucked a bouquet of bells of Ireland for Catherine.

When he arrived at the inn, it was like entering a mausoleum. It was cool and quiet, with only one man behind the counter. Davis was already with Miss Briggs, so Edward waited in the parlor. After Davis was finished with his ministrations, he came and informed Edward that Miss Briggs would see him in her rooms.

Edward knocked and was admitted by her lady's maid. Catherine reclined on a sofa, wrapped in a deep-blue-and-white quilt with a smaller bandage around her head. As he entered, her face lit with a gentle, warm smile that crinkled her eyes and pierced his heart.

"You will forgive me. I am not in the habit of entertaining men in my rooms, but Davis was adamant that I stay here to rest today, and I must know what happened last night. He refused to tell me anything."

Edward pulled a chair closer to the sofa and presented the bouquet of flowers to her.

She inhaled their scent, closing her eyes. "It has been many years since I smelled these. Excluding the other day, of course. Thank you. They are exquisite." Catherine handed them to her maid and excused her from the room.

He explained the events of the evening. She pressed him whenever he tried to gloss over points that were embarrassing or difficult, and he obliged by telling her all. When he told of removing the dress, he said, "I apologize, but your dress and other articles are ruined. I will, of course, replace them and buy you several more in repayment of their loan."

"I always disliked that dress anyway. It made me look sickly, and it was quite warm. On a balmy evening like last night, you must have been sweltering."

Edward waved his hand as if to erase the past. "Let us not discuss it anymore." He pulled a slip of paper from his pocket. "Have your dressmaker send the bill to me at this address for whatever you would like to purchase."

"Thank you, but you need to tell me the rest of the story."

He continued with the story until he finished with the earl's shot and plummet from the cliff and Livingstone's death.

She gazed at him for a long moment, lost in the maze of her own thoughts. "I am glad you were able to avenge the death of your father."

The last words stung, but Edward held her gaze and swallowed the lump forming in his throat. He took her hand in his. "I could not have done it without your help. If you had not been there at the site, if you had not gasped when you did, I would be dead right now. I owe you my life, and the fact that you were injured on my behalf..."

He looked down at their hands and wrestled with all he could not say.

Catherine returned her hand to her own lap. "Did you bring the paper?"

Edward already missed the warmth of her hand in his as he looked up. "Of course."

"Shall we?" She pulled an envelope from a nearby table and walked to the fire in the grate. He joined her, and they exchanged papers.

They both threw their papers in the fire.

Edward took her hands again. "Thank you. For everything."

The weight of their thoughts pressed them into silence for a while. When Edward realized he was alone with her in her room, he dropped her hands. "I should go. I am indebted to you in more ways than I can count. Thank you."

He crossed the hall and knocked on her father's door. John looked comfortable, sitting in a rocking chair with a cup of tea by the window.

"There you are! I've been waiting to see you. Your Davis has been a godsend. The draught he concocted brought me relief from that cursed headache, and now I am well. But tell me of your adventure. There is gossip flying about, and I will have the truth of it."

Once again, Edward told the shortened version of the tale. He apologized to John for his daughter's injuries, which John rejected.

"I have no doubt she brought it on herself. She has a habit of that."

Edward left feeling both relieved that his ordeal was over and saddened that his investigations with Catherine were at an end.

Chapter Forty Nine

The next day before lunch, Edward went to Baba to thank him for his help.

Baba's reaction was as expected. "I'm glad you didn't make me regret it."

Edward understood that was heartfelt appreciation from Baba, and he was happy for it. He knew their working relationship would be easier, and he was grateful to not have to endure another wrathful tirade from him.

Over the course of the afternoon, several dignitaries came to see the excavation and to hear whatever breathless gossip they could. Edward shared nothing of what he knew and was surprised to hear how the story had been embellished in one day. It was no use to correct anyone now, as the fiction was far more interesting than the truth. He smiled to himself, musing about how unrecognizable the story would be three days hence.

When another carriage rolled up to the dig site, Edward sighed and asked Asim to again take over his duties as he greeted whoever had arrived.

As he approached the carriage, de Lesseps stepped out.

Edward quickened his step. "Sir, I was not expecting you today."

"I want to see all that you have done here."

He showed him the entire site. De Lesseps shared how impressed he was with the care Edward had taken on the project and the extraordinary artwork they had found. When they were at the farthest end of the excavation, de Lesseps looked out over the Aegean.

"There is another reason I am here today. I have received word from our engineer that the cost for the latest steam shovel will be fifty percent larger than what had been budgeted, and we need several of them. Without a large cash infusion, the company will have difficulty meeting that need." He turned to Edward. "Despite the exceptional work you have done here, I cannot continue to fund the archaeological dig. I am sorry. I owe a debt of gratitude to you, but I cannot repay it through continued funding of the excavation."

Edward took a deep breath. He knew at the outset this project would not last forever, and yet he was stunned when the end came. Through his daze, he shook de Lesseps's hand. "Of course, sir. I understand. Thank you for the opportunity to be a part of this monumental project."

"The pleasure has been mine." He hesitated. "I will need you to secure the site from looters until someone else can fund further excavation."

"Of course, sir."

"I will also prepare a recommendation for whatever archaeological project you wish." He shook Edward's hand. "I am sure you have things to think about. I can see myself back to the carriage. Goodbye, and thank you." De Lesseps walked back toward his carriage.

Edward turned to stare out over the sea and let the breeze blow through his mind. He had done well here, but now he needed a new plan for the future. He thought of the papers to be written about his work here and the lectures to be given. Despite the abbreviated timeframe, despite the odds against the project, despite James's and Livingstone's efforts, he had been successful.

And although the work had only begun, he had no doubt that the story of these people would be known and his work would continue. As the seeds of a plan for what his life would hold for him grew, he relaxed, knowing he was making the right decision.

Soft footsteps padded behind him, and he turned as Asim approached.

"Is something wrong, sir?"

"De Lesseps has ended the excavation. With the cost of the steam shovels, there is no money to continue the dig."

Asim sighed. "I'm sorry, sir."

They stood together, admiring the view, each lost in their own thoughts.

At length, Edward said, "Let us go and tell the others, and tomorrow we will begin the work of securing the site."

After work, Edward and Henri returned to Edward's home. They sat by the fire, and Henri told him that de Lesseps had invited him to return to Damietta on his personal yacht. Henri was thrilled about the honor.

"I am happy for you, Henri. When do you leave?"

"We leave in the morning."

The air seemed to leave the room. It had been two years since Henri had walked back into his life, and even after all that time, he had proven himself a devoted friend.

"Henri..."

His friend leaned toward him. "I know. I have been an incredible friend to you, giving you the opportunity to make a name for yourself in archaeology, not to mention leading you so well across the dance floor, but please, let us not have any dramatic goodbyes. We will see each other again soon. I promise to invite you to visit me and my family in France next spring, and I will visit you in London as well. Although I must say the warmth of Damietta makes me dread those dreary London days."

Edward smiled. "All right, no dramatic goodbyes. But I owe you more than I can say, and I promise I will find a way to repay the debt."

Edward and Henri stood and Henri gave Edward a hug and a kiss on each cheek.

Until next time, my friend. *Bon chance.*"

"Until next time."

It took several more days to catalog the discoveries they'd made and to prepare them for shipment. It was agreed that certain items would be sent to de Lesseps's offices while others would go to the Museum of Antiquities in Athens.

With the excavation ending and diminished hopes of marrying Francine off to Edward, Aunt Inez decided it was time for them to move on as well. After their last meal together, he escorted the two women to their inn, and Inez suggested Edward take Francine on one last stroll about the square, which he obliged by offering his arm.

The twilight was deepening over the calm water, and as they neared the far end of the square, they could see a few fishing boats with lanterns in the cove below.

Edward asked, "This may be an impertinent question, but what were you thinking, following Fontaine behind the orchestra?"

Francine gasped. "But how did you—"

"I was there. In disguise. That is all I am willing to say about it. I wanted to come to your aid, knowing he was a man of low character, but could not. I am only glad you were able to get away. But I question why you put yourself in that position in the first place."

Francine stammered, "I... I... have been wondering that myself. I have no idea what motivated me to do something so foolish."

"I thought you were committed to Roger."

"I am. At least I want to be. I do not know. Fontaine was so foreign. So charming. I felt so at ease with him."

"He is a practiced deceiver. I hope you know now that you should be wary of characters like him. So what of Roger?"

"I have learned enough to know that in these instances, taking the hardest path is usually the best in the long run. I will write to him and confess what happened. Whether we continue at that point will be up to him, but he will know the truth of it. And I will either know the depth of his love for me or will receive my just deserts for my capriciousness. I am prepared for either, but would prefer the former."

"Then you have grown a bit."

They stood and watched the boats at the docks before he walked her back to the inn and said his goodbyes.

At the end of the last day of work, Edward gave both Asim and Gahiji letters of recommendation for their exemplary work on the project and, as promised, wrote to the director of antiquities in Egypt recommending them for work there.

Early the next afternoon, when the work site was properly secured with fences, Edward thanked his workers before dismissing them, along with Patros, back to the quarry operation.

After they left, he re-entered the site, walked to the room with the goddess mural, and sat at her feet one last time. Leaving weighed on his heart, but his own resolve pushed against it as he vowed to continue his work.

As he sat there, Patros walked in. "What are your plans from here?"

"I leave in the morning."

Patros looked grim. "I'll miss working with you, Edward. You were as green as the spring grass when you first came here, but you've grown on me."

"Thank you for everything. And please, thank your family for all their hospitality. They were a great comfort to me during the more trying times."

He went to shake Patros's hand, but Patros grabbed him in a bear hug. "It has been an honor to know you. I hope you come back someday."

Edward hugged him back rather awkwardly. "I am honored to know you, and I plan to come back and continue this work, so I assure you, you are not done with me yet."

Patros's eyes crinkled with his smile. "Next time let us have less adventure?"

As Edward walked to the door, he said, "It would be hard to have more."

Chapter Fifty

Edward went to visit the Briggses that evening. When he arrived, John was walking about with no apparent lingering effects from his illness.

John ushered him into the front parlor. "Come. Have a drink with me. Catherine told me of your plans to leave. We are leaving for business in France tomorrow, and of course will send an invitation when the time is appropriate."

Edward sat in one of the chairs facing the hearth while John poured the whiskey. Handing Edward his glass, John said, "I understand the tours were a resounding success. I have heard from several guests in the hotel dining room that they look forward to returning to see your progress in the future."

Edward stared deep into his glass. "Thank you for the kind words, John, but as of a few days ago, work has stopped on the project due to lack of funding."

"I am sorry but not surprised to hear that. I assume you have plans to secure other funding to continue your work, and I, for one, will be happy to help in that endeavor when the time comes." Raising his glass, he said, "Let us drink to your continued discovery and good fortune on this project."

They touched glasses and drank. The warmth of the whiskey drew Edward's thoughts away from the past.

"Thank you. That is generous of you. I do plan to continue the project. I will contact my friends at Oxford. It might be a nice way to assist in garnering English support for the canal."

John looked askance.

"The canal is coming, John, and to be quite honest, it will be sooner rather than later. England has tried for years to stop it and has failed. It is time to take a seat at the table or go hungry."

Smiling, John said, "Just like your father. And despite our disagreement on this particular topic, I still plan to assist your need of funding."

The sparkle in John's eye told Edward this offer was made, at least in part, due to his "involvement" with Catherine. Edward had put down his glass and leaned forward, steeling himself for what must be said next, when Catherine entered the room.

"I thought I heard voices in here."

They both stood and welcomed her to join them. Edward kissed her hands, and as she seated herself by the fire, John said, "If you will both excuse me, I must oversee the packing. Despite how often we travel, my man always requires a bit of oversight on proper storage of certain items. I look forward to seeing you again soon, Edward."

They shook hands, and Edward was left with the words to end his courtship to Catherine still in his mouth. He stared at the closed door, unsure of how to proceed, when Catherine cleared her throat.

Edward turned to face her. The royal blue of her dress gave her eyes the appearance of the Sea of Crete itself, deep blue and inviting. "You look much better. How is your wound?"

"I am much better, as is my father, thanks to Davis." She looked into his eyes. "But how are you?"

He was caught off guard by this simple question. The weight of it all flooded him again, and catching his breath, he looked away so she could not see the sorrow sting his eyes.

In a low voice, she said, "Do not run away from grief, it is the contrast that allows us to fully feel joy. I can only imagine how recent events have reopened old wounds."

Her words pierced his heart, and he walked toward the window to avoid the directness of her gaze. Her insightfulness was a dangerous thing. He stared into the garden, its buds a mystery in the gathering darkness. He took a deep breath and faced her. "That, and it has opened new ones, as I will always have the memory of wearing that dress."

They both laughed, and as he retook his seat by the fire, she said, "I am glad you came today. My father and I are leaving for France. I would like him to visit with his physician. His headaches are worsening, and I am concerned for him."

"He said he was returning for business reasons."

"Oh, he has business everywhere, and I have no doubt he will be as busy as ever. However, we are returning to France because I insist that we see his doctor."

"Is there anything I can do?"

"No. It may be nothing, but I want to be sure. But what of you? What will you do now?"

As Edward told her of the end of the archaeological project, the gears of his resolve clicked, and the seeds of the plan he had begun blossomed fully formed in his mind. "First, I will return to London and sell the house in town. It is too large for me and filled with the ghosts of a life I no longer have. I need to move among the living. Besides, I prefer a warmer clime to dreary London. I may leave England; I have not decided. Then I will solicit funds to continue my work here. We have only scratched the surface of this site, and much more work needs to be done."

Her eyes sparkled at his words. "Your plan sounds like an excellent one. I hope our paths may cross again."

Edward sighed. "Speaking of which, I planned to tell your father that I have released you from our 'arrangement' before his hasty retreat. I admit it is not a conversation I relish having. I never wished to deceive him, and the fact that I have weighs on my mind."

"I hope this is not too bold, but if it makes no difference to you, I would appreciate it if you would not end our arrangement yet." She held up a hand. "Before you protest, my reasons are not only based in self-interest. Although my life is easier without my father trying to marry me off, I am also worried for him. His health is worsening, and I do not want him to worry with trying to find a husband for me when he should be focused on his health. These past few days, even though he was in pain, he has been happier than I have seen him in some time. I do not want to take that from him, even if it means maintaining a pretense we would both rather drop."

Edward rubbed the back of his neck. "The longer we pretend, the harder that conversation will be. For all of us."

"Please, you must understand, it would be a great kindness to him and to me. When he is better, he will take this news in stride. But his health is precarious, and I do not want to jeopardize it with difficult tidings. I promise that I will release you from this arrangement without argument should you desire to court someone. I know we have had difficulty trusting each other in the past, but given all that has transpired, I believe we are past that now."

Sighing, Edward said, "I do not wish to bring anguish to your father, especially if he is not well. I will agree to this, with one condition."

"Name it."

"Please be safe."

Catherine raised her right hand. "I solemnly swear I will endeavor to be safe." Smiling, she continued, "And please let us know when you are in France. We would enjoy seeing you under less trying conditions."

Edward came to her and took her hands in his. The warmth of her small hands flooded his, and he was struck that such strength resided in her. "Until we meet again, and thank you for everything."

"Until we meet again."

THE END

Thank you for reading The Bones of Santorini. If you liked it, please **leave a review**. You can also order Book 2 of The Edward Tyrington Mysteries–**The Skulls of Malgrange**. Also, please join my community at www.joniswift.com and get my newsletter for fun stories, sneak previews, release information, and sometimes, free mysteries!

Acknowledgments

This project has been a long one for me and there are many people to thank for their help along the way. My husband has been invaluable in giving me space to follow my dreams, encouragement that I was not wasting my time, and hard criticism when it was needed. I am forever in his debt. I also need to thank my editor Kristen, who consistently improves my books, and Naomi Kappel whose encouragement has been so important. My proofreader's extraordinaire Naomi and Kimberley – thank you! I'd also like to thank J. D. Allen, who read a very early version of this book and encouraged me to keep writing. Finally, I'd like to thank my ARC tribe! Y'all are the best and I appreciate you more than you know.

Printed in Great Britain
by Amazon

The BONES *of* SANTORINI

A destitute gentleman, an unusual woman and a Victorian murder mystery that might kill them both.

Suez Canal, Egypt and Santorini Greece – 1863, Nothing had gone according to plan for Edward Tyrington since his father squandered the family fortune and abruptly died. Edward accepted a job with the Suez Canal Company as Chief Archaeologist to replenish his coffers, but when the Operations Manager of the Company is murdered things become decidedly worse.

When an unidentified man is murdered, this time at Edward's archeological site, Edward becomes the prime suspect for both murders. Thus begins his turbulent alliance with the unusual Catherine Briggs who proves to be both reckless and cunning in her efforts to clear his name. With corrupt police and international forces in play, time is running out to catch the murderer. If they fail, Edward will either be the next victim, or the man who will hang for the crimes.

"The Bones of Santorini is a rich assortment of history, culture, politics romance, and espionage, all brought to life by incredible character building and scene setting… This is historical fiction at its finest."

- Reader's Favorite 5-Star Reviews

Joni Swift was raised in New York and has loved mysteries since her firs Agatha Christie novel. She is passionate about travel, the environment hiking and loves any kind of adventure. When she isn't writing she usually hiking in the mountains or planning her next vacation.

ISBN 9798987403310
9 798987 403310
900